CLIFFSCOMPLETE

Chopin's

The Awakening

Edited and commentary by Sheri Metzger

Adjunct professor Honors Program/Lecturer English department
University of New Mexico

Complete Text + Commentary + Glossary

Hungry Minds™

Hungry Minds, Inc.
An International Data Group Company
Foster City, CA • Chicago, IL • Indianapolis, IN • New York, NY

CLIFFSCOMPLETE

Chopin's

The Awakening

About the Author
Sheri Metzger is an experienced author and lecturer who teaches regular and honors Literature and Composition classes at the University of New Mexico.

Publisher's Acknowledgments
Editorial
Project Editor: Kathleen A. Dobie
Acquisitions Editor: Gregory W. Tubach
Copy Editor: Mary Fales
Illustrator: DD Dowden
Editorial Manager: Christine Meloy Beck
Special Help: Jim Heaney, Jennifer Young
Production
Proofreader: Vicki Broyles
Hungry Minds Indianapolis Production Services

CliffsComplete Chopin's *The Awakening*
Published by
Hungry Minds, Inc.
909 Third Avenue
New York, NY 10022
www.hungryminds.com (Hungry Minds Web site)
www.cliffsnotes.com (CliffsNotes Web site)

Libray of Congress Contron Number: 2001087532

ISBN: 0-7645-8728-5

Printed in the United States of America

10 9 8 7 6 5 4 3 2 1

1O/SX/QS/QR/IN

Distributed in the United States by Hungry Minds, Inc.

Distributed by CDG Books Canada Inc. for Canada; by Transworld Publishers Limited in the United Kingdom; by IDG Norge Books for Norway; by IDG Sweden Books for Sweden; by IDG Books Australia Publishing Corporation Pty. Ltd. for Australia and New Zealand; by TransQuest Publishers Pte Ltd. for Singapore, Malaysia, Thailand, Indonesia, and Hong Kong; by Gotop Information Inc. for Taiwan; by ICG Muse, Inc. for Japan; by Norma Comunicaciones S.A. for Columbia; by Intersoft for South Africa; by Eyrolles for France; by International Thomson Publishing for Germany, Austria and Switzerland; by Distribuidora Cuspide for Argentina; by LR International for Brazil; by Galileo Libros for Chile; by Ediciones ZETA S.C.R. Ltda. for Peru; by WS Computer Publishing Corporation, Inc., for the Philippines; by Contemporanea de Ediciones for Venezuela; by Express Computer Distributors for the Caribbean and West Indies; by Micronesia Media Distributor, Inc. for Micronesia; by Grupo Editorial Norma S.A. for Guatemala; by Chips Computadoras S.A. de C.V. for Mexico; by Editorial Norma de Panama S.A. for Panama; by American Bookshops for Finland. Authorized Sales Agent: Anthony Rudkin Associates for the Middle East and North Africa.

For general information on Hungry Minds' products and services please contact our Customer Care department; within the U.S. at 800-762-2974, outside the U.S. at 317-572-3993 or fax 317-572-4002.

For sales inquiries and resellers information, including discounts, premium and bulk quantity sales and foreign language translations please contact our Customer Care department at 800-434-3422, fax 317-572-4002 or write to Hungry Minds, Inc., Attn: Customer Care department, 10475 Crosspoint Boulevard, Indianapolis, IN 46256.

For information on licensing foreign or domestic rights, please contact our Sub-Rights Customer Care department at 650-653-7098.

For information on using Hungry Minds' products and services in the classroom or for ordering examination copies, please contact our Educational Sales department at 800-434-2086 or fax 317-572-4005.

Please contact our Public Relations department at 212-884-5163 for press review copies or 212-884-5000 for author interviews and other publicity information or fax 212-884-5400.

For authorization to photocopy items for corporate, personal, or educational use, please contact Copyright Clearance Center, 222 Rosewood Drive, Danvers, MA 01923, or fax 978-750-4470.

is a trademark of
Hungry Minds· Hungry Minds, Inc.

CLIFFSCOMPLETE

Chopin's

The Awakening
CONTENTS AT A GLANCE

CLIFFSCOMPLETE

Chopin's

The Awakening

TABLE OF CONTENTS

Kate Chopin's
THE AWAKENING

INTRODUCTION TO KATE CHOPIN

Childhood

Catherine O'Flaherty (Kate Chopin) was born in St. Louis on February 8, 1850, to an Irish father and a French mother. Chopin's father, Thomas, had one son, George, who was 4 years old when his mother died. Thomas O'Flaherty needed a wife to care for his young son, and within months, he married a young Creole woman, Eliza Faris, who was 23 years younger than her very practical older husband. Within a few years, Thomas and Eliza O'Flaherty had several children, including Tom; Catherine (known as Katie), who was two years younger than Tom; Marie (who apparently died as a small child); and Jane (known as Jennie), who was three years younger than Katie. For some unexplained reason, Katie was sent to boarding school when she was 5 years old, but only two months later, her father, Thomas, was killed in a bridge collapse, and Katie was brought back home to live. Because she did not return to boarding school after an initial period of mourning, biographers assume that a conflict with her father had initiated Katie's earlier banishment from home. Within a year of her father's death, Katie's younger sister, Jane, also died. Eliza O'Flaherty was now a young widow with two children to raise.

Instead of being raised in the midst of a nineteenth-century patriarchal home, Katie was raised by women—her mother, grandmother, and great-grandmother. Her mother's sisters also lived in this household of women. The influence of her Irish father disappeared, and Katie's personality was formed, in large part, under the authority of Creole women, in a household where many of the inhabitants spoke French instead of English. In addition to her female relatives, the household also contained a slave woman and her two young daughters, so Katie's older brother, Tom, was virtually the only male in the household. Little is known of Kate's half-brother George's whereabouts during this period; he does not receive notice from Chopin's biographers until his capture during the Civil War. Emily Toth, a recent Chopin biographer, refers to Tom only as still being in the household. George was possibly at home, too, but he is not mentioned. Ten years older than Kate, he was 15 when their father died, so he may have been sent off to school.

Katie's education was guided by her great-grandmother, Victoire Charleville, who insisted that the child be educated in the style of a proper French-woman. This education included lessons in French and music, both of which young Katie mastered very well. When she was 7 years old, Katie was finally enrolled in a Catholic day school, the same school where she had been sent at age 5 by her father. In additional to the expected subjects—penmanship, history, literature, and science—Katie learned needle-point and sewing, lessons considered necessary for a young woman.

Katie remained at the Sacred Heart Academy for several years, even though the school was forced to close intermittently during the years of the Civil War. When Katie was 13, her great-grandmother died; one month later, her most beloved older half-brother, George, who had joined the Confederate Army, died of typhoid fever. Katie may have seen the Union

Army as a reasonable target for her grief and anger. Clearly, the O'Flaherty women were Confederate sympathizers, and when 13-year-old Katie tore down a Union flag and refused to return it, she was arrested. The intervention of a Union-supporting neighbor facilitated Katie's release from jail, but other threats from Union soldiers followed, and eventually the family home was occupied by Union soldiers, who found only women with no means of defense. Tom had been sent away to school, and Katie, as a young teenager, was the only child remaining at home. Whenever possible, she retreated from the soldiers by taking refuge in books. Years later, Kate Chopin's experiences during the Civil War provided the material for a number of her short stories, many of which focused on women's lives during the war.

Marriage

Kate graduated from high school at age 17 from the Sacred Heart Academy. At 18, Kate made her debut into St. Louis society. She was described as beautiful but also clever and honest—traits at odds with the custom of the day insisting that women be demur and quiet. Kate played the piano and read books, and she prepared to find a husband, which was the goal of any young debutante. At some point during this time, Kate met Oscar Chopin. Her mother had earlier taken her to New Orleans, but whether Kate met Oscar in New Orleans is not known. Oscar, who was almost eight years older than Kate, was in St. Louis to learn the banking business, and meanwhile, he began courting Kate. On June 8, 1870, Kate married Oscar Chopin, a man who indicated in every way that he was prepared to love Kate for her intelligence. He was also prepared to allow her more freedom than a young wife, at that time, typically received.

After the wedding, the newlyweds honeymooned in Europe for three months and then returned to the United States. They made their home in New Orleans, where Oscar worked as a cotton factor, someone who loaned money to planters and sold their cotton. Kate was already pregnant when the couple returned from their honeymoon. Like Adèle Ratignolle in *The*

Awakening, Kate spent much of her marriage pregnant. The Chopin's first child, a boy, Jean, was born in May, 1871. Within 5 years, Kate gave birth to three more boys: Oscar in 1873, George in 1874, and Frederick in 1876. When she gave birth to Frederick in 1876, Kate was not yet 25 years old.

Another son, Felix, was born in 1878, and in 1879, Kate finally gave birth to a girl, Marie. Kate's family was now complete. All Chopin's children survived, escaping the infectious diseases that threatened all children of the period. However, Kate, who had been one of five children, was the only surviving child of Thomas and Eliza O'Flaherty: Her remaining sibling—her older brother, Tom, was killed in an accident in 1874.

When Kate was pregnant with her daughter in 1879, the Chopins moved to Cloutierville, Louisiana.

Kate Chopin with her first four sons.
Missouri Historical Society, St. Louis

The move was necessitated by Oscar's financial problems: The family could no longer afford to live in New Orleans. In Cloutierville, Oscar opened a general store, and the family lived in a simpler manner than they had in New Orleans. Kate, however, was considered a bit scandalous by small town standards. She lifted her skirts a bit too high and revealed her ankles, and she wore fancy clothes from New Orleans and smoked Cuban cigarettes. In spite of Kate's eccentricities, or perhaps because of them, Oscar was popular and well liked. Unfortunately, three years later, in 1882, Kate's husband died after contracting swamp fever (probably malaria). At 31, Kate was a widow with six small children, the oldest not yet 11.

Career

Oscar's death left Kate Chopin without an income and in serious debt. She tried to run Oscar's many business

Clouterville house; now the Bayou Folk Museum.
Bayou Folk Museum

interests, but eventually, had to auction much of the property to settle the estate's debts. However, within two years, Kate had paid her husband's debts and was managing to support and raise her children without assistance—an unusual accomplishment for a woman in late nineteenth-century Louisiana. In 1883, Kate left Cloutierville and moved back into her mother's home in St. Louis. Within a year, Kate's mother was dead, and Kate moved into her own home.

In 1888, Kate Chopin published a short story, "Lilia. Polka for Piano," in a local newspaper. The following year, Chopin published her first real literary work, a poem titled "If It Might Be," in a journal called *America*. The same year, Chopin also wrote the short stories "Wiser than a God" and "A Point at Issue!" Both of these stories deal with women trying to redefine their roles in society and within marriage. She also began a novel, and she was taking notes for

other stories. Chopin was regularly setting aside time to write, treating her writing as a career. She kept a careful record of her writing and her publishing successes, as well as the money she was paid for each piece. She also became acquainted with editors.

There was a market for stories about the *New Woman*: a single, professional woman who had created a life separate from the traditional role of wife and mother. Chopin had developed many friendships with such women since her return to St. Louis, so she had ready source material for her stories. The New Woman was a hot topic not only among these women but also among editors. Thus, Chopin found an easy target audience. Biographer Emily Toth suggests that the New Woman was a melding of real women and the media. The New Woman was strong and independent and not defined by marriage or a husband's expectations. Many of these women chose not to marry and instead shared their lives and homes with other single women. Chopin tried to strike a balance in her writings on the New Woman. She was ever aware that men controlled publishing. She tried to make her characters strong enough to appeal to the New Woman market, but at the same time, not strong enough to offend the male publishers. It was a delicate balance to achieve.

Early writings

Chopin's first novel, *At Fault*, was published in 1890 at her own expense after she failed to find a publisher who would accept it. The local reviews were generally kind, and they brought Chopin some of the literary attention she needed. The national reviews, however, were not as friendly; some of them attacked the novel's realism and language. Although Chopin failed to sell sufficient copies of her first novel to make a profit, she achieved what she had set out to do: She got noticed. Chopin continued to write. The short story "For Marse Chouchoute" was published in *Youth's Companion* in 1891, and "Desiree's Baby," another short story, was published in *Vogue* in 1893. After a collection of Chopin's short stories titled *Bayou Folk* was published in 1894 by Houghton Mifflin Company, Chopin finally became a literary success.

Kate Chopin in 1893.
Missouri Historical Society, St. Louis

Chopin based her stories on the locations and on the people she knew best. The locales for her stories are St. Louis, New Orleans, and Cloutierville—all towns in which she had lived—and the characters (and their situations) are the inhabitants of these towns. She characterized her aunt's marriages, her mother's death, her friends, her friends' husbands, and her husband's business acquaintances—essentially, she portrayed anyone or any event she found interesting. For instance, when Kate and Oscar lived in New Orleans and summered in Grande Isle, she used the experience as part of the

setting for *The Awakening*. Chopin paid attention to the people and to the events that went on around her, and the details found their way into her work. The reviews of *Bayou Folk* often referred to her stories, and the people in them, as "quaint." Because she was writing about the Creole population, which was considered exotic, most reviewers did not see that Chopin was saying some important things about marriage, battered wives, and abusive husbands. Few of the northern reviews noticed or understood her criticism of men: The traditions and morals of Creole culture were foreign to many areas of the United States. Reviewers were not able to clearly understand Chopin's criticism of men until *The Awakening* was published in 1899.

Chopin continued to write short stories for publication in magazines. Some of these stories include "Story of an Hour" (*Vogue*, 1894) and "Tante Cat'rinette" (*Atlantic*, 1894). These stories focused on women rather than on women and men. Later in 1894, Chopin's essay, "Western Association of Writers," was published in *Critic*. Also in 1894, the *Writer* featured Chopin's first national profile. Chopin was clearly becoming a professionally disciplined writer. However, not everything was going well, and her successes were balanced by disappointments and tragedies. In 1895, publishers rejected Chopin's translations of Guy de Maupassant's works, and in 1897, her grandmother's death coincided with the publication of *A Night in Acadie*, a collection of Chopin's short stories. But Chopin wanted to write a novel; in 1897, she began writing *The Awakening*.

Reaction to the novel

As the nineteenth century neared its close, Kate Chopin had enjoyed moderate success as a writer, and she was even considered somewhat trendy in publishing circles. But she wanted to write something different. She wanted to reach beyond the provincial topics that most women writers were allowed to use in their work, so she signed with a new publisher, Way & Williams, who gave Chopin's *The Awakening* a title suggestive of sexuality. The title was not lost on the public or on the watch guards of the nation's morality—book critics. As a result of the novel's publication in 1899, Chopin went from having a little regional notoriety to being a media sensation. In general, women liked the novel, but men, who were the gatekeepers of public morality, were deeply offended. Chopin's story of a woman who leaves her husband and children, who sets up her own household, and who has an affair, was too suggestive and frightening for many men to contemplate. No proper or conventional woman chose to leave her children, and men did not want to consider the possibility. The critics were savage. They argued that the book's heroine, Edna, was a selfish and wicked woman with too much time on her hands and that she was a woman more boring than bored.

Chopin's friends rallied around her and sent letters of encouragement, but the book's banning by libraries distressed Chopin, who worried that the book would have no lasting success. The bad reviews continued, and eventually, Chopin issued a response, but nothing seemed to help. Later the same year, her publisher cancelled the contract to publish her next book. The reasons for the cancellation are unknown, and Chopin apparently destroyed the letter. However, from the controversy surrounding *The Awakening*'s publication (and which continued unabated for most of the next year), Chopin's publisher may have simply wanted to distance himself from the controversial author.

Later years

With the controversy surrounding publication of *The Awakening*, Kate Chopin's literary career was essentially over. She continued to write, though not as prolifically as before, and she sold some short pieces, but only a few of her stories were published. Chopin's writing career lasted just over 10 years. With so much controversy surrounding her work, Chopin's health suffered, perhaps from depression. In 1903, her daughter-in-law died in childbirth, and so did the child she was carrying. Chopin's son, Jean, suffered a breakdown and returned to his mother's house to live.

In 1904, Chopin returned from a day at the World's Fair, which was held that year in St. Louis, with a severe headache. A few days later, she died at the age of 53. Chopin's obituaries praised her work as a writer, but barely mentioned *The Awakening*, except to refer to the novel as not her best work.

Chopin's novel virtually disappeared after her death, and it was not rediscovered by the public until a new edition of her work was published in 1969, 65 years after her death. Now, thanks in large part to

Kate Chopin in 1899.
Missouri Historical Society, St. Louis

women's studies programs, Chopin is undergoing a renaissance in the academic world, and her work, especially *The Awakening*, has found an important place in the literary canon. She would no doubt be pleased that her book finally has the lasting effect she always hoped that it would have.

INTRODUCTION TO *THE AWAKENING*

When *The Awakening* was published in 1899, it was condemned by critics and much of the public. The reviews focused on one central issue: the suggestion that a married woman could or should engage in a sexual affair with a man who was not her husband. That she would willingly leave her husband and children for that man was even more frightening. It was even thought shocking that a woman should demonstrate a sexual desire for a man other than her husband—or for that matter, express a sexual desire for any man. As an American woman writer, Chopin's use of such sexual frankness was especially condemned, although a few male writers had been writing about sexuality with much less notice than Chopin did. Ultimately *The Awakening* was even banned in libraries. The resulting furor, in which her novel was labeled as scandalous, virtually ended Kate Chopin's literary career.

None of Chopin's earlier works achieved the success and notoriety of *The Awakening*. She had published many short stories and collections of stories, some of which achieved a certain critical success, but these works had not received the notice that greeted Chopin's 1899 novel. Chopin's only other novel, *At Fault*, had not been as successful as her short stories, and so prior to the publication of *The Awakening*, Chopin was known primarily as a regional writer who was admired for some of her work, but not well-known. Her obscurity changed with *The Awakening*.

The Awakening is the story of Edna Pontellier, a young mother in her late twenties who, over a period of several months, awakens to her own sexuality. The

story opens in the midst of a summer holiday on Grand Isle. Edna is an emotionally and sexually repressed outsider, with little understanding of the Creole society into which she has married. A summer flirtation with Robert Lebrun leads Edna to realize the possibilities of a life more fulfilling than her existence as a wife and mother. A foil to Edna, Madame Ratignolle (Adèle) is a close friend of Edna's. Adèle represents the ideal New Orleans mother, a model of perfect motherhood whose Madonna-like qualities Edna has no interest in emulating.

Madame Ratignolle has been married for seven

Madame Ratignolle.

years and has three children; she is expecting another child. Like Chopin, Adèle has spent almost her entire married life pregnant. And unlike Edna, she is happy with being pregnant and devoted to her children and husband.

Many feminist scholars interpret *The Awakening* as evidence of Chopin's desire for women's rights, but no evidence supports this assertion. Chopin was married to a man she deeply loved, and she enjoyed liberties that most women of the time did not. However, Chopin was interested in women's personal freedom, and the novel can be regarded as an argument for a woman's self-awareness and independence. For example, Madame Ratignolle is as happy in her marriage as Edna is dissatisfied in hers, but Edna is unable to see that she is simply different from Madame Ratignolle. Nor can Edna's husband Léonce comprehend this difference. Even Doctor Mandelet sees Edna's unhappiness as a manifestation of disease rather than a manifestation of need. Consequently, Edna can only see herself as unfit for her world. Indeed, the conflict created by trying to fit into a neatly molded existence as Léonce Pontellier's wife leads Edna on a journey toward self-destruction.

In many ways, Edna is a throwback to an earlier literary period, yet she does not fit neatly and simply into the late-nineteenth-century literary period, either. She is a romantic, derived from a literary movement that ended in the mid–nineteenth century, but she is trapped in the naturalistic influences of late-nineteenth-century literature. Nor is she a bridge between the two periods; she comes too long after the end of the former and too near the end of the latter.

Romanticism is a literary movement that began in the late eighteenth century and lasted until the middle of the nineteenth century. The Romantics sought to free the artist and the individual from the constraints and rules that governed literature and society; a stronger emphasis was placed on the importance of imagination and on individualism. Romanticism serves as a vivid contrast to *naturalism*, which emphasizes nature and society rather than the individual. According to the tenets of naturalism, humans are little more than animals, vulnerable to the influences of nature, so that actions are largely innate or the influences of environment outweigh personal choice. Edna's desire for individual rebellion attempts to recapture the ideals of Romanticism, but her existence in the late nineteenth century makes her susceptible to a movement arguing that the individual has no choice.

Chopin fits into a tradition of contemporary women writers that begins with Jane Austen and Mary Shelley and continues with Charlotte Bronté, George Eliot, and George Sand. The nineteenth century was a period of growth for women writers, and Chopin fits well into this tradition. But her influences are not limited to the canon of women writers. *The Awakening* explores many of the same issues that Henrik Ibsen explores in *The Doll's House* (1879); Nora's willingness to leave her husband and children are strangely similar to Edna's abandonment of her family. Moreover, Edna is often compared to Gustave Flaubert's *Madame Bovary* (1857) in her self-destructiveness and to Theodore Dreiser's *Sister Carrie* (1818) in her wanton sexuality.

The late nineteenth century saw the emergence of New Women writers who spoke for what was then labeled the *New Woman*. The readers of their books were women who were demanding access to higher education, career opportunities, and political and social freedom. Women wanted access to the literary and art worlds, which had been previously dominated by men. Instead of being the objects of art and literature, women wanted to be the creators, and they wanted their creations to depict their concerns. Widowed and unmarried women began living on their own—not with their families. These women were interested in a life that did not center on husbands and children. Although Chopin had been happily married prior to being widowed, and even though she was happily a mother, she saw herself as one of these New Women. This movement was not really about feminism; it was about personal freedom. Chopin was not articulating equality in salary or in the workplace. She was interested in more basic choices, such as whether a woman must marry, whether she could choose not to be a mother, or whether she could choose to support herself. Chopin's arguments were about basic personal rights, not a political agenda, so the term *feminism*, which is often applied to *The Awakening*, does not accurately reflect Chopin's intent.

The Awakening embodies many of the themes that interested the New Women—women's creativity, marriage, motherhood, and a woman's place in society. Many of Chopin's short stories deal with similar themes, and by setting them in the South and within the Creole culture, Chopin had previously deflected any serious criticism of these topics. For *The Awakening*, Chopin adopted a familiar setting and familiar themes, so she should have been safe from attack; after all, her strategy had worked many times in the past. New Orleans offered a location that seemed to suggest a world separate from most of America, and Chopin must have expected a similar response from critics who had largely ignored the potential controversy of her work. Obviously, she was completely unprepared for the reception that greeted the book. The Creole culture in New Orleans offers a set of traditions, customs, and morals that are unique to the place and time. Chopin uses this culture to create a conflict between Edna's Kentucky Presbyterian upbringing and the Catholic Creole society into which she marries. In the novel, the Creole society is warm and easygoing, but women's roles are rigidly defined within the New Orleans social construct. In the Creole tradition, married women can engage in frank sexual discussions, but every woman's actions are as rigidly controlled as they are in any other area of the country. Edna doesn't understand these rules. She equates openness in language with openness in lifestyle, and she does not comprehend the extent of her misunderstanding until it is too late.

An important element in the novel is Edna's attempt to escape the constraints and obligations of the New Orleans rigidly defined social milieu. Every move she makes is one prescribed by an unwritten tenet of society. Edna is expected to fulfill certain social obligations—for example, managing her household or being home on Tuesdays to welcome the wives of her husband's business associates. According to society, Edna's interests should reflect her husband's needs, and she should display an almost slavish devotion to her children. None of these social expectations mirror Edna's own needs, and as a result, she rebels.

Edna never fully understands the ramifications of her actions. In Kentucky, there was no ambiguity in behavior. The rules were clearer, and so were the expectations for a young woman. Edna's father and older sister always made clear what they expected of the middle daughter. But in New Orleans society, social expectations sometimes contradict with the behavior that Edna misunderstands. When she abandons her Tuesdays at home, she sees only her own desire to rebel against a meaningless and arbitrary social system; but her husband envisions a social affront that will cost him business. And later, after Edna abandons all sense of propriety to move from her husband's home into an unchaperoned house, where she entertains a man whose reputation labels him a cad, she cannot see that her actions should reflect on anyone but herself. Of course, Edna is wrong. Because she is a mother and a wife, her actions do have consequences for others besides herself. In fact, Edna's relationships with other men reveal how little she understands about her function in New Orleans society.

Edna becomes infatuated with Robert Lebrun, a charming young man who, for many years, has been idling the summers away by flirting with women. Robert epitomizes a flirt, and he is unwilling to fulfill his promises. In contrast, Alcée Arobin is far more than a flirt—he's an experienced seducer of women. Edna's willingness to accept Alcée as a lover, even after she knows that Robert is returning, convinces Edna that she is destined for a life of promiscuity. When she gives Robert the same opportunities that she provided to Alcée, Robert runs away. He is honorable, and perhaps he escapes to protect Edna (and himself). But having grown up in Creole society, he is also accustomed to merely talking about love. Edna demands much more of him. Alcée, on the other hand, bears no honor, because he is a cad. He is more than willing to move beyond talk and embrace action. However, Alcée's availability frightens Edna, who has a history of attachments to unavailable men. In the past, she had always been safe from real involvement; the men to whom she was attracted never knew of her infatuation. Léonce is unable to possess Edna because he exists in a practical world of commerce and social obligation—a world that holds no meaning for Edna.

Edna lives in a fairytale world. She cares little about reality, because she does not have any substantial responsibilities. Her husband relieves her of all responsibility, and he even makes excuses when she fails to meet his few expectations. The children have a nurse and a paternal grandmother to care for them, so Edna has no maternal demands placed upon her. Léonce makes no demands of Edna, and in fact, goes out of his way to let her do whatever she wants, as long as it does not conflict with his own desires or expectations. He takes control of all situations. Because no demands are placed on her, Edna doesn't have to demand anything of herself. All this freedom is illusionary, but the world that Edna creates within her mind is just as misleading. Edna's imagination leads her to conclude that the only acceptable reality is the loss of reality. She has no other choice.

Naturalism

Appearing at the end of the nineteenth century, *The Awakening* embodies an important literary movement—naturalism. *Naturalism* suggests a biological and socioeconomic determinism that predicts the choices that each individual makes about his or her life. The idea of choices is illusionary, because according to naturalism, each human is little more than an animal responding to innate desires. Naturalism is a cause-and-effect that determines the outcome of life—that is, nature causes humans to respond to certain events in a preordained manner that nature has already determined. Naturalism is characterized by an emphasis on the indifference of nature for human plans and by internal and external forces that shape events. For example, Edna thinks that she can make choices about her life and that these choices should have no impact on anyone else. But in truth, Edna is a mother, and nature determines that women will become mothers. Consequently, they must also become wives, and as wives, they can no longer choose. Consequently, Edna is trapped by nature into a life that is not of her choosing. She cannot escape, because society—the environmental aspect of naturalism—also prescribes certain behaviors. According to naturalism, humans bear little or no responsibility for events.

Whereas American naturalism focuses more on environmental influences, European naturalism emphasizes hereditary forces. Chopin was certainly influenced by the naturalism of George Eliot, for whom this principle was important. In *The Awakening*, European naturalism is clearly embodied in Edna, who, like her father, enjoys the horse races and likes to drink—characteristics that are likely hereditary. Biology, another element of naturalism, determines her femaleness, and it also limits her possibilities. The biological aspects of womanhood are an important theme in *The Awakening*; Edna faces biological as well as social limitations, and she fails to recognize them. Edna cannot enjoy the same freedoms as Alcée Arobin, who can seduce women and be free with his sexuality. Edna longs for personal freedom, but she is bound by social rules that condemn such behavior and cannot challenge the social order that rules her actions. Her children will suffer for her actions, and her awareness of this leads to her suicide.

Naturalism also limits Edna's possibilities. Instead of determining her own existence, naturalism—as fate—determines her life: Edna's interest in the horse races is derived from her father. However, her interest leads her to an involvement with Arobin and an affair in which her own sexual nature is revealed. This affair finally leads Edna to understand that her own sexuality cannot be suppressed, and as a result, she envisions a future where her sons will suffer for her indiscretions. On the surface, Edna's decision to accompany her father to the horse races appears as an innocent outing, but she makes the first movement in a larger plan—one that nature has always intended but that Edna has resisted—in which Edna succumbs to her own nature.

Naturalism does not concern human responsibility. The individual's nature is everything, and Edna's nature determines her destiny and, ultimately, the choices she makes. With naturalism, science determines the individual's life. The third-person narration of *The Awakening* suggests a scientist who observes Edna's life and reports her actions. However, the report is told from Edna's point of view and through the narrowness of her understanding. This point of view helps to create a compelling story of her destruction. Chopin's use of third-person narration, which typically offers an omniscient view of events, is limited by the narrowness of Edna's perspective. Instead of knowing everything, as readers may expect from a third-person narration, Chopin creates tension and mystery by limiting the readers' perspective to Edna's own understanding. Because Edna does not understand the unfolding events, the reader may find them difficult to understand as well. Edna's limitations, then, become the readers' limitations. Chopin's manipulation of point of view forces the reader into a closer reading of the text in the hopes of understanding Edna's choices.

Symbolism

Chopin makes effective use of symbolism as a way to illustrate Edna's life. The caged parrot that opens the book is a metaphor for Edna's situation.

A parrot is a wild bird that has been captured and domesticated. Like the parrot, Edna has been captured by Léonce and turned into property. Edna is kept caged and close at hand; she is useful as a means to entertain Léonce's friends and to echo Léonce's values and worth in the community. Bird imagery is also evident throughout the novel, most obviously in a meeting with Mademoiselle Reisz in which she asks Edna if her wings are strong enough to soar above the prejudices of society. And in the final pages of the novel, the bird provides a symbol of

Caged parrot.

Edna's own world in which a wounded young woman must struggle for her very existence.

The sea is also an important symbol that begins and ends the novel. By learning how to swim, Edna becomes more aware of her body and awakens to her own individuality. However, her rigid upbringing has taught her to think harshly about women who act on their impulses. Her infatuation with Robert is merely physical, but she confuses it with love, and when she succumbs to Arobin, she thinks that she is promiscuous. Thus, when she enters the sea for the final time, she disposes of her clothing, the worn-out social conventions of her society. She is reborn by the awareness of her nude body. The sea to which she returns represents the womb, the symbol of eternal life.

Edna awakens to her sexuality, to herself and her life, to her social life, and to her marriage. She awakens to the need to be in control of her life. Throughout the novel, Edna is clearly a mother by accident and not by choice. During her awakening, she longs for a choice. Edna leads a duel life; outwardly (at least initially) she appears to conform, but inwardly, she questions her life. In the end, she is unable to survive the only existence left to her. Like the bird with a broken wing that spirals toward the depths of the water, Edna spirals into an end that she cannot avoid.

Societal Influences

Another theme of *The Awakening* is the effect that a dominating, patriarchal society can have upon a woman. Edna attempts to reject this patriarchal society, but she does not have the freedom to do so. Edna cannot really leave Léonce, except emotionally. Edna does attempt to break free. First she abandons her duties by neglecting the management of their home and ignoring her social obligations. She also abandons her role as mother by allowing her sons an extended visit with their grandmother. Then she abandons her home by choosing a small house and moving her belongings out of her husband's home. But all these choices are only temporary. Edna understands that when her husband returns to town, she will be forced to return to the role that society has chosen for her: the role of wife and mother. In the end, Edna cannot escape society and her marriage; all she can do is escape her life. Patriarchy shapes her life: Léonce governs her economic life as well as her social life.

The only single woman in the novel, Mademoiselle Reisz, is successful as a single woman, but she is unpopular and unwelcome in spite of her talent. Her presence establishes that life as a single woman, even as a successful artist, still affords certain limitations. Without the social trappings of marriage to tame her, Mademoiselle Reisz is bitter and rude. A patriarchal society has no real place for a single career woman. Her success offers a threat to the tenet of patriarchy in which a woman's position is best met by marriage and motherhood. If Mademoiselle Reisz was universally admired (and, as a result, if she was happy and content with her choices), she could offer an acceptable model for other women. But her very nature, which is defined by her bitterness and rudeness toward others, makes her choices appear unappetizing to other women. She pays a huge price for her freedom: social acceptance and happiness.

Edna's world is a patriarchal world in which men control women through economic and social forces. Men provide the economic stability in women's lives, and they use this economic force to govern women's choices. Because Edna is able to earn a little bit of money though her art, which is supplemented by a small income from her mother's estate, Edna feels that she can leave her husband's house and move into a place that will be hers alone. But patriarchy is about much more than economics. Patriarchy is also about establishing rules that women must obey. Edna's husband will not accept her choice to leave their home, nor will her Catholic husband be willing to divorce her. If she refuses to return, Edna will become a social outcast with no friends and will have an existence of isolation and loneliness.

The social forces that govern Edna establish expectations based on social standing. For example, Madame Ratignolle is not forced to take part in the "at home" on Tuesday afternoons, when ladies of a certain social stature call on women of a similar standing. Her husband owns a store, and they live above the store. But in spite of her lower social standing, when Edna flaunts society and entertains Arobin alone in her new house, Madame Ratignolle cannot continue to visit her, because to do so would tarnish her own reputation. Despite certain economic differences, the rules that govern sexual impropriety are applicable for all social levels.

The events of Edna's awakening take place during the gestational period of Madame Ratignolle's pregnancy. She is only recently pregnant when the novel begins and delivers a child when the book ends. Appropriately, motherhood defines the novel's perimeters. For Edna, motherhood (and all that it represents) is a prison. Edna, who desires so much more of life, can never enjoy true freedom. In the end, the only freedom is in death—an end that Edna appears to embrace willingly.

Critical Issues

Scholars still argue about *The Awakening*, much as critics did upon its release. Is Edna justified in abandoning her responsibilities, in having what is often described as a selfish affair with another man? Is she simply self-indulgent, or a narcissist who thinks only of herself? Or is she a woman in pain, seeking to escape an intolerable existence as the property of a wealthy man who is incapable of appreciating her talents and her worth? Is she trapped between biology and society as a wife and mother, but never a woman—an individual? Chopin does not provide any easy answers. The reader is never permitted to forget Edna's children, whom she abandons and who will certainly not be better off without their mother. But Edna's end is not torturous or even very painful—or at least the reader is not expected to think so. Instead, Edna just drifts away, much as she did in life, with scarcely any final thoughts.

Throughout the novel, she has acted impetuously, often without thought and based largely on what feels right at the moment. Readers may argue that Edna is self-destructive because her attempts to assert her individuality merely isolate her from friends, husband, and children. Instead of arguing for one interpretation or the other, consider what Edna's behavior reveals about the reader. Readers bring to the text their own social, cultural, and educational position, and as a result, they perhaps find that Chopin's novel permits an opportunity to study their own values and desires. If readers sympathize with Edna and with her suicide, they can condemn the society that pushes her toward her actions. Chopin, however, never suggests that this society should be condemned. She only asks that the reader consider the complexities that color Edna's existence.

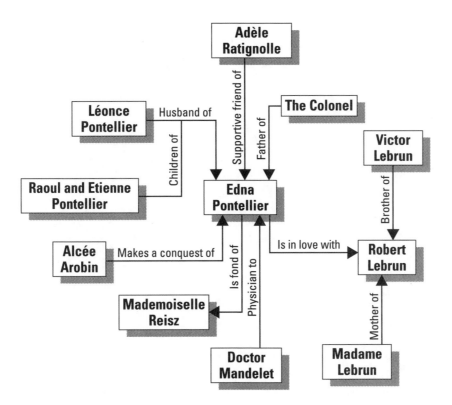

CHARACTERS IN THE NOVEL

CLIFFSCOMPLETE

KATE CHOPIN'S

THE

AWAKENING

Chapters 1–4

Edna and Léonce Pontellier and Robert Lebrun are vacationing on Grand Isle. Edna and Robert spend their time casually flirting and swimming, whereas Léonce spends his time reading and playing billiards. After returning home from playing billiards, Léonce reproaches Edna for her neglect of their children and immediately goes to sleep. In the morning, he leaves the island for the workweek in the city. With Léonce gone for the week, Edna is left to spend her days with Madame Ratignolle, another vacationer, who offers Edna friendship. The two women spend many of their days together, with Robert also present.

CHAPTER I

A green and yellow parrot, which hung in a cage outside the door, kept repeating over and over:

"Allez vous-en! **Allez vous-en! Sapristi**! That's all right!"

He could speak a little Spanish, and also a language which nobody understood, unless it was the mocking-bird that hung on the other side of the door, whistling his fluty notes out upon the breeze with maddening persistence.

Mr. Pontellier, unable to read his newspaper with any degree of comfort, arose with an expression and an exclamation of disgust.

He walked down the gallery and across the narrow "bridges" which connected the Lebrun cottages one with the other. He had been seated before the door of the main house. The parrot and the mockingbird were the property of Madame Lebrun, and they had the right to make all the noise they wished. Mr. Pontellier had the privilege of quitting their society when they ceased to be entertaining.

He stopped before the door of his own cottage, which was the fourth one from the main building and next to the last. Seating himself in a wicker rocker which was there, he once more applied himself to the task of reading the newspaper. The day was Sunday; the paper was a day old. The Sunday papers had not yet reached **Grand Isle**. He was already acquainted with the market reports, and he glanced restlessly over the editorials and bits of news which he had not had time to read before quitting New Orleans the day before.

Mr. Pontellier wore eye-glasses. He was a man of forty, of medium height and rather slender build; he stooped a little. His hair was brown and straight, parted on one side. His beard was neatly and closely trimmed.

Notes

(Here and in the following sections, difficult words and foreign phrases are explained.)

Allez vous-en! Sapristi!: "Get out! Damn it!"

Grand Isle: an island off the Louisiana coast, about fifty miles south of New Orleans.

Once in a while he withdrew his glance from the newspaper and looked about him. There was more noise than ever over at the house. The main building was called "the house," to distinguish it from the cottages. The chattering and whistling birds were still at it. Two young girls, the Farival twins, were playing a duet from "**Zampa**" upon the piano. Madame Lebrun was bustling in and out, giving orders in a high key to a yard-boy whenever she got inside the house, and directions in an equally high voice to a dining-room servant whenever she got outside. She was a fresh, pretty woman, clad always in white with elbow sleeves. Her starched skirts crinkled as she came and went. Farther down, before one of the cottages, a lady in black was walking demurely up and down, **telling her beads**. A good many persons of the **pension** had gone over to the **Chênière Caminada** in Beaudelet's **lugger** to hear mass. Some young people were out under the water-oaks playing croquet. Mr. Pontellier's two children were there—sturdy little fellows of four and five. A **quadroon** nurse followed them about with a faraway, meditative air.

Mr. Pontellier finally lit a cigar and began to smoke, letting the paper drag idly from his hand. He fixed his gaze upon a white **sunshade** that was advancing at snail's pace from the beach. He could see it plainly between the gaunt trunks of the water-oaks and across the stretch of yellow **camomile**. The gulf looked far away, melting hazily into the blue of the horizon. The sunshade continued to approach slowly. Beneath its pink-lined shelter were his wife, Mrs. Pontellier, and young Robert Lebrun. When they reached the cottage, the two seated themselves with some appearance of fatigue upon the upper step of the porch, facing each other, each leaning against a supporting post.

"What folly! to bathe at such an hour in such heat!" exclaimed Mr. Pontellier. He himself had taken a plunge at daylight. That was why the morning seemed long to him.

"You are burnt beyond recognition," he added, looking at his wife as one looks at a valuable piece of personal property which has suffered some damage. She held up her hands, strong, shapely hands, and surveyed them critically, drawing up her **lawn sleeves** above the wrists. Looking at them reminded her of her rings, which she had given to her husband before leaving for the beach. She silently reached out to him, and he, understanding, took the rings from his vest pocket and dropped them into her open palm. She slipped them upon her fingers; then clasping her knees, she

Zampa: written by Ferdinand Herold (1971-1833), an opera in which a character drowns at sea.

telling her beads: praying on her rosary.

pension: a boarding house; a term used in France and other continental countries.

Chênière Caminada: a small island lying between Grand Isle and the Louisiana coast.

lugger: a small vessel equipped with at least one lugsail, which is a four-sided sail with the upper edge supported by a yard that is fastened obliquely to the mast.

quadroon: a person who has one black grandparent; child of a mulatto and a white.

sunshade: a parasol used for protection against sun rays.

camomile: any plant of two genera (*Anthemis* and *Matricaria*) of the composite family, with strong-smelling foliage, especially a plant (*A. nobilis*) whose dried, daisylike flower heads are used as a medicine and in making tea.

lawn sleeves: sleeves made from lawn (a fine, sheer cloth of linen or cotton).

looked across at Robert and began to laugh. The rings sparkled upon her fingers. He sent back an answering smile.

"What is it?" asked Pontellier, looking lazily and amused from one to the other. It was some utter nonsense; some adventure out there in the water, and they both tried to relate it at once. It did not seem half so amusing when told. They realized this, and so did Mr. Pontellier. He yawned and stretched himself. Then he got up, saying he had half a mind to go over to Klein's hotel and play a game of billiards.

"Come go along, Lebrun," he proposed to Robert. But Robert admitted quite frankly that he preferred to stay where he was and talk to Mrs. Pontellier.

"Well, send him about his business when he bores you, Edna," instructed her husband as he prepared to leave.

"Here, take the umbrella," she exclaimed, holding it out to him. He accepted the sunshade, and lifting it over his head descended the steps and walked away.

"Coming back to dinner?" his wife called after him. He halted a moment and shrugged his shoulders. He felt in his vest pocket; there was a ten-dollar bill there. He did not know; perhaps he would return for the early dinner and perhaps he would not. It all depended upon the company which he found over at Klein's and the size of "the game." He did not say this, but she understood it, and laughed, nodding good-by to him.

Both children wanted to follow their father when they saw him starting out. He kissed them and promised to bring them back bonbons and peanuts.

CHAPTER II

Mrs. Pontellier's eyes were quick and bright; they were a yellowish brown, about the color of her hair. She had a way of turning them swiftly upon an object and holding them there as if lost in some inward maze of contemplation or thought.

Her eyebrows were a shade darker than her hair. They were thick and almost horizontal, emphasizing the depth of her eyes. She was rather handsome than beautiful. Her face was captivating by reason of a certain frankness of expression and a contradictory subtle play of features. Her manner was engaging.

Robert rolled a cigarette. He smoked cigarettes because he could not afford cigars, he said. He had a cigar in his pocket which Mr. Pontellier had presented him with, and he was saving it for his after-dinner smoke.

This seemed quite proper and natural on his part. In coloring he was not unlike his companion. A clean-shaved face made the resemblance more pronounced than it would otherwise have been. There rested no shadow of care upon his open **countenance**. His eyes gathered in and reflected the light and languor of the summer day.

Mrs. Pontellier reached over for a palm-leaf fan that lay on the porch and began to fan herself, while Robert sent between his lips light puffs from his cigarette. They chatted incessantly: about the things around them; their amusing adventure out in the water-it had again assumed its entertaining aspect; about the wind, the trees, the people who had gone to the **Chênière**; about the children playing croquet under the oaks, and the Farival twins, who were now performing the overture to "**The Poet and the Peasant**."

Robert talked a good deal about himself. He was very young, and did not know any better. Mrs. Pontellier talked a little about herself for the same reason. Each was interested in what the other said. Robert spoke of his intention to go to Mexico in the autumn, where fortune awaited him. He was always intending to go to Mexico, but some way never got there. Meanwhile he held on to his modest position in a mercantile house in New Orleans, where an equal familiarity with English, French and Spanish gave him no small value as a clerk and correspondent.

He was spending his summer vacation, as he always did, with his mother at Grand Isle. In former times, before Robert could remember, "the house" had been a summer luxury of the Lebruns. Now, flanked by its dozen or more cottages, which were always filled with exclusive visitors from the "**Quartier Français**," it enabled Madame Lebrun to maintain the easy and comfortable existence which appeared to be her birthright.

Mrs. Pontellier talked about her father's Mississippi plantation and her girlhood home in the old Kentucky bluegrass country. She was an American woman, with a small infusion of French which seemed to have been lost in dilution. She read a letter from her sister, who was away in the East, and who had engaged herself to be married. Robert was interested, and wanted to know what manner of girls the sisters were, what the father was like, and how long the mother had been dead.

countenance: look on a person's face that shows one's nature or feelings.

Chênière: here, a proper name referring to a business, probably a gentleman's club.

The Poet and the Peasant: an overture by Franz von Suppe (1819-1895), an Austrian conductor and composer of opera, operetta, and incidental music.

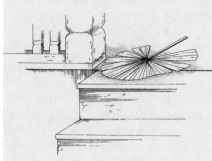

A Palm-leaf fan.

Quartier Français: French Quarter, also known as the Old Quarter; the oldest part of New Orleans and the area in which most New Orleans Creoles lived; an area whose population is predominately French rather than Creole.

When Mrs. Pontellier folded the letter it was time for her to dress for the early dinner.

"I see Léonce isn't coming back," she said, with a glance in the direction whence her husband had disappeared. Robert supposed he was not, as there were a good many New Orleans club men over at Klein's.

When Mrs. Pontellier left him to enter her room, the young man descended the steps and strolled over toward the croquet players, where, during the half-hour before dinner, he amused himself with the little Pontellier children, who were very fond of him.

CHAPTER III

It was eleven o'clock that night when Mr. Pontellier returned from Klein's hotel. He was in an excellent humor, in high spirits, and very talkative. His entrance awoke his wife, who was in bed and fast asleep when he came in. He talked to her while he undressed, telling her anecdotes and bits of news and gossip that he had gathered during the day. From his trousers pockets he took a fistful of crumpled bank notes and a good deal of silver coin, which he piled on the bureau indiscriminately with keys, knife, handkerchief, and whatever else happened to be in his pockets. She was overcome with sleep, and answered him with little half utterances.

He thought it very discouraging that his wife, who was the sole object of his existence, evinced so little interest in things which concerned him, and valued so little his conversation.

Mr. Pontellier had forgotten the bonbons and peanuts for the boys. Notwithstanding he loved them very much, and went into the adjoining room where they slept to take a look at them and make sure that they were resting comfortably. The result of his investigation was far from satisfactory. He turned and shifted the youngsters about in bed. One of them began to kick and talk about a basket full of crabs.

Mr. Pontellier returned to his wife with the information that Raoul had a high fever and needed looking after. Then he lit a cigar and went and sat near the open door to smoke it.

Mrs. Pontellier was quite sure Raoul had no fever. He had gone to bed perfectly well, she said, and nothing had ailed him all day. Mr. Pontellier was too well acquainted with fever symptoms to be mistaken. He assured her the child was **consuming** at that moment in the next room.

consuming: [now rare] wasting away; perishing.

He reproached his wife with her inattention, her habitual neglect of the children. If it was not a mother's place to look after children, whose on earth was it? He himself had his hands full with his brokerage business. He could not be in two places at once; making a living for his family on the street, and staying at home to see that no harm befell them. He talked in a monotonous, insistent way.

Mrs. Pontellier sprang out of bed and went into the next room. She soon came back and sat on the edge of the bed, leaning her head down on the pillow. She said nothing, and refused to answer her husband when he questioned her. When his cigar was smoked out he went to bed, and in half a minute he was fast asleep.

Mrs. Pontellier was by that time thoroughly awake. She began to cry a little, and wiped her eyes on the sleeve of her **peignoir**. Blowing out the candle, which her husband had left burning, she slipped her bare feet into a pair of satin **mules** at the foot of the bed and went out on the porch, where she sat down in the wicker chair and began to rock gently to and fro.

It was then past midnight. The cottages were all dark. A single faint light gleamed out from the hallway of the house. There was no sound abroad except the hooting of an old owl in the top of a water-oak, and the everlasting voice of the sea, that was not uplifted at that soft hour. It broke like a mournful lullaby upon the night.

The tears came so fast to Mrs. Pontellier's eyes that the damp sleeve of her peignoir no longer served to dry them. She was holding the back of her chair with one hand; her loose sleeve had slipped almost to the shoulder of her uplifted arm. Turning, she thrust her face, steaming and wet, into the bend of her arm, and she went on crying there, not caring any longer to dry her face, her eyes, her arms. She could not have told why she was crying. Such experiences as the foregoing were not uncommon in her married life. They seemed never before to have weighed much against the abundance of her husband's kindness and a uniform devotion which had come to be tacit and self-understood.

An indescribable oppression, which seemed to generate in some unfamiliar part of her consciousness, filled her whole being with a vague anguish. It was like a shadow, like a mist passing across her soul's summer day. It was strange and unfamiliar; it was a mood. She did not sit there inwardly upbraiding her husband, lamenting at Fate,

peignoir: a woman's loose, full dressing gown.

mules: lounging slippers that do not cover the heel.

which had directed her footsteps to the path which they had taken. She was just having a good cry all to herself. The mosquitoes made merry over her, biting her firm, round arms and nipping at her bare insteps.

The little stinging, buzzing imps succeeded in dispelling a mood which might have held her there in the darkness half a night longer.

The following morning Mr. Pontellier was up in good time to take the **rockaway** which was to convey him to the steamer at the wharf. He was returning to the city to his business, and they would not see him again at the Island till the coming Saturday. He had regained his composure, which seemed to have been somewhat impaired the night before. He was eager to be gone, as he looked forward to a lively week in **Carondelet Street**.

rockaway: a light horse-drawn carriage with four wheels, open sides, and a standing top.

Mr. Pontellier gave his wife half of the money which he had brought away from Klein's hotel the evening before. She liked money as well as most women, and, accepted it with no little satisfaction.

Carondelet Street: the center of the New Orleans financial district.

"It will buy a handsome wedding present for Sister Janet!" she exclaimed, smoothing out the bills as she counted them one by one.

"Oh! we'll treat Sister Janet better than that, my dear," he laughed, as he prepared to kiss her good-by.

The boys were tumbling about, clinging to his legs, imploring that numerous things be brought back to them. Mr. Pontellier was a great favorite, and ladies, men, children, even nurses, were always on hand to say good-by to him. His wife stood smiling and waving, the boys shouting, as he disappeared in the old rockaway down the sandy road.

A few days later a box arrived for Mrs. Pontellier from New Orleans. It was from her husband. It was filled with **friandises**, with luscious and toothsome bits—the finest of fruits, **patés**, a rare bottle or two, delicious syrups, and bonbons in abundance.

friandises: delicacies or sweetmeats, which are any sweet food or delicacy prepared with sugar or honey, as a cake, confection, preserve, etc.; specifically, a candy, candied fruit, etc.

patés: meat pies; meat pastes or spreads.

Mrs. Pontellier was always very generous with the contents of such a box; she was quite used to receiving them when away from home. The pates and fruit were brought to the dining-room; the bonbons were passed around. And the ladies, selecting with dainty and discriminating fingers and a little greedily, all declared that Mr. Pontellier was the best husband in the world. Mrs. Pontellier was forced to admit that she knew of none better.

CHAPTER IV

It would have been a difficult matter for Mr. Pontellier to define to his own satisfaction or any one else's wherein his wife failed in her duty toward their children. It was something which he felt rather than perceived, and he never voiced the feeling without subsequent regret and ample atonement.

If one of the little Pontellier boys took a tumble whilst at play, he was not apt to rush crying to his mother's arms for comfort; he would more likely pick himself up, wipe the water out of his eyes and the sand out of his mouth, and go on playing. Tots as they were, they pulled together and stood their ground in childish battles with doubled fists and uplifted voices, which usually prevailed against the other mother-tots. The quadroon nurse was looked upon as a huge encumbrance, only good to button up waists and panties and to brush and part hair; since it seemed to be a law of society that hair must be parted and brushed.

In short, Mrs. Pontellier was not a mother-woman. The mother-women seemed to prevail that summer at Grand Isle. It was easy to know them, fluttering about with extended, protecting wings when any harm, real or imaginary, threatened their precious brood. They were women who idolized their children, worshiped their husbands, and esteemed it a holy privilege to efface themselves as individuals and grow wings as ministering angels.

Many of them were delicious in the role; one of them was the embodiment of every womanly grace and charm. If her husband did not adore her, he was a brute, deserving of death by slow torture. Her name was Adèle Ratignolle. There are no words to describe her save the old ones that have served so often to picture the bygone heroine of romance and the fair lady of our dreams. There was nothing subtle or hidden about her charms; her beauty was all there, flaming and apparent: the spun-gold hair that comb nor confining pin could restrain; the blue eyes that were like nothing but sapphires; two lips that pouted, that were so red one could only think of cherries or some other delicious crimson fruit in looking at them. She was growing a little stout, but it did not seem to detract an iota from the grace of every step, pose, gesture. One would not have wanted her white neck a mite less full or her beautiful arms more slender. Never were hands more exquisite than hers, and it was a joy to look at them when she threaded her needle or adjusted her gold thimble to her taper middle finger as she sewed away on the little night-drawers or fashioned a bodice or a bib.

Madame Ratignolle was very fond of Mrs. Pontellier, and often she took her sewing and went over to sit with her in the afternoons. She was sitting there the afternoon of the day the box arrived from New Orleans. She had possession of the rocker, and she was busily engaged in sewing upon a diminutive pair of night-drawers.

She had brought the pattern of the drawers for Mrs. Pontellier to cut out—a marvel of construction, fashioned to enclose a baby's body so effectually that only two small eyes might look out from the garment, like an Eskimo's. They were designed for winter wear, when treacherous drafts came down chimneys and insidious currents of deadly cold found their way through key-holes.

Mrs. Pontellier's mind was quite at rest concerning the present material needs of her children, and she could not see the use of anticipating and making winter night garments the subject of her summer meditations. But she did not want to appear unamiable and uninterested, so she had brought forth newspapers, which she spread upon the floor of the gallery, and under Madame Ratignolle's directions she had cut a pattern of the impervious garment.

Robert was there, seated as he had been the Sunday before, and Mrs. Pontellier also occupied her former position on the upper step, leaning listlessly against the post. Beside her was a box of bonbons, which she held out at intervals to Madame Ratignolle.

That lady seemed at a loss to make a selection, but finally settled upon a stick of nougat, wondering if it were not too rich; whether it could possibly hurt her. Madame Ratignolle had been married seven years. About every two years she had a baby. At that time she had three babies, and was beginning to think of a fourth one. She was always talking about her "**condition**." Her "condition" was in no way apparent, and no one would have known a thing about it but for her persistence in making it the subject of conversation.

condition: here, the condition of being pregnant.

Robert started to reassure her, asserting that he had known a lady who had subsisted upon nougat during the entire— but seeing the color mount into Mrs. Pontellier's face he checked himself and changed the subject.

Mrs. Pontellier, though she had married a **Creole**, was not thoroughly at home in the society of Creoles; never before had she been thrown so intimately among them. There

Creole: a person descended from the original French settlers of Louisiana, especially of the New Orleans area.

were only Creoles that summer at Lebrun's. They all knew each other, and felt like one large family, among whom existed the most amicable relations. A characteristic which distinguished them and which impressed Mrs. Pontellier most forcibly was their entire absence of prudery. Their freedom of expression was at first incomprehensible to her, though she had no difficulty in reconciling it with a lofty chastity which in the Creole woman seems to be inborn and unmistakable.

Never would Edna Pontellier forget the shock with which she heard Madame Ratignolle relating to old Monsieur Farival the harrowing story of one of her **accouchements,** withholding no intimate detail. She was growing accustomed to like shocks, but she could not keep the mounting color back from her cheeks. Oftener than once her coming had interrupted the droll story with which Robert was entertaining some amused group of married women.

A book had gone the rounds of the **pension**. When it came her turn to read it, she did so with profound astonishment. She felt moved to read the book in secret and solitude, though none of the others had done so,—to hide it from view at the sound of approaching footsteps. It was openly criticised and freely discussed at table. Mrs. Pontellier gave over being astonished, and concluded that wonders would never cease.

accouchements: childbirth.

pension: in France and other continental countries, a boardinghouse

COMMENTARY

The Awakening is told from Edna's point of view, although Chopin occasionally shifts viewpoints to provide Léonce's thoughts. However, the narrative is always in the objective third person and is not a first-person account of the events or of the character's actions and thoughts. This style of narration allows the reader to observe and understand the characters rather than simply judge their behavior, as the more intimate first-person narration sometimes permits. In the first chapter, the reader observes Léonce watching his wife, but most often, the narration is from Edna's point of view. This novel is clearly her story—the story of a young woman's search for her own identity.

The story opens with a caged parrot screaming, "Allez vous-en! Allez vous-en! Sapristi!"—a phrase mixed with French and Spanish that means "Get out! Get out! Damn it!" The caged-bird metaphor establishes

an important theme of Chopin's novel: Edna is confined by a gilded cage that restricts her to the rules of society and to an existence that only appreciates her beauty. The bars of Edna's cage confine her to a life as a fancy ornament, little more than décor. Like the parrot, Edna is valued for her beauty, and when she defiantly speaks out, hardly anyone understands the words she speaks. The mocking bird, whose purpose is to sing and entertain, further emphasizes Edna's lack of opportunity.

A recurring motif in *The Awakening*, bird symbolism is represented by the caged existence of the parrot as well as by the birds that freely soar above the beach. In Victorian New Orleans society, women are generally marked by their physical attributes and by their abilities to entertain, but they possess little more freedom than the freedom accorded to the caged birds.

The first chapters of *The Awakening* serve as a means to introduce the novel's main characters. The reader first meets Léonce Pontellier, a man of little patience. Even the bird's calling irritates him and causes him to retreat to the silence of the Pontellier's cottage. He portrays a rather ordinary businessman, who, in this initial chapter, occupies himself with observing his wife's appearance after she returns from swimming.

Edna's husband, Léonce.

Whereas Edna returns happy and relaxed after her swimming lesson, Léonce focuses on propriety and, especially, on social position. His exclamation, "You are burnt beyond recognition," is quickly explained by Chopin as the response of a man who "looks at a valuable piece of personal property [that] has suffered some damage." The wives of successful New Orleans businessmen cannot be mistaken for servants, whose sun-burned faces and arms suggest domestic or garden work. Even on vacation, Edna cannot forget her responsibilities to her husband's social stature, and Léonce obviously never forgets.

The Pontelliers are comfortable in their relationship. When Edna extends her hand, Léonce knows to return her wedding rings, which she had earlier removed. In fact, Edna says little in this initial scene. Although Edna and Léonce can comfortably communicate without words, their lack of communication suggests an unhappy marriage in which the participants rarely speak. Their comfortable silence is merely an illusion of happiness. Léonce happily spends his evenings with friends, instead of returning to dine with his wife and children, and Edna is content that he does not return. Underneath the surface, issues more important than Edna's sunburn need to be addressed. Edna is merely an object—an object to be owned by her husband.

Edna is described as handsome and captivating, and Robert, whose appearance is a mirror image of Edna's, clearly finds her so. Their conversations are filled with laughter and with the giggling of conspirators. For Robert, flirting is a way to entertain himself during the summer; his flirtation with Edna is just one in a long series of casual summertime flirtations. Léonce's casual acceptance of Robert's attentions toward Edna and his willingness to give his wife over to the attentions of a younger man reflect his understanding of Creole social conventions.

Edna enjoys the attentions and the conversation of a man close to her own age. Her comfort with Robert's attentions is vastly different from the negligent comfort that exists in her marriage. The conversation between Edna and Robert is one of contented friends, whereas the discussion between Edna and Léonce is one of indifferent spouses.

After an evening of gambling with friends, Léonce returns to the cottage in a lively and talkative mood. Even though Edna is sleeping, he wakes her. He is completely unaware that she exists as an individual separate from him. Chopin emphasizes Léonce's selfish concern for his own needs and his inability to see his wife as having a life separate from his own. Léonce, in his thoughts, complains that Edna, "the sole object of his existence, evince[s] so little interest in things which [concern] him, and value[s] so little his conversation." But in truth, Léonce has many other interests, one of which is his blatant desire to spend his evenings with friends. However, he clearly expects Edna to have no interests other than her husband and children. Léonce is so completely focused on his own desires that he initiates an argument with Edna over their child's health. The child is fine, but the argument is not really about the child. According to Léonce, Edna fails to behave as a proper New Orleans mother. His accusations leave no doubt that Edna is not measuring up to her husband's ideals, and if Edna's tears are any indication, Léonce is not living up to Edna's expectations, either. The gifts that soon arrive for Edna are meant to provide an apology, but they do not erase the injury that Léonce has caused her.

This argument is not the first time that Léonce has complained to Edna about her failed duty to their children. Edna knows that she is not a "mother-woman," whom Chopin describes with the bird metaphor as "fluttering about with extended, protecting wings when any harm, real or imaginary, threatened [its] precious broad." Chopin also describes the mother-women as "women who idolized their children, worshipped their husbands, and esteemed it a holy privilege to efface themselves as individuals and grow wings as ministering angels." Edna recognizes that she is different from the other women who spend their summer at Grand Isle, doting on husbands and children. Edna is more complex than these women; she has desires and needs beyond those of other wives and mothers. Edna's children also sense their mother's distance and don't waste their time running to their mother for comfort after small childhood injuries. Although Edna can be protective and comforting of her children, they don't define her existence or limit her potential. Edna's strength is her independence, which can also provide a positive model for her children.

Compared to Adèle Ratignolle, Edna can see her own inadequacies as a mother. Chopin describes Madame Ratignolle in much the same manner that a Renaissance poet may describe an ideal woman as a blazon of beauty—a metaphor of an ideal woman that begins with the top of her head, moves downward over her face, and ends at her waist. The blazon describes excessive beauty that is far beyond the ordinary. Likewise, Chopin's description begins with Adèle's gold-spun hair, moves to her sapphire blue eyes and her pouting lips that remind Edna of delicious cherries, and then lingers on her exquisite hands. Reaching back to the Renaissance poets, Chopin uses a rhetorical device most often associated with the unattainable perfection of the ideal woman. For Edna, Madam Ratignolle is the unattainable ideal.

She is the perfect mother-woman that Edna can never be—nor does she want to be. Whereas Adèle represents the ideal New Orleans–Creole wife and mother, Edna represents what was newly regarded during Chopin's period as the New Woman, a woman with desires and needs that extended beyond the home and into a more independent sphere. Unfortunately for Edna, no other kind of woman is acceptable in New Orleans society, which is Adèle's world, the world of the mother-woman.

Madame Ratignolle is the kind of mother who constantly thinks about her family and devotes every waking moment toward making her children happy and safe. In contrast, Edna spends little time thinking about her children, and she is simply content to enjoy the summer on Grand Isle by taking pleasure in the moment and by not planning ahead. Madame Ratignolle, however, always plans ahead: She is already preparing for winter. Whenever she visits Edna, Madame Ratignolle always carries her sewing so she can work on winter garments for her children.

Edna, on the other hand, sees no purpose in this work, but because she is genuinely fond of Madame Ratignolle, she dutifully copies patterns that she will never use. Although Edna does not dislike sewing, she "cannot see the use of anticipating and making winter night garments the subject of her summer meditations." The servants, if anyone, will make clothing for the Pontellier children. Later in the novel, Chopin provides ample evidence of the differences between Edna and the mother-woman, but in this scene, she anticipates the crux of Edna's dilemma: She is ill-suited for the role in which she has been cast.

Kate Chopin's *The Awakening* begins and ends on Grand Isle. This setting appears idyllic with the seductiveness of summer heat, the lush vegetation, and the long hours of unstructured freedom. The many trees provide momentary shade for the children to play.

To Edna, who has been bound by the rigid confines of New Orleans society, Grand Isle is an Eden, a paradise where freedom is an illusion and where she does not quite belong. Edna is an outsider, a woman whose interests do not center on family and social obligation. Edna is not a Creole, is not from an old New Orleans family, and is not accustomed to the rules that govern this society.

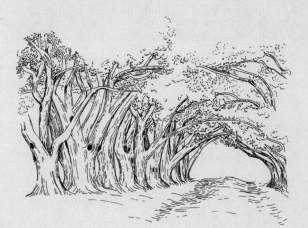

Water oaks.

Although the rules of social obligation are relaxed during this summer period, important rules still apply to social behavior—rules that Edna does not understand. The Creoles have a freedom of expression that is unfamiliar to Edna; they can discuss intimate details in a way that is completely unthinkable for someone with Edna's rigid Presbyterian upbringing. The casual flirting that she allows Robert to indulge in with her is a custom that should not be taken seriously.

Notes

Chapters 5–6

Edna, Robert, and Madame Ratignolle spend the summer afternoon together. When Robert teasingly professes his love for Madame Ratignolle, she plays along by pretending to ignore him but all the time responding to his teasing. Edna, however, is uncomfortable with this Creole flirting, but she listens and concentrates on trying to draw a likeness of Madame Ratignolle. Edna grows bored as the afternoon advances, and Robert urges her to go for a swim. Initially, Edna declines but is easily convinced to change her mind. Later, she wonders why she had first declined and then agreed. Edna begins to realize that something different is happening to her. She is beginning to awaken to the possibilities that the world has to offer her.

CHAPTER V

They formed a congenial group sitting there that summer afternoon—Madame Ratignolle sewing away, often stopping to relate a story or incident with much expressive gesture of her perfect hands; Robert and Mrs. Pontellier sitting idle, exchanging occasional words, glances or smiles which indicated a certain advanced stage of intimacy and **camaraderie**.

He had lived in her shadow during the past month. No one thought anything of it. Many had predicted that Robert would devote himself to Mrs. Pontellier when he arrived. Since the age of fifteen, which was eleven years before, Robert each summer at Grand Isle had constituted himself the devoted attendant of some fair dame or damsel. Sometimes it was a young girl, again a widow; but as often as not it was some interesting married woman.

For two consecutive seasons he lived in the sunlight of Mademoiselle Duvigné's presence. But she died between summers; then Robert posed as an inconsolable, prostrating himself at the feet of Madame Ratignolle for whatever crumbs of sympathy and comfort she might be pleased to vouchsafe.

Mrs. Pontellier liked to sit and gaze at her fair companion as she might look upon a faultless Madonna.

"Could any one fathom the cruelty beneath that fair exterior?" murmured Robert. "She knew that I adored her once, and she let me adore her. It was `Robert, come; go; stand up; sit down; do this; do that; see if the baby sleeps; my thimble, please, that I left God knows where. Come and read **Daudet** to me while I sew.'"

NOTES

camaraderie: loyalty and warm, friendly feeling among comrades; comradeship.

Sewing implements.

Daudet: Alphonse Daudet (1840–97), a French novelist of the naturalist school.

"Par exemple! I never had to ask. You were always there under my feet, like a troublesome cat."

"You mean like an adoring dog. And just as soon as Ratignolle appeared on the scene, then it was like a dog. '**Passez! Adieu! Allez vous-en!**'"

Passez! adieu! allez vous-en!: Go on! Good-bye! Go away!

"Perhaps I feared to make Alphonse jealous," she interjoined, with excessive naïveté. That made them all laugh. The right hand jealous of the left! The heart jealous of the soul! But for that matter, the Creole husband is never jealous; with him the **gangrene** passion is one which has become dwarfed by disuse.

gangrene: decay of tissue in a part of the body when the blood supply is obstructed by injury, disease, etc. In this case, the implication is that there is little to feed passion, and hence, little to feed jealousy.

Meanwhile Robert, addressing Mrs. Pontellier, continued to tell of his one time hopeless passion for Madame Ratignolle; of sleepless nights, of consuming flames till the very sea sizzled when he took his daily plunge. While the lady at the needle kept up a little running, contemptuous comment:

"**Blagueur—farceur—gros bête, va!**"

Blaguer—farceur—grose bête, va!: Comedian! Clown! Silly beast, away with you!

He never assumed this seriocomic tone when alone with Mrs. Pontellier. She never knew precisely what to make of it; at that moment it was impossible for her to guess how much of it was jest and what proportion was earnest. It was understood that he had often spoken words of love to Madame Ratignolle, without any thought of being taken seriously. Mrs. Pontellier was glad he had not assumed a similar role toward herself. It would have been unacceptable and annoying.

Mrs. Pontellier had brought her sketching materials, which she sometimes dabbled with in an unprofessional way. She liked the dabbling. She felt in it satisfaction of a kind which no other employment afforded her.

She had long wished to try herself on Madame Ratignolle. Never had that lady seemed a more tempting subject than at that moment, seated there like some sensuous Madonna, with the gleam of the fading day enriching her splendid color.

Robert crossed over and seated himself upon the step below Mrs. Pontellier, that he might watch her work. She handled her brushes with a certain ease and freedom which came, not from long and close acquaintance with them, but from a natural aptitude. Robert followed her work with close attention, giving forth little ejaculatory expressions of appreciation in French, which he addressed to Madame Ratignolle.

"Mais ce n'est pas mal! Elle s'y connait, elle a de la force, oui."

During his oblivious attention he once quietly rested his head against Mrs. Pontellier's arm. As gently she repulsed him. Once again he repeated the offense. She could not but believe it to be thoughtlessness on his part; yet that was no reason she should submit to it. She did not remonstrate, except again to repulse him quietly but firmly. He offered no apology.

The picture completed bore no resemblance to Madame Ratignolle. She was greatly disappointed to find that it did not look like her. But it was a fair enough piece of work, and in many respects satisfying.

Mrs. Pontellier evidently did not think so. After surveying the sketch critically she drew a broad smudge of paint across its surface, and crumpled the paper between her hands.

The youngsters came tumbling up the steps, the quadroon following at the respectful distance which they required her to observe. Mrs. Pontellier made them carry her paints and things into the house. She sought to detain them for a little talk and some pleasantry. But they were greatly in earnest. They had only come to investigate the contents of the bon-bon box. They accepted without murmuring what she chose to give them, each holding out two chubby hands scoop-like, in the vain hope that they might be filled; and then away they went.

The sun was low in the west, and the breeze soft and languorous that came up from the south, charged with the seductive odor of the sea. Children, freshly **befurbelowed**, were gathering for their games under the oaks. Their voices were high and penetrating.

Madame Ratignolle folded her sewing, placing thimble, scissors, and thread all neatly together in the roll, which she pinned securely. She complained of faintness. Mrs. Pontellier flew for the cologne water and a fan. She bathed Madame Ratignolle's face with cologne, while Robert plied the fan with unnecessary vigor.

The spell was soon over, and Mrs. Pontellier could not help wondering if there were not a little imagination responsible for its origin, for the rose tint had never faded from her friend's face.

She stood watching the fair woman walk down the long line of galleries with the grace and majesty which queens

Mais ce n'est pas mal! Elle s'y connait, elle a de la force, oui: But that's not bad at all! She knows what she's doing, she has a talent.

befurbelowed: trimmed with flounces or ruffles.

are sometimes supposed to possess. Her little ones ran to meet her. Two of them clung about her white skirts, the third she took from its nurse and with a thousand endearments bore it along in her own fond, encircling arms. Though, as everybody well knew, the doctor had forbidden her to lift so much as a pin!

"Are you going bathing?" asked Robert of Mrs. Pontellier. It was not so much a question as a reminder.

"Oh, no," she answered, with a tone of indecision. "I'm tired; I think not." Her glance wandered from his face away toward the Gulf, whose sonorous murmur reached her like a loving but imperative entreaty.

"Oh, come!" he insisted. "You mustn't miss your bath. Come on. The water must be delicious; it will not hurt you. Come."

He reached up for her big, rough straw hat that hung on a peg outside the door, and put it on her head. They descended the steps, and walked away together toward the beach. The sun was low in the west and the breeze was soft and warm.

CHAPTER VI

Edna Pontellier could not have told why, wishing to go to the beach with Robert, she should in the first place have declined, and in the second place have followed in obedience to one of the two contradictory impulses which impelled her.

A certain light was beginning to dawn dimly within her,— the light which, showing the way, forbids it.

At that early period it served but to bewilder her. It moved her to dreams, to thoughtfulness, to the shadowy anguish which had overcome her the midnight when she had abandoned herself to tears.

In short, Mrs. Pontellier was beginning to realize her position in the universe as a human being, and to recognize her relations as an individual to the world within and about her. This may seem like a ponderous weight of wisdom to descend upon the soul of a young woman of twenty-eight—perhaps more wisdom than the Holy Ghost is usually pleased to **vouchsafe** to any woman.

But the beginning of things, of a world especially, is necessarily vague, tangled, chaotic, and exceedingly disturbing. How few of us ever emerge from such beginning! How many souls perish in its tumult!

vouchsafe: to be gracious enough or condescend to give or grant.

The voice of the sea is seductive; never ceasing, whispering, clamoring, murmuring, inviting the soul to wander for a spell in abysses of solitude; to lose itself in mazes of inward contemplation.

The voice of the sea speaks to the soul. The touch of the sea is sensuous, enfolding the body in its soft, close embrace.

COMMENTARY

These chapters reveal the progression of Robert's courtship. The glances and exchanges between Edna and Robert indicate a "certain advanced stage of intimacy and camaraderie." Clearly, Robert and Edna have formed an attachment during the course of the summer. Robert's custom is to seek out a woman and make her the center of his attentions. Robert himself describes his devoted attentions to Mademoiselle Duvigné and to Madame Ratignolle in past summers. After the former woman's death, Robert "posed as inconsolable." The very use of the word "posed" implies his insincerity, so the reader is always aware of his duplicity. In turn, Robert's tone when talking with Adèle—Madame Ratignolle—is light and easy, never serious. Alphonse Ratignolle was never jealous of Robert's attentions to his wife, nor is Léonce jealous of Robert's attentions to Edna. Like the casual discussion of sexual matters, which is centered on children and motherhood, this casual flirting is harmless entertainment.

Robert's behavior with Edna, however, is more serious. Edna is discernibly uncomfortable with this type of flirting, so he leaves behind the easy banter that he usually uses when addressing a woman. He does not assume a "serio-comic" tone with Edna, and as a result, she mistakes Robert's attentions for serious courtship. She does not understand the rules of this kind of social engagement.

The harmless flirting between Adèle and Robert that opens the beginning of Chapter 5 shows the reader that these harmless flirtations are the ordinary, accepted manner of Creole life. Robert courts Madame Ratignolle, but they recognize that courtship is a rhetorical exercise, little more than formulaic. In Creole society, such flirting is, in fact, an important part of Creole life that

Edna sketching.

Edna fails to understand. For Edna, flirting is a precursor to courtship, which may lead to a serious relationship, but in Creole society, this flirting is most closely defined as social discourse, only slightly different than ordinary conversation. Robert describes his passion for Madame Ratignolle as "hopeless." Edna has never experienced hopeless passions, certainly not in her marriage.

As Edna, Robert, and Madame Ratignolle sit together, Edna sketches her friend, who she describes as a "faultless" Madonna.

Although Edna has a "natural aptitude" for painting, she merely "dabbles" in her art; she does not take it seriously. The picture that she paints of Adèle proves unsatisfactory, and Edna destroys it. But because Edna does possesses a natural talent, the reason that she is so disappointed with the painting is worth considering. Edna, whom Chopin describes as handsome rather than beautiful, lacks the perfect beauty of Madame Ratignolle. But more importantly, Edna thinks that she fails to measure up to Adèle's perfect, mother-woman image. An image is not reality, and again, Edna is deceived by convention. By referring to Adèle as a fault-less Madonna, Edna makes obvious her own feelings of inadequacy when measured against such excellence. No wonder Edna destroys a painting that cannot capture the idealistic perfection of her vision of Madame Ratignolle—a painting cannot capture what does not exist.

Although Edna initially declines Robert's invitation to swim, she allows him to coax her into taking an evening swim, which is really what she wanted to do all along. Although Chapter 6 covers only one short page, it offers a crucial scene in which Edna finally begins to awaken to her own individuality. Chopin writes that Edna is "beginning to realize her position in the universe as a human being, and to recognize her relations as an individual to the world within and about her."

Edna has always been someone's property. As a young girl and later as a young woman, Edna was her father's property. When she married, she became Léonce's property. For the first time in her life, Edna is beginning to realize that she is more than an object of ownership. The sensual, soft, warm breezes and the sun moving toward the horizon combine with the seduc-tiveness of the sea to make Edna aware of herself and her body in ways that she has not previously experi-enced. Edna is awakening to herself and to the possi-bilities that extend beyond the life she knows as the wife of Léonce and the mother of Raul and Etienne.

Edna and Robert leave for their swim after the other mothers have returned to their evening chores. Edna watches as Madame Ratignolle's children move natu-rally into her enveloping arms. Edna's children are with their nurse, so she is freed of the motherly duties that occupy other women. Edna makes her first transition into behavior that deviates from the ordinary; she freely swims in the evening, when none of the other women will swim. Overtly, swimming with Robert is acceptable; they frequently swim together during the day. But one gets the sense that Edna's activity is not quite proper. Having once experienced the freedom that Grand Isle offers, returning to her conventional life as wife and mother becomes even more difficult for Edna, and she slowly moves toward the unconventional as her story progresses.

Edna and Robert walking togther.
Everett Collection

Notes

Notes

Chapters 7–8

Edna and Madame Ratignolle spend the afternoon at the beach. The children, as well as Robert, have been left behind. For Edna, this encounter is one of reflection and closeness with a woman friend. Edna spends much of the afternoon reflecting on her childhood, her marriage to Léonce, and her role as a mother. Soon, the quiet afternoon is interrupted by the arrival of Robert and the children. On the way back to the cottages, Madame Ratignolle warns Robert to cease his flirtation with Edna, who may take Robert's meaningless flirting seriously.

CHAPTER VII

Mrs. Pontellier was not a woman given to confidences, a characteristic hitherto contrary to her nature. Even as a child she had lived her own small life all within herself. At a very early period she had apprehended instinctively the dual life—that outward existence which conforms, the inward life which questions.

That summer at Grand Isle she began to loosen a little the mantle of reserve that had always enveloped her. There may have been—there must have been—influences, both subtle and apparent, working in their several ways to induce her to do this; but the most obvious was the influence of Adèle Ratignolle. The excessive physical charm of the Creole had first attracted her, for Edna had a sensuous susceptibility to beauty. Then the candor of the woman's whole existence, which every one might read, and which formed so striking a contrast to her own habitual reserve—this might have furnished a link. Who can tell what metals the gods use in forging the subtle bond which we call sympathy, which we might as well call love.

The two women went away one morning to the beach together, arm in arm, under the huge white sunshade. Edna had prevailed upon Madame Ratignolle to leave the children behind, though she could not induce her to relinquish a diminutive roll of needlework, which Adèle begged to be allowed to slip into the depths of her pocket. In some unaccountable way they had escaped from Robert.

The walk to the beach was no inconsiderable one, consisting as it did of a long, sandy path, upon which a sporadic and tangled growth that bordered it on either side made frequent and unexpected inroads. There were acres of yellow camomile reaching out on either hand. Further away still, vegetable gardens abounded, with frequent small plantations of orange or lemon trees intervening. The dark green clusters glistened from afar in the sun.

Notes

The women were both of goodly height, Madame Ratignolle possessing the more feminine and matronly figure. The charm of Edna Pontellier's physique stole insensibly upon you. The lines of her body were long, clean and symmetrical; it was a body which occasionally fell into splendid poses; there was no suggestion of the trim, stereotyped **fashion-plate** about it. A casual and indiscriminating observer, in passing, might not cast a second glance upon the figure. But with more feeling and discernment he would have recognized the noble beauty of its modeling, and the graceful severity of poise and movement, which made Edna Pontellier different from the crowd.

fashion-plate: a fashionably dressed person.

She wore a cool **muslin** that morning—white, with a waving vertical line of brown running through it; also a white linen **collar** and the big straw hat which she had taken from the peg outside the door. The hat rested any way on her yellow-brown hair, that waved a little, was heavy, and clung close to her head.

muslin: any of various strong, often sheer cotton fabrics of plain weave; especially a heavy variety used for sheets, pillowcases, etc.

collar: a cloth band or folded-over piece attached to the neck of a garment.

Madame Ratignolle, more careful of her complexion, had twined a gauze veil about her head. She wore doeskin gloves, with **gauntlets** that protected her wrists. She was dressed in pure white, with a fluffiness of ruffles that became her. The draperies and fluttering things which she wore suited her rich, luxuriant beauty as a greater severity of line could not have done.

gauntlets: long gloves with flaring cuffs that cover the lower part of the arm.

There were a number of bath-houses along the beach, of rough but solid construction, built with small, protecting galleries facing the water. Each house consisted of two compartments, and each family at Lebrun's possessed a compartment for itself, fitted out with all the essential paraphernalia of the bath and whatever other conveniences the owners might desire. The two women had no intention of bathing; they had just strolled down to the beach for a walk and to be alone and near the water. The Pontellier and Ratignolle compartments adjoined one another under the same roof.

Mrs. Pontellier had brought down her key through force of habit. Unlocking the door of her bath-room she went inside, and soon emerged, bringing a rug, which she spread upon the floor of the **gallery**, and two huge hair pillows covered with **crash**, which she placed against the front of the building.

gallery: a veranda or porch.

crash: a coarse cotton or linen cloth with a plain, loose weave, used for towels, curtains, clothes, etc.

The two seated themselves there in the shade of the porch, side by side, with their backs against the pillows and their feet extended. Madame Ratignolle removed her veil, wiped her face with a rather delicate handkerchief, and fanned herself with the fan which she always carried suspended somewhere about her person by a long, narrow ribbon. Edna removed her collar and opened her dress at the throat. She took the fan from Madame Ratignolle and began to fan both herself and her companion. It was very warm, and for a while they did nothing but exchange remarks about the heat, the sun, the glare. But there was a breeze blowing, a choppy, stiff wind that whipped the water into froth. It fluttered the skirts of the two women and kept them for a while engaged in adjusting, readjusting, tucking in, securing hair-pins and hat-pins. A few persons were sporting some distance away in the water. The beach was very still of human sound at that hour. The lady in black was reading her morning devotions on the porch of a neighboring bathhouse. Two young lovers were exchanging their hearts' yearnings beneath the children's tent, which they had found unoccupied.

Edna Pontellier, casting her eyes about, had finally kept them at rest upon the sea. The day was clear and carried the gaze out as far as the blue sky went; there were a few white clouds suspended idly over the horizon. A **lateen sail** was visible in the direction of Cat Island, and others to the south seemed almost motionless in the far distance.

"Of whom—of what are you thinking?" asked Adèle of her companion, whose countenance she had been watching with a little amused attention, arrested by the absorbed expression which seemed to have seized and fixed every feature into a statuesque repose.

"Nothing," returned Mrs. Pontellier, with a start, adding at once: "How stupid! But it seems to me it is the reply we make instinctively to such a question. Let me see," she went on, throwing back her head and narrowing her fine eyes till they shone like two vivid points of light. "Let me see. I was really not conscious of thinking of anything; but perhaps I can retrace my thoughts."

"Oh! never mind!" laughed Madame Ratignolle. "I am not quite so exacting. I will let you off this time. It is really too hot to think, especially to think about thinking."

"But for the fun of it," persisted Edna. "First of all, the sight of the water stretching so far away, those motionless sails against the blue sky, made a delicious picture that I just wanted to sit and look at. The hot wind beating in my

lateen sail: designating or of a triangular, fore-and-aft-rigged sail attached to a long yard suspended from a short mast.

face made me think—without any connection that I can trace of a summer day in Kentucky, of a meadow that seemed as big as the ocean to the very little girl walking through the grass, which was higher than her waist. She threw out her arms as if swimming when she walked, beating the tall grass as one strikes out in the water. Oh, I see the connection now!"

"Where were you going that day in Kentucky, walking through the grass?"

"I don't remember now. I was just walking diagonally across a big field. My sun-bonnet obstructed the view. I could see only the stretch of green before me, and I felt as if I must walk on forever, without coming to the end of it. I don't remember whether I was frightened or pleased. I must have been entertained.

"Likely as not it was Sunday," she laughed; "and I was running away from prayers, from the Presbyterian service, read in a spirit of gloom by my father that chills me yet to think of."

"And have you been running away from prayers ever since, ma chère?" asked Madame Ratignolle, amused.

"No! oh, no!" Edna hastened to say. "I was a little unthinking child in those days, just following a misleading impulse without question. On the contrary, during one period of my life religion took a firm hold upon me; after I was twelve and until—until—why, I suppose until now, though I never thought much about it—just driven along by habit. But do you know," she broke off, turning her quick eyes upon Madame Ratignolle and leaning forward a little so as to bring her face quite close to that of her companion, "sometimes I feel this summer as if I were walking through the green meadow again; idly, aimlessly, unthinking and unguided."

Madame Ratignolle laid her hand over that of Mrs. Pontellier, which was near her. Seeing that the hand was not withdrawn, she clasped it firmly and warmly. She even stroked it a little, fondly, with the other hand, murmuring in an undertone, "**Pauvre chérie**."

Pauvre chérie: poor dear.

The action was at first a little confusing to Edna, but she soon lent herself readily to the Creole's gentle caress. She was not accustomed to an outward and spoken expression of affection, either in herself or in others. She and her younger sister, Janet, had quarreled a good deal through force of unfortunate habit. Her older sister, Margaret, was matronly and dignified, probably from having assumed matronly and housewifely responsibilities too early in life, their mother having died when they were quite young, Margaret was not effusive; she was practical. Edna had had an occasional girl friend, but whether accidentally or not, they seemed to have been all of one type—the self-contained. She never realized that the reserve of her own character had much, perhaps everything, to do with this. Her most intimate friend at school had been one of rather exceptional intellectual gifts, who wrote fine-sounding essays, which Edna admired and strove to imitate; and with her she talked and glowed over the English classics, and sometimes **held religious and political controversies**.

held . . . controversies: conducted a lengthy discussion of an important question in which opposing opinions clash.

Edna often wondered at one propensity which sometimes had inwardly disturbed her without causing any outward show or manifestation on her part. At a very early age—perhaps it was when she traversed the ocean of waving grass—she remembered that she had been passionately enamored of a dignified and sad-eyed cavalry officer who visited her father in Kentucky. She could not leave his presence when he was there, nor remove her eyes from his face, which was something like Napoleon's, with a lock of black hair failing across the forehead. But the cavalry officer melted imperceptibly out of her existence.

At another time her affections were deeply engaged by a young gentleman who visited a lady on a neighboring plantation. It was after they went to Mississippi to live. The young man was engaged to be married to the young lady, and they sometimes called upon Margaret, driving over of afternoons in a buggy. Edna was a little miss, just merging into her teens; and the realization that she herself was nothing, nothing, nothing to the engaged young man was a bitter affliction to her. But he, too, went the way of dreams.

She was a grown young woman when she was overtaken by what she supposed to be the climax of her fate. It was when the face and figure of a great **tragedian** began to haunt her imagination and stir her senses. The persistence of the infatuation lent it an aspect of genuineness. The hopelessness of it colored it with the lofty tones of a great passion.

tragedian: a writer of tragedies or an actor of tragedy.

The picture of the tragedian stood enframed upon her desk. Any one may possess the portrait of a tragedian without exciting suspicion or comment. (This was a sinister reflection which she cherished.) In the presence of others she expressed admiration for his exalted gifts, as she handed the photograph around and dwelt upon the fidelity of the likeness. When alone, she sometimes picked it up and kissed the cold glass passionately.

Her marriage to Léonce Pontellier was purely an accident, in this respect resembling many other marriages which masquerade as the decrees of Fate. It was in the midst of her secret great passion that she met him. He fell in love, as men are in the habit of doing, and pressed his suit with an earnestness and an ardor which left nothing to be desired. He pleased her; his absolute devotion flattered her. She fancied there was a sympathy of thought and taste between them, in which fancy she was mistaken. Add to this the violent opposition of her father and her sister Margaret to her marriage with a Catholic, and we need seek no further for the motives which led her to accept Monsieur Pontellier for her husband.

The acme of bliss, which would have been a marriage with the tragedian, was not for her in this world. As the devoted wife of a man who worshiped her, she felt she would take her place with a certain dignity in the world of reality, closing the **portals** forever behind her upon the realm of romance and dreams.

But it was not long before the tragedian had gone to join the cavalry officer and the engaged young man and a few others; and Edna found herself face to face with the realities. She grew fond of her husband, realizing with some unaccountable satisfaction that no trace of passion or excessive and fictitious warmth colored her affection, thereby threatening its dissolution.

She was fond of her children in an uneven, impulsive way. She would sometimes gather them passionately to her heart; she would sometimes forget them. The year before they had spent part of the summer with their grandmother Pontellier in Iberville. Feeling secure regarding their happiness and welfare, she did not miss them except with an occasional intense longing. Their absence was a sort of relief, though she did not admit this, even to herself. It seemed to free her of a responsibility which she had blindly assumed and for which Fate had not fitted her.

Edna did not reveal so much as all this to Madame Ratignolle that summer day when they sat with faces turned to the sea. But a good part of it escaped her. She had put her head down on Madame Ratignolle's shoulder.

portals: doorways, gates, or entrances, especially large and imposing ones.

She was flushed and felt intoxicated with the sound of her own voice and the unaccustomed taste of candor. It muddled her like wine, or like a first breath of freedom.

There was the sound of approaching voices. It was Robert, surrounded by a troop of children, searching for them. The two little Pontelliers were with him, and he carried Madame Ratignolle's little girl in his arms. There were other children beside, and two nurse-maids followed, looking disagreeable and resigned.

The women at once rose and began to shake out their **draperies** and relax their muscles. Mrs. Pontellier threw the cushions and rug into the bath-house. The children all scampered off to the awning, and they stood there in a line, gazing upon the intruding lovers, still exchanging their vows and sighs. The lovers got up, with only a silent protest, and walked slowly away somewhere else.

draperies: clothing arranged in loose folds.

The children possessed themselves of the tent, and Mrs. Pontellier went over to join them.

Madame Ratignolle begged Robert to accompany her to the house; she complained of cramp in her limbs and stiffness of the joints. She leaned draggingly upon his arm as they walked.

CHAPTER VIII

"Do me a favor, Robert," spoke the pretty woman at his side, almost as soon as she and Robert had started their slow, homeward way. She looked up in his face, leaning on his arm beneath the encircling shadow of the umbrella which he had lifted.

"Granted; as many as you like," he returned, glancing down into her eyes that were full of thoughtfulness and some speculation.

"I only ask for one; let Mrs. Pontellier alone."

"**Tiens**!" he exclaimed, with a sudden, boyish laugh. "**Voilà que Madame Ratignolle est jalouse!**"

Tiens! Voilà que Madame Ratignolle est jalouse!: Finally! It appears that Madame Ratignolle is jealous!

"Nonsense! I'm in earnest; I mean what I say. Let Mrs. Pontellier alone."

"Why?" he asked; himself growing serious at his companion's solicitation.

"She is not one of us; she is not like us. She might make the unfortunate blunder of taking you seriously."

His face flushed with annoyance, and taking off his soft hat he began to beat it impatiently against his leg as he walked. "Why shouldn't she take me seriously?" he demanded sharply. "Am I a comedian, a clown, a jack-in-the-box? Why shouldn't she? You Creoles! I have no patience with you! Am I always to be regarded as a feature of an amusing **programme**? I hope Mrs. Pontellier does take me seriously. I hope she has discernment enough to find in me something besides the **blagueur**. If I thought there was any doubt—"

"Oh, enough, Robert!" she broke into his heated outburst. "You are not thinking of what you are saying. You speak with about as little reflection as we might expect from one of those children down there playing in the sand. If your attentions to any married women here were ever offered with any intention of being convincing, you would not be the gentleman we all know you to be, and you would be unfit to associate with the wives and daughters of the people who trust you."

Madame Ratignolle had spoken what she believed to be the law and the gospel. The young man shrugged his shoulders impatiently.

"Oh! well! That isn't it," slamming his hat down vehemently upon his head. "You ought to feel that such things are not flattering to say to a fellow."

"Should our whole intercourse consist of an exchange of compliments? **Ma foi!**"

"It isn't pleasant to have a woman tell you—" he went on, unheedingly, but breaking off suddenly: "Now if I were like Arobin—you remember Alcée Arobin and that story of the consul's wife at Biloxi?" And he related the story of Alcée Arobin and the consul's wife; and another about the tenor of the French Opera, who received letters which should never have been written; and still other stories, grave and gay, till Mrs. Pontellier and her possible propensity for taking young men seriously was apparently forgotten.

Madame Ratignolle, when they had regained her cottage, went in to take the hour's rest which she considered helpful. Before leaving her, Robert begged her pardon for the impatience—he called it rudeness—with which he had received her well-meant caution.

"You made one mistake, Adèle," he said, with a light smile; "there is no earthly possibility of Mrs. Pontellier ever taking me seriously. You should have warned me against taking myself seriously. Your advice might then have carried some

programme: the acts, speeches, musical pieces, etc. that make up an entertainment, ceremony, etc.

blagueur: a tobacco pouch.

Ma foi!: Indeed! (literally "my goodness").

weight and given me subject for some reflection. **Au revoir**. But you look tired," he added, solicitously. "Would you like a cup of **bouillon**? Shall I stir you a **toddy**? Let me mix you a toddy with a drop of Angostura."

Au revoir: good-bye.

bouillon: a clear broth, usually of beef.

toddy: a drink of brandy, whiskey, etc., with hot water, sugar, and often spices.

She acceded to the suggestion of bouillon, which was grateful and acceptable. He went himself to the kitchen, which was a building apart from the cottages and lying to the rear of the house. And he himself brought her the golden-brown bouillon, in a dainty **Sèvres** cup, with a flaky cracker or two on the saucer.

Sèvres: a type of fine French porcelain.

She thrust a bare, white arm from the curtain which shielded her open door, and received the cup from his hands. She told him he was a **bon garçon**, and she meant it. Robert thanked her and turned away toward "the house."

bon garçon: good boy (or good waiter).

The lovers were just entering the grounds of the pension. They were leaning toward each other as the water-oaks bent from the sea. There was not a particle of earth beneath their feet. Their heads might have been turned upside-down, so absolutely did they tread upon blue **ether**. The lady in black, creeping behind them, looked a trifle paler and more jaded than usual. There was no sign of Mrs. Pontellier and the children. Robert scanned the distance for any such apparition. They would doubtless remain away till the dinner hour. The young man ascended to his mother's room. It was situated at the top of the house, made up of odd angles and a queer, sloping ceiling. Two broad dormer windows looked out toward the Gulf, and as far across it as a man's eye might reach. The furnishings of the room were light, cool, and practical.

ether: the upper regions of space; clear sky.

Madame Lebrun was busily engaged at the sewing-machine. A little black girl sat on the floor, and with her hands worked the **treadle** of the machine. The Creole woman does not take any chances which may be avoided of imperiling her health.

treadle: a lever or pedal moved by the foot as to turn a wheel.

Robert went over and seated himself on the broad sill of one of the dormer windows. He took a book from his pocket and began energetically to read it, judging by the precision and frequency with which he turned the leaves. The sewing-machine made a resounding clatter in the room; it was of a ponderous, by-gone make. In the lulls, Robert and his mother exchanged bits of desultory conversation.

"Where is Mrs. Pontellier?"

"Down at the beach with the children."

"I promised to lend her the **Goncourt**. Don't forget to take it down when you go; it's there on the bookshelf over the

Goncourt: Edmond Louis Antoine Huot de Goncourt (1822–96); French novelist and art critic.

small table." Clatter, clatter, clatter, bang! for the next five or eight minutes.

"Where is Victor going with the rockaway?"

"The rockaway? Victor?"

"Yes; down there in front. He seems to be getting ready to drive away somewhere."

"Call him." Clatter, clatter!

Robert uttered a shrill, piercing whistle which might have been heard back at the wharf.

"He won't look up."

Madame Lebrun flew to the window. She called "Victor!" She waved a handkerchief and called again. The young fellow below got into the vehicle and started the horse off at a gallop.

Madame Lebrun went back to the machine, crimson with annoyance. Victor was the younger son and brother—a **tête montée**, with a temper which invited violence and a will which no ax could break.

"Whenever you say the word I'm ready to thrash any amount of reason into him that he's able to hold."

"If your father had only lived!" Clatter, clatter, clatter, clatter, bang! It was a fixed belief with Madame Lebrun that the conduct of the universe and all things pertaining thereto would have been manifestly of a more intelligent and higher order had not Monsieur Lebrun been removed to other spheres during the early years of their married life.

"What do you hear from Montel?" Montel was a middle-aged gentleman whose vain ambition and desire for the past twenty years had been to fill the void which Monsieur Lebrun's taking off had left in the Lebrun household. Clatter, clatter, bang, clatter!

"I have a letter somewhere," looking in the machine drawer and finding the letter in the bottom of the workbasket. "He says to tell you he will be in Vera Cruz the beginning of next month,"—clatter, clatter!—"and if you still have the intention of joining him"—bang! clatter, clatter, bang!

"Why didn't you tell me so before, mother? You know I wanted—"Clatter, clatter, clatter!

"Do you see Mrs. Pontellier starting back with the children? She will be in late to luncheon again. She never starts to get ready for luncheon till the last minute." Clatter, clatter! "Where are you going?"

"Where did you say the Goncourt was?"

tête montée: a hot-headed person.

COMMENTARY

Robert is not the only person with whom Edna forms an alliance during the summer vacation at Grand Isle. This section focuses on Edna's growing friendship with, and affection for, Madame Ratignolle. Chopin suggests that, because of Edna's sensibility for beauty, "the excessive physical charm of the Creole" first attracted her to Adèle. But Edna is more attracted to Adèle's entire being, one that seems entirely different from her own. In the intimacy of friendship, Edna is able to loosen her inhibitions and share her life. No doubt, Adèle's warmth and her willingness to share her own thoughts help Edna relax.

Chopin offers a contrast between the two women by describing Adèle in a gown of flowing white, with ruffles and a gauze veil to protect her from the sun. Adèle's gown suits her matronly appearance but is also a sensual gown that drapes and flows around her Creole body. Adèle also covers her head, face, and hands, taking great pains to protect her "more feminine" figure from the effects of the sun. Adèle is also newly pregnant, so her looser gown, though designed to hide any obvious suggestion of her condition, also reveals her earthy sensuality—something that Edna takes great pains to hide. In contrast, Edna more rigidly and severely dressed; she also wears white, but without the softness of ruffles or gauze. Edna wears a more structured gown, one with a collar to close off her body and with lines designed to suppress the sensuality that Madame Ratignolle's looser gown suggests. The image of Edna's gown overtly represents propriety, but although Edna's clothing accentuates her poise and "noble beauty," she does not fit the "stereotyped fashion-plate." Chopin suggests that Edna's dress does not contradict the formality of her position in life, her grace of movement makes her stand out from the crowd.

When Edna begins to talk about her life, she also begins to loosen her gown and remove her collar. This act symbolizes the opening of Edna's life and her defiance of the rigid forces that control her life.

As Edna tells Adèle her story, the two lovers and the woman in black move on the edge of the scene. These three characters reappear throughout the time at Grand Isle. The lovers are passionate and unrestrained in their obvious love for one another. Moving in unison, the pair represents a singular force that Edna has never experienced. Edna is awakening to the possibility of passion, and the two lovers are a constant reminder of what may come to exist between her and another man, possibly even Robert.

The woman in black serves several purposes. Clearly a widow, she is a reminder of death. She offers Edna a picture of her own possible future after her husband dies; Edna may also face a future alone, clad in black, a figure isolated and on the margins of society. The woman in black also suggests the conventional role of the chaperone because she accompanies the young lovers while they move about the island. Here again is the kind of role to which lonely widows are relegated. Creole society may be passionate, but it is also governed by rigid rules. The woman in black, lingering while Edna tells her story, functions as a reminder of the controls and expectations that all women must observe. Combined, these characters—the lovers and the woman in black—serve to remind Edna of the opportunity for love and passion, while at the same time, they remind her of social conventions and of a world in which time is not infinite.

Sitting along the beach with Madame Ratignolle reminds Edna of her childhood, and she recalls the tall Kentucky grasses of her home. This conversation is important because it reveals many of the reasons for Edna's prudish behavior and helps account for her actions during the coming months. Edna's father, the colonel, is never mentioned by name, but he is identified with uncompromising rigidity. His sermons frightened her as a child, and he offered no answering affection to diminish her fright. When Adèle takes Edna's hand, Edna is confused by the gesture. Obviously, Edna is not used to being caressed. Her father defined himself through his sermons and not through a gentle touch. Edna does not know this kind of touch, and as the scene with Adèle suggests, Edna is unfamiliar with such affections.

During her conversation with Adèle, Edna reveals that she is concerned about her propensity to become "passionately enamoured" of unattainable men. Her first object of infatuation was a young cavalry officer. Her next infatuation was with a young man who was engaged to another woman. Eventually, this young man was replaced by the picture of a tragedian, a man whom she had never met, yet whose image consumed her passions. Edna has been infatuated with three different men, all of whom she can never possess; these men "went the way of dreams." And indeed, her infatuations have all been the material of fantasy, including her affection for Léonce. Edna supposed that they shared a "sympathy of thought," but in truth, they share little in common. More importantly, Léonce and Edna come from disparate backgrounds that cannot be reconciled. Edna describes the ideal marriage as a union with the tragedian, a man (like her father) who makes a living in drama and role-playing. In her relationships with men, Edna has always relied upon her imagination rather than upon reality and knowledge.

The intimate discussion between Edna and Adèle is interrupted by the arrival of Robert and the children. When Edna and Adèle walk to the beach for a quiet morning together, Edna must convince her friend to leave the children behind. For Edna, children are encumbrances and are best left to their nurses. The voices of the children are an intrusion for Edna, even though their nurse is also present to care for them. Edna is an unconventional mother, one who is "fond of her children in an uneven, impulsive way." But when her children are away, Edna is rarely concerned for them, and instead, she welcomes their extended visits to their paternal grandmother.

Edna's relationship to her husband has some striking similarities to her relationship with her children. She is certainly fond of them, but Edna's affection for Léonce and her children never suggests love. And even her fondness for her husband appears to be eroding during the summer.

Adèle purposefully asks Robert to walk with her back to the cottages so she can suggest that he leave Edna alone. Edna's confidences to Adèle suggest a vulnerability that worries her. Instead of complying, Robert is angered by the suggestion that he may be the same sort of man as Alcée Arobin, a rogue who preys on women. This section provides the reader with two important pieces of information. First, Alcée Arobin is introduced, along with the news about what kind of man he is. Note that Alcée reappears later in the novel, and this early warning foreshadows the danger Edna faces.

The second surprise is Robert's anger. Thus far, he has always been good natured and easygoing. But in this scene, he is injured by Madame Ratignolle's suggestion. Perhaps he is hurt by the suggestion that he is not completely honorable. But more likely, Madame Ratignolle's words serve as a reminder of the emptiness and pointlessness of his life. Robert is 26 years old, and he has spent the last several summers with the women at Grand Isle. The men go into the city every week to work, but Robert does not. Instead, he lounges around during the summer, chatting with women and flirting with the woman whom he selects for his summer entertainment.

After Madame Ratignolle speaks to Robert, the lovers reappear and are even more united, and the woman in black also reappears and is even "paler and more jaded than usual." These characters foreshadow the passion and consequences to come.

Chapters 9–10

On a Saturday evening, the summer visitors gather for an evening of entertainment. After dancing, Robert entices Mademoiselle Reisz to play the piano. The pianist's efforts elicit a sensuous and passionate response from Edna, who listens from the porch. After the entertainment, everyone walks to the beach for a moonlit swim, and Edna finally swims with ease.

CHAPTER IX

Every light in the hall was ablaze; every lamp turned as high as it could be without smoking the chimney or threatening explosion. The lamps were fixed at intervals against the wall, encircling the whole room. Some one had gathered orange and lemon branches, and with these fashioned graceful festoons between. The dark green of the branches stood out and glistened against the white muslin curtains which draped the windows, and which puffed, floated, and flapped at the capricious will of a stiff breeze that swept up from the Gulf.

It was Saturday night a few weeks after the intimate conversation held between Robert and Madame Ratignolle on their way from the beach. An unusual number of husbands, fathers, and friends had come down to stay over Sunday; and they were being suitably entertained by their families, with the material help of Madame Lebrun. The dining tables had all been removed to one end of the hall, and the chairs ranged about in rows and in clusters. Each little family group had had its say and exchanged its domestic gossip earlier in the evening. There was now an apparent disposition to relax; to widen the circle of confidences and give a more general tone to the conversation.

Many of the children had been permitted to sit up beyond their usual bedtime. A small band of them were lying on their stomachs on the floor looking at the colored sheets of the comic papers which Mr. Pontellier had brought down. The little Pontellier boys were permitting them to do so, and making their authority felt.

Music, dancing, and a recitation or two were the entertainments furnished, or rather, offered. But there was nothing systematic about the programme, no appearance of pre-arrangement nor even premeditation.

At an early hour in the evening the Farival twins were prevailed upon to play the piano. They were girls of fourteen, always clad in the Virgin's colors, blue and white, having been **dedicated to the Blessed Virgin** at their baptism. They played a duet from "Zampa," and at the earnest

NOTES

dedicated to the Blessed Virgin: committed to becoming a nun.

solicitation of every one present followed it with the overture to "The Poet and the Peasant."

"Allez vous-en! Sapristi!" shrieked the parrot outside the door. He was the only being present who possessed sufficient candor to admit that he was not listening to these gracious performances for the first time that summer. Old Monsieur Farival, grandfather of the twins, grew indignant over the interruption, and insisted upon having the bird removed and consigned to regions of darkness. Victor Lebrun objected; and his decrees were as immutable as those of Fate. The parrot fortunately offered no further interruption to the entertainment, the whole venom of his nature apparently having been cherished up and hurled against the twins in that one impetuous outburst.

Later a young brother and sister gave recitations, which every one present had heard many times at winter evening entertainments in the city.

A little girl performed a skirt dance in the center of the floor. The mother played her accompaniments and at the same time watched her daughter with greedy admiration and nervous apprehension. She need have had no apprehension. The child was mistress of the situation. She had been properly dressed for the occasion in black tulle and black silk tights. Her little neck and arms were bare, and her hair, artificially crimped, stood out like fluffy black plumes over her head. Her poses were full of grace, and her little black-shod toes twinkled as they shot out and upward with a rapidity and suddenness which were bewildering.

But there was no reason why every one should not dance. Madame Ratignolle could not, so it was she who gaily consented to play for the others. She played very well, keeping excellent waltz time and infusing an expression into the strains which was indeed inspiring. She was keeping up her music on account of the children, she said; because she and her husband both considered it a means of brightening the home and making it attractive.

Almost every one danced but the twins, who could not be induced to separate during the brief period when one or the other should be whirling around the room in the arms of a man. They might have danced together, but they did not think of it.

The children were sent to bed. Some went submissively; others with shrieks and protests as they were dragged away. They had been permitted to sit up till after the ice-cream, which naturally marked the limit of human indulgence.

The ice-cream was passed around with cake—gold and silver cake arranged on platters in alternate slices; it had been made and frozen during the afternoon back of the kitchen by two black women, under the supervision of Victor. It was pronounced a great success—excellent if it had only contained a little less vanilla or a little more sugar, if it had been frozen a degree harder, and if the salt might have been kept out of portions of it. Victor was proud of his achievement, and went about recommending it and urging every one to partake of it to excess.

After Mrs. Pontellier had danced twice with her husband, once with Robert, and once with Monsieur Ratignolle, who was thin and tall and swayed like a reed in the wind when he danced, she went out on the gallery and seated herself on the low window-sill, where she commanded a view of all that went on in the hall and could look out toward the Gulf. There was a soft **effulgence** in the east. The moon was coming up, and its mystic shimmer was casting a million lights across the distant, restless water.

effulgence: great brightness; radiance; brilliance.

"Would you like to hear Mademoiselle Reisz play?" asked Robert, coming out on the porch where she was. Of course Edna would like to hear Mademoiselle Reisz play; but she feared it would be useless to entreat her.

"I'll ask her," he said. "I'll tell her that you want to hear her. She likes you. She will come." He turned and hurried away to one of the far cottages, where Mademoiselle Reisz was shuffling away. She was dragging a chair in and out of her room, and at intervals objecting to the crying of a baby, which a nurse in the adjoining cottage was endeavoring to put to sleep. She was a disagreeable little woman, no longer young, who had quarreled with almost every one, owing to a temper which was self-assertive and a disposition to trample upon the rights of others. Robert prevailed upon her without any too great difficulty.

She entered the hall with him during a lull in the dance. She made an awkward, imperious little bow as she went in. She was a homely woman, with a small **weazened** face and body and eyes that glowed. She had absolutely no taste in dress, and wore a batch of rusty black lace with a bunch of artificial violets pinned to the side of her hair.

weazened: (wizened) shriveled, withered.

"Ask Mrs. Pontellier what she would like to hear me play," she requested of Robert. She sat perfectly still before the piano, not touching the keys, while Robert carried her message to Edna at the window. A general air of surprise and genuine satisfaction fell upon every one as they saw the pianist enter. There was a settling down, and a prevailing air of expectancy everywhere. Edna was a trifle embarrassed at being thus signaled out for the imperious little woman's favor. She would not dare to choose, and begged that Mademoiselle Reisz would please herself in her selections.

Edna was what she herself called very fond of music. Musical strains, well rendered, had a way of evoking pictures in her mind. She sometimes liked to sit in the room of mornings when Madame Ratignolle played or practiced. One piece which that lady played Edna had entitled "Solitude." It was a short, plaintive, minor strain. The name of the piece was something else, but she called it "Solitude." When she heard it there came before her imagination the figure of a man standing beside a desolate rock on the seashore. He was naked. His attitude was one of hopeless resignation as he looked toward a distant bird winging its flight away from him.

Another piece called to her mind a dainty young woman clad in an **Empire gown**, taking mincing dancing steps as she came down a long avenue between tall hedges. Again, another reminded her of children at play, and still another of nothing on earth but a demure lady stroking a cat.

The very first chords which Mademoiselle Reisz struck upon the piano sent a keen tremor down Mrs. Pontellier's spinal column. It was not the first time she had heard an artist at the piano. Perhaps it was the first time she was ready, perhaps the first time her being was tempered to take an impress of the abiding truth.

She waited for the material pictures which she thought would gather and blaze before her imagination. She waited in vain. She saw no pictures of solitude, of hope, of longing, or of despair. But the very passions themselves were aroused within her soul, swaying it, lashing it, as the waves daily beat upon her splendid body. She trembled, she was choking, and the tears blinded her.

Mademoiselle had finished. She arose, and bowing her stiff, lofty bow, she went away, stopping for neither, thanks nor applause. As she passed along the gallery she patted Edna upon the shoulder.

"Well, how did you like my music?" she asked. The young woman was unable to answer; she pressed the hand of the pianist convulsively. Mademoiselle Reisz perceived her agitation and even her tears. She patted her again upon the shoulder as she said:

M. Reisz playing the piano.

Empire gown: designating a gown in the style of the French Empire period under Napoleon, with a flowing skirt, a short waist, a bodice cut low so as to bare the neck and shoulders, and short, puffed sleeves.

"You are the only one worth playing for. Those others? Bah!" and she went shuffling and sidling on down the gallery toward her room.

But she was mistaken about "those others." Her playing had aroused a fever of enthusiasm. "What passion!" "What an artist!" "I have always said no one could play **Chopin** like Mademoiselle Reisz!" "That last prelude! **Bon Dieu**! It shakes a man!"

It was growing late, and there was a general disposition to disband. But some one, perhaps it was Robert, thought of a bath at that mystic hour and under that mystic moon.

CHAPTER X

At all events Robert proposed it, and there was not a dissenting voice. There was not one but was ready to follow when he led the way. He did not lead the way, however, he directed the way; and he himself loitered behind with the lovers, who had betrayed a disposition to linger and hold themselves apart. He walked between them, whether with malicious or mischievous intent was not wholly clear, even to himself.

The Pontelliers and Ratignolles walked ahead; the women leaning upon the arms of their husbands. Edna could hear Robert's voice behind them, and could sometimes hear what he said. She wondered why he did not join them. It was unlike him not to. Of late he had sometimes held away from her for an entire day, redoubling his devotion upon the next and the next, as though to make up for hours that had been lost. She missed him the days when some pretext served to take him away from her, just as one misses the sun on a cloudy day without having thought much about the sun when it was shining.

The people walked in little groups toward the beach. They talked and laughed; some of them sang. There was a band playing down at Klein's hotel, and the strains reached them faintly, tempered by the distance. There were strange, rare odors abroad—a tangle of the sea smell and of weeds and damp, new-plowed earth, mingled with the heavy perfume of a field of white blossoms somewhere near. But the night sat lightly upon the sea and the land. There was no weight of darkness; there were no shadows. The white light of the moon had fallen upon the world like the mystery and the softness of sleep.

Chopin: Frédéric François Chopin (1810–49); Polish composer and pianist, lived in France after 1831.

Bon Dieu!: Good God!

Most of them walked into the water as though into a native element. The sea was quiet now, and swelled lazily in broad billows that melted into one another and did not break except upon the beach in little foamy crests that coiled back like slow, white serpents.

Edna had attempted all summer to learn to swim. She had received instructions from both the men and women; in some instances from the children. Robert had pursued a system of lessons almost daily; and he was nearly at the point of discouragement in realizing the futility of his efforts. A certain ungovernable dread hung about her when in the water, unless there was a hand near by that might reach out and reassure her.

But that night she was like the little tottering, stumbling, clutching child, who of a sudden realizes its powers, and walks for the first time alone, boldly and with over-confidence. She could have shouted for joy. She did shout for joy, as with a sweeping stroke or two she lifted her body to the surface of the water.

A feeling of exultation overtook her, as if some power of significant import had been given her to control the working of her body and her soul. She grew daring and reckless, overestimating her strength. She wanted to swim far out, where no woman had swum before.

Her unlooked-for achievement was the subject of wonder, applause, and admiration. Each one congratulated himself that his special teachings had accomplished this desired end.

"How easy it is!" she thought. "It is nothing," she said aloud; "why did I not discover before that it was nothing. Think of the time I have lost splashing about like a baby!" She would not join the groups in their sports and bouts, but intoxicated with her newly conquered power, she swam out alone.

She turned her face seaward to gather in an impression of space and solitude, which the vast expanse of water, meeting and melting with the moonlit sky, conveyed to her excited fancy. As she swam she seemed to be reaching out for the unlimited in which to lose herself.

Once she turned and looked toward the shore, toward the people she had left there. She had not gone any great distance that is, what would have been a great distance for an experienced swimmer. But to her unaccustomed vision the stretch of water behind her assumed the aspect of a barrier which her unaided strength would never be able to overcome.

A quick vision of death smote her soul, and for a second of time appalled and enfeebled her senses. But by an effort she rallied her staggering faculties and managed to regain the land.

She made no mention of her encounter with death and her flash of terror, except to say to her husband, "I thought I should have perished out there alone."

"You were not so very far, my dear; I was watching you," he told her.

Edna went at once to the bath-house, and she had put on her dry clothes and was ready to return home before the others had left the water. She started to walk away alone. They all called to her and shouted to her. She waved a dissenting hand, and went on, paying no further heed to their renewed cries which sought to detain her.

"Sometimes I am tempted to think that Mrs. Pontellier is **capricious**," said Madame Lebrun, who was amusing herself immensely and feared that Edna's abrupt departure might put an end to the pleasure.

capricious: subject to caprices, tending to change abruptly and without apparent reason, erratic, flighty.

"I know she is," assented Mr. Pontellier; "sometimes, not often."

Edna had not traversed a quarter of the distance on her way home before she was overtaken by Robert.

"Did you think I was afraid?" she asked him, without a shade of annoyance.

"No; I knew you weren't afraid."

"Then why did you come? Why didn't you stay out there with the others?"

"I never thought of it."

"Thought of what?"

"Of anything. What difference does it make?"

"I'm very tired," she uttered, complainingly.

"I know you are."

"You don't know anything about it. Why should you know? I never was so exhausted in my life. But it isn't unpleasant. A thousand emotions have swept through me to-night. I don't comprehend half of them. Don't mind what I'm saying; I am just thinking aloud. I wonder if I shall ever be stirred again as Mademoiselle Reisz's playing moved me to-night. I wonder if any night on earth will ever again be like this one. It is like a night in a dream. The people about me are like some uncanny, half-human beings. There must be spirits abroad to-night."

"There are," whispered Robert, "Didn't you know this was the twenty-eighth of August?"

"The twenty-eighth of August?"

"Yes. On the twenty-eighth of August, at the hour of midnight, and if the moon is shining—the moon must be shining—a spirit that has haunted these shores for ages rises up from the Gulf. With its own penetrating vision the spirit seeks some one mortal worthy to hold him company, worthy of being exalted for a few hours into realms of the semi-celestials. His search has always hitherto been fruitless, and he has sunk back, disheartened, into the sea. But to-night he found Mrs. Pontellier. Perhaps he will never wholly release her from the spell. Perhaps she will never again suffer a poor, unworthy earthling to walk in the shadow of her divine presence."

"Don't banter me," she said, wounded at what appeared to be his flippancy. He did not mind the entreaty, but the tone with its delicate note of **pathos** was like a reproach. He could not explain; he could not tell her that he had penetrated her mood and understood. He said nothing except to offer her his arm, for, by her own admission, she was exhausted. She had been walking alone with her arms hanging limp, letting her white skirts trail along the dewy path. She took his arm, but she did not lean upon it. She let her hand lie listlessly, as though her thoughts were elsewhere—somewhere in advance of her body, and she was striving to overtake them.

Robert assisted her into the hammock which swung from the post before her door out to the trunk of a tree.

"Will you stay out here and wait for Mr. Pontellier?" he asked.

"I'll stay out here. Good-night."

"Shall I get you a pillow?"

"There's one here," she said, feeling about, for they were in the shadow.

"It must be soiled; the children have been tumbling it about."

"No matter." And having discovered the pillow, she adjusted it beneath her head. She extended herself in the hammock with a deep breath of relief. She was not a **supercilious** or an over-dainty woman. She was not much given to reclining in the hammock, and when she did so it was with no cat-like suggestion of voluptuous ease, but

pathos: the quality in something experienced or observed which arouses feelings of pity, sorrow, sympathy, or compassion.

supercilious: disdainful or contemptuous, full of or characterized by pride or scorn, haughty.

with a beneficent **repose** which seemed to invade her whole body.

repose: restful tranquility.

"Shall I stay with you till Mr. Pontellier comes?" asked Robert, seating himself on the outer edge of one of the steps and taking hold of the hammock rope which was fastened to the post.

"If you wish. Don't swing the hammock. Will you get my white shawl which I left on the window-sill over at the house?"

"Are you chilly?"

"No; but I shall be presently."

"Presently?" he laughed. "Do you know what time it is? How long are you going to stay out here?"

"I don't know. Will you get the shawl?"

"Of course I will," he said, rising. He went over to the house, walking along the grass. She watched his figure pass in and out of the strips of moonlight. It was past midnight. It was very quiet.

When he returned with the shawl she took it and kept it in her hand. She did not put it around her.

"Did you say I should stay till Mr. Pontellier came back?"

"I said you might if you wished to."

He seated himself again and rolled a cigarette, which he smoked in silence. Neither did Mrs. Pontellier speak. No multitude of words could have been more significant than those moments of silence, or more pregnant with the first-felt throbbings of desire.

When the voices of the bathers were heard approaching, Robert said good-night. She did not answer him. He thought she was asleep. Again she watched his figure pass in and out of the strips of moonlight as he walked away.

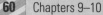

COMMENTARY

The evening event is an informal social gathering. The children are allowed to stay up past their bedtimes, and some of them provide entertainment. The Farival twins play the piano, but the parrot interrupts the ensemble. Then other children give performances, including a young girl who dances with aplomb.

Madame Ratignolle, who is unable to participate in vigorous activity, plays the piano so everyone can dance. The beauty of her playing contrasts with the playing of the Farival twins, whose clamorous music inspires the parrot's shrieks. Adèle tells the audience that she is "keeping up with her music on account of the children," and she and her husband agree that music brightens their home. Unlike Edna, who wishes to paint because it creates something in her life that satisfies an individual need, Adèle sees no reason for artistic endeavors unless they befit her mother-woman role. Chopin describes Adèle's playing as "inspiring," but this talent is unimportant to Madame Ratignolle; only its function to her family is important. Madame Ratignolle's playing is significant for another reason as well—it provides a dramatic contrast to Mademoiselle Reisz's playing, which soon follows.

After Edna dances for a brief time, she chooses to sit outside to enjoy the brightness of the rising moon and the light breeze coming off the water. Despite Madame Ratignolle's earlier advice to leave Edna alone, Robert joins her on the porch.

When Edna doubts that Mademoiselle Reisz will play for her, Robert plays the gallant and promises to bring Mademoiselle Reisz to perform. Mademoiselle Reisz is the premier pianist on Grand Isle, but she is a disagreeable woman who must be persuaded before she agrees to play. An unmarried woman without children or social position, Mademoiselle Reisz can devote herself to her music. But Chopin's description of her indicates that she pays a significant price for her art. Mademoiselle Reisz is quarrelsome and self-assertive, in a way that is clearly not an attribute. Moreover, she is homely and is poorly and unfashionably dressed.

Music and, in particular, Mademoiselle Reisz play an important role in Edna's awakening. Edna frequently identifies sensuality in music. She even describes images of a naked man, but she is also so attuned to music that, when she hears certain pieces, she is able to conjure images of life that interpret the music. Edna's body responds to the emotional sway of music; she hears and sees images that other listeners may miss. Madame Reisz's talent gives an authority to Edna's life. The older woman can create art with her playing, and she seems to reject the society that entraps Edna. She not only reminds Edna of all the beauty and sensuality that is missing from her own life, but Mademoiselle Reisz promises the possibility of a future where art and creativity are valued as much as motherhood.

Mademoiselle Reisz is a model of what Edna can expect of a single woman who rejects marriage in favor of art. She also provides a stark contrast to Madame Ratignolle. Although her playing is inspired, Madame Ratignolle can be gracious, beautiful, and talented because she has no career. Thus, her beauty is always partnered with her mother-woman image. Mademoiselle Reisz, however, has no husband or children; music is her career. As a result, she is described as having no positive attributes, except for her talent. Chopin is clearly pointing to the paradox that awaits a single woman. If she succeeds in her career, she is left alone, barren, and unattractive.

Edna's response to music is sensual, and in one particular selection previously played by Madame Ratignolle, she regarded the music as sexual. She envisioned a naked man, who longingly glanced "toward a distant bird winging its flight away from him." Edna was that bird, who has now been captured by a man — namely, her husband. On this particular evening, though, Edna's response to Mademoiselle Reisz's music is more pronounced; she emerges from the depths of her body. Edna experiences passions that are "aroused within her soul, swaying it, lashing it."

While the rest of the assembled guests acknowledge Mademoiselle Reisz's playing, the pianist ignores the others and focuses on Edna. Her awareness of Edna's emotional response foreshadows the role that she plays later in Edna's romantic attachment to Robert. Mademoiselle Reisz's music is the catalyst that completes Edna's awakening, but she is also the instrument that alters Edna's life—in this scene, when she responds to Robert's pleas and agrees to play, and later, when she serves as Edna's confessor and contact for Robert's letters.

Although Mademoiselle Reisz finishes playing late in the evening, the group quickly moves toward the beach for a moonlit swim. Chopin says that "perhaps" Robert suggested the swim, and he was certainly the one who directed them all toward the beach. Just as Robert took control by convincing Mademoiselle Reisz to play, he appears to assume command of the situation. If anything, Madame Ratignolle's conversation with Robert has resulted in a more aggressive response toward Edna, and toward everyone else.

While the group walks to the beach, Robert separates the lovers by walking between them. Chopin writes that whether his actions are made with "malicious or mischievous intent [is] not wholly clear." What is clear, though, is that Robert has changed. He is no longer the careless young man who spends his summers

Edna and Robert walking along the sea.

wooing unavailable women, and he does not join the party while they walk toward the beach, as he would have in the past.

Edna notices the change, which confuses her. She remarks that Robert often stays away from her for a whole day and then "[redoubles] his devotion upon the next and the next." Whether Robert is playing a game is not clear, but he is obviously enjoying his conquest of Edna. After all, the previous objects of his attention have not taken him seriously. Now, however, the beautiful wife of a successful New Orleans businessman has clearly become infatuated with him, and perhaps she has even fallen in love. Robert cannot easily ignore the feelings of power that this idea provides.

He wants to be successful—with the money, the power, and the lifestyle that Edna's husband enjoys. But Robert is the son of Madame Lebrun, a woman who rents cottages to the wealthy, and a woman who, in the winter, will no longer be host or guest at their fashionable New Orleans parties. For now, Robert has the

affections of a wealthy society woman, and he vacillates between the sensible choice of leaving Edna alone and the riskier one of continuing toward a possible seduction. Robert may be making a good-faith effort to stay away from Edna, as Madame Ratignolle has requested, but the power her infatuation gives him makes it difficult to adhere to these principles.

When the group arrives at the beach, something again happens to change Edna's life. She has been trying to learn to swim all summer but has not been successful. But with her passions aflame, Edna is suddenly able to swim, and as a result, she realizes a new kind of freedom. In the water, she experiences a "feeling of exultation" that makes her feel reckless and daring. She wants to swim farther than any woman has ever swum. In the water, Edna is free of the conventions of her life. By swimming farther, she can dare more and risk more, but most importantly, she is alone. She is not fettered to her husband or her children, and she is not restrained by land—there is only the water. The water, with its buoyancy, feels different than it did when she was only able to splash about in the shallow parts. Now she experiences a sensual awareness of the water as it moves against her body and offers even more freedom than she had previously experienced.

Edna ignores everyone else and swims out alone, but at one point, she looks toward the shore and is frightened to see how far she is from land. Although Edna becomes afraid when she experiences a quick vision of death, she finds the strength to overcome her panic swims back toward the shore.

In this scene, Edna is aware of two significant powers. One is an awareness of death that initially "appalled and enfeebled her senses." The second is an awareness of her own power. Although she is momentarily afraid, Edna is able to rally her strength and swim back; she proves to herself that she can survive.

When Edna returns to shore, however, Léonce is dismissive of Edna's momentary confrontation with risk.

On the way back to the cottage, Robert joins Edna and begins to tell her an old Creole story in which magic and moonlight come together in a spirit, and on this evening, they have reached out for Edna. Perhaps because the story is so exaggerated, Edna thinks that Robert is teasing her, and she is angry. She senses that, like her husband, Robert is yet another man who fails to take her seriously.

When they arrive back at the Pontellier cottage, Robert assists Edna to the hammock on the porch, where she indicates she will rest for a while.

Robert asks twice if he should stay with her, and Edna replies that he should decide. Although Robert stays until the rest of the party returns from the beach, Edna and Robert do not speak. But their silence does speak—at least for Edna. Chopin describes the sexual tension between them as "pregnant with the first-felt throbbings of desire." When Robert leaves, Edna does not answer his good night, but she is very aware of his departure.

During the course of the evening, the music has awakened Edna's passions, and swimming amid the freedom of the water has made her aware of her body in ways that she has never before experienced. Robert's story of magic and spirits may have angered Edna, but clearly, the story is true in ways that Robert may not understand. Edna has experienced a magical evening, one that has changed her forever.

Edna in hammock.
Everett Collection

Notes

Chapters 11–14

Following the late evening swim, the tension between the Pontelliers becomes more obvious when Edna asserts some independence. Edna awakens early and summons Robert to accompany her to the Chênière. Edna becomes faint during the morning services, and then Robert takes her to Madame Antoine's to recover. After a nap and dinner, Edna and Robert return to the cottages late in the evening. Léonce has left the cottage, and after the children go to sleep, Edna is left alone to think about the day.

CHAPTER XI

"What are you doing out here, Edna? I thought I should find you in bed," said her husband, when he discovered her lying there. He had walked up with Madame Lebrun and left her at the house. His wife did not reply.

"Are you asleep?" he asked, bending down close to look at her.

"No." Her eyes gleamed bright and intense, with no sleepy shadows, as they looked into his.

"Do you know it is past one o'clock? Come on," and he mounted the steps and went into their room.

"Edna!" called Mr. Pontellier from within, after a few moments had gone by.

"Don't wait for me," she answered. He thrust his head through the door.

"You will take cold out there," he said, irritably. "What folly is this? Why don't you come in?"

"It isn't cold; I have my shawl."

"The mosquitoes will devour you."

"There are no mosquitoes."

She heard him moving about the room; every sound indicating impatience and irritation. Another time she would have gone in at his request. She would, through habit, have yielded to his desire; not with any sense of submission or obedience to his compelling wishes, but unthinkingly, as we walk, move, sit, stand, go through the daily treadmill of the life which has been portioned out to us.

"Edna, dear, are you not coming in soon?" he asked again, this time fondly, with a note of entreaty.

"No; I am going to stay out here."

"This is more than folly," he blurted out. "I can't permit you to stay out there all night. You must come in the house instantly."

With a writhing motion she settled herself more securely in the hammock. She perceived that her will had blazed up, stubborn and resistant. She could not at that moment have done other than denied and resisted. She wondered if her husband had ever spoken to her like that before, and if she had submitted to his command. Of course she had; she remembered that she had. But she could not realize why or how she should have yielded, feeling as she then did.

"Léonce, go to bed," she said "I mean to stay out here. I don't wish to go in, and I don't intend to. Don't speak to me like that again; I shall not answer you."

Mr. Pontellier had prepared for bed, but he slipped on an extra garment. He opened a bottle of wine, of which he kept a small and select supply in a buffet of his own. He drank a glass of the wine and went out on the gallery and offered a glass to his wife. She did not wish any. He drew up the rocker, hoisted his slippered feet on the rail, and proceeded to smoke a cigar. He smoked two cigars; then he went inside and drank another glass of wine. Mrs. Pontellier again declined to accept a glass when it was offered to her. Mr. Pontellier once more seated himself with elevated feet, and after a reasonable interval of time smoked some more cigars.

Edna began to feel like one who awakens gradually out of a dream, a delicious, **grotesque**, impossible dream, to feel again the realities pressing into her soul. The physical need for sleep began to overtake her; the exuberance which had sustained and exalted her spirit left her helpless and yielding to the conditions which crowded her in.

The stillest hour of the night had come, the hour before dawn, when the world seems to hold its breath. The moon hung low, and had turned from silver to copper in the sleeping sky. The old owl no longer hooted, and the water-oaks had ceased to moan as they bent their heads.

Edna arose, cramped from lying so long and still in the hammock. She tottered up the steps, clutching feebly at the post before passing into the house.

"Are you coming in, Léonce?" she asked, turning her face toward her husband.

"Yes, dear," he answered, with a glance following a misty puff of smoke. "Just as soon as I have finished my cigar."

grotesque: ludicrously eccentric or strange; ridiculous; absurd.

CHAPTER XII

She slept but a few hours. They were troubled and feverish
hours, disturbed with dreams that were intangible, that
eluded her, leaving only an impression upon her half-
awakened senses of something unattainable. She was up and
dressed in the cool of the early morning. The air was invigorating and steadied somewhat her faculties. However, she
was not seeking refreshment or help from any source, either
external or from within. She was blindly following whatever
impulse moved her, as if she had placed herself in alien
hands for direction, and freed her soul of responsibility.

Most of the people at that early hour were still in bed and
asleep. A few, who intended to go over to the Chênière for
mass, were moving about. The lovers, who had laid their
plans the night before, were already strolling toward the
wharf. The lady in black, with her Sunday prayer-book,
velvet and gold-clasped, and her Sunday silver beads, was
following them at no great distance. Old Monsieur Farival
was up, and was more than half inclined to do anything
that suggested itself. He put on his big straw hat, and taking his umbrella from the stand in the hall, followed the
lady in black, never overtaking her.

The little negro girl who worked Madame Lebrun's sewing-
machine was sweeping the galleries with long, absent-
minded strokes of the broom. Edna sent her up into the
house to awaken Robert.

"Tell him I am going to the Chênière. The boat is ready;
tell him to hurry."

He had soon joined her. She had never sent for him before.
She had never asked for him. She had never seemed to
want him before. She did not appear conscious that she
had done anything unusual in commanding his presence.
He was apparently equally unconscious of anything
extraordinary in the situation. But his face was suffused
with a quiet glow when he met her.

They went together back to the kitchen to drink coffee.
There was no time to wait for any nicety of service. They
stood outside the window and the cook passed them their
coffee and a roll, which they drank and ate from the
window-sill. Edna said it tasted good.

She had not thought of coffee nor of anything. He told her
he had often noticed that she lacked forethought.

"Wasn't it enough to think of going to the Chênière and
waking you up?" she laughed. "Do I have to think of

everything?—as Léonce says when he's in a bad humor. I don't blame him; he'd never be in a bad humor if it weren't for me."

They took a short cut across the sands. At a distance they could see the curious procession moving toward the wharf—the lovers, shoulder to shoulder, creeping; the lady in black, gaining steadily upon them; old Monsieur Farival, losing ground inch by inch, and a young barefooted Spanish girl, with a red kerchief on her head and a basket on her arm, bringing up the rear.

Robert knew the girl, and he talked to her a little in the boat. No one present understood what they said. Her name was Mariequita. She had a round, sly, piquant face and pretty black eyes. Her hands were small, and she kept them folded over the handle of her basket. Her feet were broad and coarse. She did not strive to hide them. Edna looked at her feet, and noticed the sand and slime between her brown toes.

Beaudelet grumbled because Mariequita was there, taking up so much room. In reality he was annoyed at having old Monsieur Farival, who considered himself the better sailor of the two. But he would not quarrel with so old a man as Monsieur Farival, so he quarreled with Mariequita. The girl was deprecatory at one moment, appealing to Robert. She was saucy the next, moving her head up and down, making "eyes" at Robert and making "mouths" at Beaudelet.

The lovers were all alone. They saw nothing, they heard nothing. The lady in black was counting her beads for the third time. Old Monsieur Farival talked incessantly of what he knew about handling a boat, and of what Beaudelet did not know on the same subject.

Edna liked it all. She looked Mariequita up and down, from her ugly brown toes to her pretty black eyes, and back again.

"Why does she look at me like that?" inquired the girl of Robert.

"Maybe she thinks you are pretty. Shall I ask her?"

"No. Is she your sweetheart?"

"She's a married lady, and has two children."

"Oh! well! Francisco ran away with Sylvano's wife, who had four children. They took all his money and one of the children and stole his boat."

"Shut up!"

"Does she understand?"

"Oh, hush!"

"Are those two married over there—leaning on each other?"

"Of course not," laughed Robert.

"Of course not," echoed Mariequita, with a serious, confirmatory bob of the head.

The sun was high up and beginning to bite. The swift breeze seemed to Edna to bury the sting of it into the pores of her face and hands. Robert held his umbrella over her. As they went cutting sidewise through the water, the sails bellied taut, with the wind filling and overflowing them. Old Monsieur Farival laughed sardonically at something as he looked at the sails, and Beaudelet swore at the old man under his breath.

Sailing across the bay to the Chênière Caminada, Edna felt as if she were being borne away from some anchorage which had held her fast, whose chains had been loosening—had snapped the night before when the mystic spirit was abroad, leaving her free to drift whithersoever she chose to set her sails. Robert spoke to her incessantly; he no longer noticed Mariequita. The girl had shrimps in her bamboo basket. They were covered with Spanish moss. She beat the moss down impatiently, and muttered to herself sullenly.

"Let us go to **Grande Terre** to-morrow?" said Robert in a low voice.

"What shall we do there?"

"Climb up the hill to the old fort and look at the little wriggling gold snakes, and watch the lizards sun themselves."

She gazed away toward Grande Terre and thought she would like to be alone there with Robert, in the sun, listening to the ocean's roar and watching the slimy lizards writhe in and out among the ruins of the old fort.

"And the next day or the next we can sail to the Bayou Brulow," he went on.

"What shall we do there?"

"Anything—cast bait for fish."

"No; we'll go back to Grande Terre. Let the fish alone."

"We'll go wherever you like," he said. "I'll have Tonie come over and help me patch and trim my boat. We shall not need Beaudelet nor any one. Are you afraid of the **pirogue**?"

Grande Terre: an island close to Grand Isle, off the coast of Louisiana.

pirogue: a dugout canoe.

"Oh, no."

"Then I'll take you some night in the pirogue when the moon shines. Maybe your Gulf spirit will whisper to you in which of these islands the treasures are hidden—direct you to the very spot, perhaps."

"And in a day we should be rich!" she laughed. "I'd give it all to you, the pirate gold and every bit of treasure we could dig up. I think you would know how to spend it. Pirate gold isn't a thing to be hoarded or utilized. It is something to squander and throw to the four winds, for the fun of seeing the golden specks fly."

"We'd share it, and scatter it together," he said. His face flushed.

They all went together up to the quaint little **Gothic** church of Our Lady of Lourdes, gleaming all brown and yellow with paint in the sun's glare.

Gothic: designating, of, or related to a style of architecture developed in Western Europe between the 12th and 16th centuries and characterized by the use of ribbed vaulting, flying buttresses, pointed arches, steep, high roofs, etc. *Gothic church.*

Only Beaudelet remained behind, tinkering at his boat, and Mariequita walked away with her basket of shrimps, casting a look of childish ill humor and reproach at Robert from the corner of her eye.

CHAPTER XIII

A feeling of oppression and drowsiness overcame Edna during the service. Her head began to ache, and the lights on the altar swayed before her eyes. Another time she might have made an effort to regain her composure; but her one thought was to quit the stifling atmosphere of the church and reach the open air. She arose, climbing over Robert's feet with a muttered apology. Old Monsieur Farival, flurried, curious, stood up, but upon seeing that Robert had followed Mrs. Pontellier, he sank back into his seat. He whispered an anxious inquiry of the lady in black, who did not notice him or reply, but kept her eyes fastened upon the pages of her velvet prayer-book.

"I felt giddy and almost overcome," Edna said, lifting her hands instinctively to her head and pushing her straw hat up from her forehead. "I couldn't have stayed through the service." They were outside in the shadow of the church. Robert was full of solicitude.

"It was folly to have thought of going in the first place, let alone staying. Come over to Madame Antoine's; you can rest there." He took her arm and led her away, looking anxiously and continuously down into her face.

How still it was, with only the voice of the sea whispering through the reeds that grew in the salt-water pools! The long line of little gray, weather-beaten houses nestled peacefully among the orange trees. It must always have been God's day on that low, drowsy island, Edna thought. They stopped, leaning over a jagged fence made of **sea-drift**, to ask for water. A youth, a mild-faced **Acadian**, was drawing water from the cistern, which was nothing more than a rusty buoy, with an opening on one side, sunk in the ground. The water which the youth handed to them in a tin pail was not cold to taste, but it was cool to her heated face, and it greatly revived and refreshed her.

Madame Antoine's cot was at the far end of the village. She welcomed them with all the native hospitality, as she would have opened her door to let the sunlight in. She was fat, and walked heavily and clumsily across the floor. She could speak no English, but when Robert made her understand that the lady who accompanied him was ill and desired to rest, she was all eagerness to make Edna feel at home and to **dispose** of her comfortably.

The whole place was immaculately clean, and the big, four-posted bed, snow-white, invited one to repose. It stood in a small side room which looked out across a narrow grass plot toward the shed, where there was a disabled boat lying keel upward.

Madame Antoine had not gone to mass. Her son Tonie had, but she supposed he would soon be back, and she invited Robert to be seated and wait for him. But he went and sat outside the door and smoked. Madame Antoine busied herself in the large front room preparing dinner. She was boiling **mullets** over a few red coals in the huge fireplace.

Edna, left alone in the little side room, loosened her clothes, removing the greater part of them. She bathed her face, her neck and arms in the basin that stood between the windows. She took off her shoes and stockings and stretched herself in the very center of the high, white bed. How luxurious it felt to rest thus in a strange, quaint bed, with its sweet country odor of laurel lingering about the sheets and mattress! She stretched her strong limbs that ached a little. She ran her fingers through her loosened hair for a while. She looked at her round arms as she held them straight up and rubbed them one after the other, observing closely, as if it were something she saw for the first time,

sea-drift: driftwood, wood drifting in the water, or that has been washed ashore.

Acadian: Descendant of the French Canadians who in 1755 left Acadia, a former French colony (1604–1713) on the northeast coast of North America.

dispose: to arrange (matters).

mullets: any of a family of edible, spiny-finned percoid fishes, both freshwater and marine, having a small mouth and feeble teeth; especially, a striped species.

the fine, firm quality and texture of her flesh. She clasped her hands easily above her head, and it was thus she fell asleep.

She slept lightly at first, half awake and drowsily attentive to the things about her. She could hear Madame Antoine's heavy, scraping tread as she walked back and forth on the sanded floor. Some chickens were clucking outside the windows, scratching for bits of gravel in the grass. Later she half heard the voices of Robert and Tonie talking under the shed. She did not stir. Even her eyelids rested numb and heavily over her sleepy eyes. The voices went on—Tonie's slow, Acadian drawl, Robert's quick, soft, smooth French. She understood French imperfectly unless directly addressed, and the voices were only part of the other drowsy, muffled sounds lulling her senses.

When Edna awoke it was with the conviction that she had slept long and soundly. The voices were hushed under the shed. Madame Antoine's step was no longer to be heard in the adjoining room. Even the chickens had gone elsewhere to scratch and cluck. The mosquito bar was drawn over her; the old woman had come in while she slept and let down the bar. Edna arose quietly from the bed, and looking between the curtains of the window, she saw by the slanting rays of the sun that the afternoon was far advanced. Robert was out there under the shed, reclining in the shade against the **sloping keel** of the overturned boat. He was reading from a book. Tonie was no longer with him. She wondered what had become of the rest of the party. She peeped out at him two or three times as she stood washing herself in the little basin between the windows.

sloping keel: The keel is the chief timber or steel piece extending along the entire length of the bottom of a boat or ship and supporting the frame; it sometimes protrudes beneath the hull. This description refers to the shape of the keel.

Madame Antoine had laid some coarse, clean towels upon a chair, and had placed a box of poudre de riz within easy reach. Edna dabbed the powder upon her nose and cheeks as she looked at herself closely in the little distorted mirror which hung on the wall above the basin. Her eyes were bright and wide awake and her face glowed.

When she had completed her toilet she walked into the adjoining room. She was very hungry. No one was there. But there was a cloth spread upon the table that stood against the wall, and a **cover** was laid for one, with a crusty brown loaf and a bottle of wine beside the plate. Edna bit a piece from the brown loaf, tearing it with her strong, white teeth. She poured some of the wine into the glass and drank it down. Then she went softly out of doors, and plucking an

cover: a tablecloth and setting for a meal, especially for one person.

orange from the low-hanging bough of a tree, threw it at Robert, who did not know she was awake and up.

An illumination broke over his whole face when he saw her and joined her under the orange tree.

"How many years have I slept?" she inquired. "The whole island seems changed. A new race of beings must have sprung up, leaving only you and me as past relics. How many ages ago did Madame Antoine and Tonie die? and when did our people from Grand Isle disappear from the earth?"

He familiarly adjusted a ruffle upon her shoulder.

"You have slept precisely one hundred years. I was left here to guard your slumbers; and for one hundred years I have been out under the shed reading a book. The only evil I couldn't prevent was to keep a broiled fowl from drying up."

"If it has turned to stone, still will I eat it," said Edna, moving with him into the house. "But really, what has become of Monsieur Farival and the others?"

"Gone hours ago. When they found that you were sleeping they thought it best not to awake you. Any way, I wouldn't have let them. What was I here for?"

"I wonder if Léonce will be uneasy!" she speculated, as she seated herself at table.

"Of course not; he knows you are with me," Robert replied, as he busied himself among sundry pans and covered dishes which had been left standing on the hearth.

"Where are Madame Antoine and her son?" asked Edna.

"Gone to **Vespers**, and to visit some friends, I believe. I am to take you back in Tonie's boat whenever you are ready to go."

He stirred the smoldering ashes till the broiled fowl began to sizzle afresh. He served her with no mean repast, dripping the coffee anew and sharing it with her. Madame Antoine had cooked little else than the mullets, but while Edna slept Robert had foraged the island. He was childishly gratified to discover her appetite, and to see the relish with which she ate the food which he had procured for her.

"Shall we go right away?" she asked, after draining her glass and brushing together the crumbs of the crusty loaf.

"The sun isn't as low as it will be in two hours," he answered.

"The sun will be gone in two hours."

"Well, let it go; who cares!"

Vespers: the sixth of the seven canonical hours; evening prayer.

They waited a good while under the orange trees, till Madame Antoine came back, panting, waddling, with a thousand apologies to explain her absence. Tonie did not dare to return. He was shy, and would not willingly face any woman except his mother.

It was very pleasant to stay there under the orange trees, while the sun dipped lower and lower, turning the western sky to flaming copper and gold. The shadows lengthened and crept out like stealthy, grotesque monsters across the grass.

Edna and Robert both sat upon the ground—that is, he lay upon the ground beside her, occasionally picking at the hem of her muslin gown.

Madame Antoine seated her fat body, broad and squat, upon a bench beside the door. She had been talking all the afternoon, and had wound herself up to the storytelling pitch.

And what stories she told them! But twice in her life she had left the Chênière Caminada, and then for the briefest span. All her years she had squatted and waddled there upon the island, gathering legends of the Baratarians and the sea. The night came on, with the moon to lighten it. Edna could hear the whispering voices of dead men and the click of muffled gold.

When she and Robert stepped into Tonie's boat, with the red lateen sail, misty spirit forms were prowling in the shadows and among the reeds, and upon the water were phantom ships, speeding to cover.

CHAPTER XIV

The youngest boy, Etienne, had been very naughty, Madame Ratignolle said, as she delivered him into the hands of his mother. He had been unwilling to go to bed and had made a scene; whereupon she had taken charge of him and pacified him as well as she could. Raoul had been in bed and asleep for two hours.

The youngster was in his long white nightgown, that kept tripping him up as Madame Ratignolle led him along by the hand. With the other chubby fist he rubbed his eyes, which were heavy with sleep and ill humor. Edna took him in her arms, and seating herself in the rocker, began to coddle and caress him, calling him all manner of tender names, soothing him to sleep.

It was not more than nine o'clock. No one had yet gone to bed but the children.

Léonce had been very uneasy at first, Madame Ratignolle said, and had wanted to start at once for the Chênière. But Monsieur Farival had assured him that his wife was only overcome with sleep and fatigue, that Tonie would bring her safely back later in the day; and he had thus been dissuaded from crossing the bay. He had gone over to Klein's, looking up some cotton broker whom he wished to see in regard to securities, exchanges, stocks, bonds, or something of the sort, Madame Ratignolle did not remember what. He said he would not remain away late. She herself was suffering from heat and oppression, she said. She carried a bottle of salts and a large fan. She would not consent to remain with Edna, for Monsieur Ratignolle was alone, and he detested above all things to be left alone.

When Etienne had fallen asleep Edna bore him into the back room, and Robert went and lifted the mosquito bar that she might lay the child comfortably in his bed. The quadroon had vanished. When they emerged from the cottage Robert bade Edna good-night.

"Do you know we have been together the whole livelong day, Robert—since early this morning?" she said at parting.

"All but the hundred years when you were sleeping. Good-night."

He pressed her hand and went away in the direction of the beach. He did not join any of the others, but walked alone toward the Gulf.

Edna stayed outside, awaiting her husband's return. She had no desire to sleep or to retire; nor did she feel like going over to sit with the Ratignolles, or to join Madame Lebrun and a group whose animated voices reached her as they sat in conversation before the house. She let her mind wander back over her stay at Grand Isle; and she tried to discover wherein this summer had been different from any and every other summer of her life. She could only realize that she herself—her present self—was in some way different from the other self. That she was seeing with different eyes and making the acquaintance of new conditions in herself that colored and changed her environment, she did not yet suspect.

She wondered why Robert had gone away and left her. It did not occur to her to think he might have grown tired of being with her the livelong day. She was not tired, and she felt that he was not. She regretted that he had gone. It was so much more natural to have him stay when he was not absolutely required to leave her.

As Edna waited for her husband she sang low a little song that Robert had sung as they crossed the bay. It began with "Ah! **Si tu savais**," and every verse ended with "si tu savais."

Robert's voice was not pretentious. It was musical and true. The voice, the notes, the whole refrain haunted her memory.

Si tu savais: if you knew.

COMMENTARY

Edna is still lying in the hammock when Léonce Pontellier arrives at the cottage. When he discovers that she is awake, he reminds her of the time and orders her to come to bed in the same way that a parent reminds a child of his or her bedtime and orders that child to bed. However, Edna is not a child, and she is no longer the compliant wife. When Léonce speaks to her, Edna replies as his equal—a point that Chopin makes clear. When Léonce imperiously demands that Edna come inside the house, she declines, and tells him never again to speak to her in such a manner. Léonce refers to his wife's disobedience as "folly."

While he prepares for bed, Léonce's restlessness reveals not only his impatience with his wife, but how unaccustomed he is to Edna's defiance. Edna had always acquiesced "through habit . . . unthinkingly." Her obedience is innate in the way that people "walk, move, sit, stand, go through the daily treadmill of . . . life." In the past, Edna's obedience was automatic; she has now awakened to her own desires, including thinking for herself. Although Edna is tired, she refuses to go to bed, and thus, she refuses to obey her husband.

When Léonce moves from demanding Edna's obedience to imploring her to come inside, Edna again resists. Obviously, Edna is no more moved by his pleas than she was moved by his demands. Léonce is a businessman, and people who work for him also obey him. According to Léonce, his wife should be as obedient as any employee, but she is not. The confrontation between husband and wife quickly becomes a struggle for authority. In part, Léonce is shocked at the behavior of his wife. Her submissiveness is gone. She looks at him and speaks to him as an equal, and Léonce responds the only way he can—with anger. Léonce tells Edna that he cannot permit her to stay on the porch all night, and he resolves to wait her out. Otherwise, he would abdicate

control by allowing Edna to win. In the hours that pass, Edna begins to feel the strength and euphoria from the previous evening dissolve in the realities of her life; she "yield[s] to the conditions [that] crowd her in." She really has no choice but to go into the house, and when she enters and asks whether Léonce is joining her, he declines. In any struggle for power, Léonce will obviously be a formidable foe.

Although Edna has slept only a few hours, she leaves the cottage and sends a servant to awaken Robert. Edna has changed. She has never before asked for Robert; she had simply accepted his presence. Now she has summoned him, and as a result, her action signifies a new relationship between them. Chopin emphasizes this new relationship by repeating, "She had never sent for him . . . She had never asked for him . . . She had never seemed to want him." These thoughts are all new for Edna, and they reveal how significantly Edna has changed. Just as Léonce commanded Edna to come inside the night before, Edna has commanded Robert to join her, and she has told him to hurry. Clearly, the transformation of the previous evening was not a momentary whim. When Edna and Robert arrive at the wharf, they are joined by the ever-lurking lovers and the woman in black. These three disparate characters have been witnesses all summer to Edna's burgeoning relationship with Robert.

Edna and Robert are joined in the boat with others from the island, including the Spanish girl, Mariequita. She asks whether Edna and Robert are lovers. Her question is not condemning, because in Mariequita's world, married women can have lovers and often do. Her assumption that Edna is Robert's lover reveals how different the relationship has become. Edna is no longer the proper married woman, whose behavior is beyond reproach. In comparing Edna to a local woman who left

COMMENTARY

Sailboat at sea.

her husband and four children to run away with another man, Mariequita is acknowledging the sexual tension that exists between Edna and Robert. Robert is intently aware that Edna has changed. He suggests taking a trip the next day to Grande Terre so they can watch wriggling snakes and lizards writhing in the hot sun. The sexual imagery is obvious. Edna agrees, and she even suggests taking a second trip on the following day. Her mood is light and joyous, and she joins in easily with Robert's teasing. The trip away from Grand Isle has made Edna feel as if she is free from the shackles that have constrained her. If the sailboat has made Edna feel free from the island and her obligations, the Gothic church, and all that it represents, chokes her spirit.

Edna finds the church service oppressive because of its representation of ancient rituals and tenets. The church represents the old Edna, who vowed to obey when she married. Moreover, the church and its services represent the conventional orderly life that Edna now finds overwhelming. Suddenly, Edna finds that the "stifling atmosphere" of the church is too much to

tolerate. When Edna feels faint, she leaves the church instead of fighting for her composure. This action foreshadows that Edna will not be restrained by the conventions of society.

Edna finds a small bit of sanctuary at Madame Antoine's, where a comfortable bed awaits her. Left alone, Edna loosens her clothing, going so far as to "remov[e] the greater part of them." Edna is acutely aware of her body, just as she was during her swim the previous evening. She sees, as if for the first time, her limbs and her skin; she notices her body's strength and the firmness of her flesh. For Edna, a great period of time seems to elapse when she sleeps. Although she awakes late afternoon, Edna feels like she is again reborn. After asking how many years have passed since she slept, Edna suggests that a "new race of beings must have sprung up, leaving only you and me as past relics," and she asks, "when did our people from Grand Isle disappear from the earth?" For Edna, she fantasizes that she and Robert have been left alone and that Léonce may have disappeared. Robert touches Edna "familiarly" and easily jokes that she has been asleep for 100 years. But Edna's question about Grand Isle proclaims her awareness that she cannot so easily escape her life as well as the people waiting for her to return to the island.

Edna has awakened hungry, and she eats with the gusto of someone who has been starved, and certainly, Edna has been starved. She has awakened to her own sexuality, and having discovered her own body, her desire to feed all parts of her body is heightened. Although Edna inquires whether Léonce may be worried, Chopin uses the word "speculated" to imply that the answer is of little concern to Edna. She and Robert make no move to return to Grand Isle, and they linger on the island until midevening. For Edna, the time is to be enjoyed. She is free of Léonce and her children, and she is in no hurry to return to the bondage of her life. In fact, she never even mentions her children. For Edna, even the return trip seems infused with magical spirits.

This magic is quickly dispelled with the arrival on Grand Isle. Madame Ratignolle has been attending to Edna's children, and the oldest one has gone to bed. Edna seemingly feels no guilt for inconveniencing her dearest friend, who admits to suffering from "heat and oppression," the same conditions that drove Edna from the church earlier. But for Madame Ratignolle, these

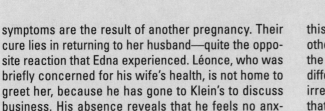

symptoms are the result of another pregnancy. Their cure lies in returning to her husband—quite the opposite reaction that Edna experienced. Léonce, who was briefly concerned for his wife's health, is not home to greet her, because he has gone to Klein's to discuss business. His absence reveals that he feels no anxiousness at his wife's absence. Robert soon leaves, and Edna is left alone to think about the day just passed.

While she waits on the porch for Léonce's return, Edna replays the summer's events in her mind. She recognizes that she has somehow changed, but she is unable to remember any particular moment "wherein this summer ha[s] been different from any and every other summer of her life." Edna does not yet realize that the summer has not been different at all. Instead, she is different. Within the past few days, her life has changed irrevocably. She regrets Robert's departure, thinking that his presence in her life is "natural." Ironically, Edna sings the refrain, "if you only knew." Unlike Edna, Robert knows that Edna is different, and consequently, this knowledge has changed him. When he leaves, instead of joining the other visitors, Robert turns toward the beach for a solitary walk and a chance to think. How much he has changed will soon be evident to Edna.

Notes

Chapters 15–16

Edna enters the dining room for dinner and learns that Robert is leaving for Mexico the same evening. Edna is surprised and upset and returns to her cottage, where Robert later finds her. After Robert tells her good-bye, Edna realizes that she is infatuated with him. Edna misses Robert and takes every opportunity to talk about him. The time at Grand Isle is ending, and to help pass the time, Edna spends extra time practicing her swimming, but she is no longer enjoying her summer at Grand Isle.

CHAPTER XV

When Edna entered the dining-room one evening a little late, as was her habit, an unusually animated conversation seemed to be going on. Several persons were talking at once, and Victor's voice was predominating, even over that of his mother. Edna had returned late from her bath, had dressed in some haste, and her face was flushed. Her head, set off by her dainty white gown, suggested a rich, rare blossom. She took her seat at table between old Monsieur Farival and Madame Ratignolle.

As she seated herself and was about to begin to eat her soup, which had been served when she entered the room, several persons informed her simultaneously that Robert was going to Mexico. She laid her spoon down and looked about her bewildered. He had been with her, reading to her all the morning, and had never even mentioned such a place as Mexico. She had not seen him during the afternoon; she had heard some one say he was at the house, upstairs with his mother. This she had thought nothing of, though she was surprised when he did not join her later in the afternoon, when she went down to the beach.

She looked across at him, where he sat beside Madame Lebrun, who presided. Edna's face was a blank picture of bewilderment, which she never thought of disguising. He lifted his eyebrows with the pretext of a smile as he returned her glance. He looked embarrassed and uneasy. "When is he going?" she asked of everybody in general, as if Robert were not there to answer for himself.

"To-night!" "This very evening!" "Did you ever!" "What possesses him!" were some of the replies she gathered, uttered simultaneously in French and English.

"Impossible!" she exclaimed. "How can a person start off from Grand Isle to Mexico at a moment's notice, as if he were going over to Klein's or to the wharf or down to the beach?"

NOTES

"I said all along I was going to Mexico; I've been saying so for years!" cried Robert, in an excited and irritable tone, with the air of a man defending himself against a swarm of stinging insects.

Madame Lebrun knocked on the table with her knife handle.

"Please let Robert explain why he is going, and why he is going to-night," she called out. "Really, this table is getting to be more and more like **Bedlam** every day, with everybody talking at once. Sometimes—I hope God will forgive me—but positively, sometimes I wish Victor would lose the power of speech."

Bedlam: any place or condition of noise and confusion.

Victor laughed sardonically as he thanked his mother for her holy wish, of which he failed to see the benefit to anybody, except that it might afford her a more ample opportunity and license to talk herself.

Monsieur Farival thought that Victor should have been taken out in mid-ocean in his earliest youth and drowned. Victor thought there would be more logic in thus disposing of old people with an established claim for making themselves universally obnoxious. Madame Lebrun grew a trifle hysterical; Robert called his brother some sharp, hard names.

"There's nothing much to explain, mother," he said; though he explained, nevertheless—looking chiefly at Edna—that he could only meet the gentleman whom he intended to join at Vera Cruz by taking such and such a steamer, which left New Orleans on such a day; that Beaudelet was going out with his lugger-load of vegetables that night, which gave him an opportunity of reaching the city and making his vessel in time.

"But when did you make up your mind to all this?" demanded Monsieur Farival.

"This afternoon," returned Robert, with a shade of annoyance.

"At what time this afternoon?" persisted the old gentleman, with nagging determination, as if he were cross-questioning a criminal in a court of justice.

"At four o'clock this afternoon, Monsieur Farival," Robert replied, in a high voice and with a lofty air, which reminded Edna of some gentleman on the stage.

She had forced herself to eat most of her soup, and now she was picking the flaky bits of a **court bouillon** with her fork.

court bouillon: an aromatic liquid used especially for poaching fish and made by cooking white wine, water, onions, celery, carrots, and herbs together.

The lovers were profiting by the general conversation on Mexico to speak in whispers of matters which they rightly considered were interesting to no one but themselves. The lady in black had once received a pair of prayer-beads of curious workmanship from Mexico, with very special **indulgence** attached to them, but she had never been able to ascertain whether the indulgence extended outside the Mexican border. Father Fochel of the Cathedral had attempted to explain it; but he had not done so to her satisfaction. And she begged that Robert would interest himself, and discover, if possible, whether she was entitled to the indulgence accompanying the remarkably curious Mexican prayer-beads.

Madame Ratignolle hoped that Robert would exercise extreme caution in dealing with the Mexicans, who, she considered, were a treacherous people, unscrupulous and revengeful. She trusted she did them no injustice in thus condemning them as a race. She had known personally but one Mexican, who made and sold excellent tamales, and whom she would have trusted implicitly, so soft-spoken was he. One day he was arrested for stabbing his wife. She never knew whether he had been hanged or not.

Victor had grown hilarious, and was attempting to tell an anecdote about a Mexican girl who served chocolate one winter in a restaurant in Dauphine Street. No one would listen to him but old Monsieur Farival, who went into convulsions over the droll story.

Edna wondered if they had all gone mad, to be talking and clamoring at that rate. She herself could think of nothing to say about Mexico or the Mexicans.

"At what time do you leave?" she asked Robert.

"At ten," he told her. "Beaudelet wants to wait for the moon."

"Are you all ready to go?"

"Quite ready. I shall only take a hand-bag, and shall pack my trunk in the city."

He turned to answer some question put to him by his mother, and Edna, having finished her black coffee, left the table.

She went directly to her room. The little cottage was **close** and stuffy after leaving the outer air. But she did not mind; there appeared to be a hundred different things demanding her attention indoors. She began to set the toilet-stand to rights, grumbling at the negligence of the quadroon, who

indulgence: a partial or complete remission, under conditions specified by the Catholic church, of divine temporal punishment that may otherwise still be due for sin committed but forgiven.

close: here, confined or confining; narrow.

was in the adjoining room putting the children to bed. She gathered together stray garments that were hanging on the backs of chairs, and put each where it belonged in closet or bureau drawer. She changed her gown for a more comfortable and **commodious** wrapper. She rearranged her hair, combing and brushing it with unusual energy. Then she went in and assisted the quadroon in getting the boys to bed.

commodious: offering plenty of room; spacious; roomy.

They were very playful and inclined to talk—to do anything but lie quiet and go to sleep. Edna sent the quadroon away to her supper and told her she need not return. Then she sat and told the children a story. Instead of soothing it excited them, and added to their wakefulness. She left them in heated argument, speculating about the conclusion of the tale which their mother promised to finish the following night.

The little black girl came in to say that Madame Lebrun would like to have Mrs. Pontellier go and sit with them over at the house till Mr. Robert went away. Edna returned answer that she had already undressed, that she did not feel quite well, but perhaps she would go over to the house later. She started to dress again, and got as far advanced as to remove her peignoir. But changing her mind once more she resumed the peignoir, and went outside and sat down before her door. She was overheated and irritable, and fanned herself energetically for a while. Madame Ratignolle came down to discover what was the matter.

"All that noise and confusion at the table must have upset me," replied Edna, "and moreover, I hate shocks and surprises. The idea of Robert starting off in such a ridiculously sudden and dramatic way! As if it were a matter of life and death! Never saying a word about it all morning when he was with me."

"Yes," agreed Madame Ratignolle. "I think it was showing us all—you especially—very little consideration. It wouldn't have surprised me in any of the others; those Lebruns are all given to heroics. But I must say I should never have expected such a thing from Robert. Are you not coming down? Come on, dear; it doesn't look friendly."

"No," said Edna, a little sullenly. "I can't go to the trouble of dressing again; I don't feel like it."

"You needn't dress; you look all right; fasten a belt around your waist. Just look at me!"

"No," persisted Edna; "but you go on. Madame Lebrun might be offended if we both stayed away."

Madame Ratignolle kissed Edna good-night, and went away, being in truth rather desirous of joining in the general and animated conversation which was still in progress concerning Mexico and the Mexicans.

Somewhat later Robert came up, carrying his hand-bag.

"Aren't you feeling well?" he asked.

"Oh, well enough. Are you going right away?"

He lit a match and looked at his watch. "In twenty minutes," he said. The sudden and brief flare of the match emphasized the darkness for a while. He sat down upon a stool which the children had left out on the porch.

"Get a chair," said Edna.

"This will do," he replied. He put on his soft hat and nervously took it off again, and wiping his face with his handkerchief, complained of the heat.

"Take the fan," said Edna, offering it to him.

"Oh, no! Thank you. It does no good; you have to stop fanning some time, and feel all the more uncomfortable afterward."

"That's one of the ridiculous things which men always say. I have never known one to speak otherwise of fanning. How long will you be gone?"

"Forever, perhaps. I don't know. It depends upon a good many things."

"Well, in case it shouldn't be forever, how long will it be?"

"I don't know."

"This seems to me perfectly preposterous and uncalled for. I don't like it. I don't understand your motive for silence and mystery, never saying a word to me about it this morning." He remained silent, not offering to defend himself. He only said, after a moment:

"Don't part from me in any ill humor. I never knew you to be out of patience with me before."

"I don't want to part in any ill humor," she said. "But can't you understand? I've grown used to seeing you, to having you with me all the time, and your action seems unfriendly, even unkind. You don't even offer an excuse for it. Why, I was planning to be together, thinking of how pleasant it would be to see you in the city next winter."

"So was I," he blurted. "Perhaps that's the—" He stood up suddenly and held out his hand. "Good-by, my dear Mrs. Pontellier; good-by. You won't—I hope you won't completely forget me." She clung to his hand, striving to detain him.

"Write to me when you get there, won't you, Robert?" she entreated.

"I will, thank you. Good-by."

How unlike Robert! The merest acquaintance would have said something more emphatic than "I will, thank you; good-by," to such a request.

He had evidently already taken leave of the people over at the house, for he descended the steps and went to join Beaudelet, who was out there with an oar across his shoulder waiting for Robert. They walked away in the darkness. She could only hear Beaudelet's voice; Robert had apparently not even spoken a word of greeting to his companion.

Edna bit her handkerchief convulsively, striving to hold back and to hide, even from herself as she would have hidden from another, the emotion which was troubling— tearing—her. Her eyes were brimming with tears.

For the first time she recognized the symptoms of infatuation which she had felt **incipiently** as a child, as a girl in her earliest teens, and later as a young woman. The recognition did not lessen the reality, the poignancy of the revelation by any suggestion or promise of instability. The past was nothing to her; offered no lesson which she was willing to heed. The future was a mystery which she never attempted to penetrate. The present alone was significant; was hers, to torture her as it was doing then with the biting conviction that she had lost that which she had held, that she had been denied that which her impassioned, newly awakened being demanded.

CHAPTER XVI

"Do you miss your friend greatly?" asked Mademoiselle Reisz one morning as she came creeping up behind Edna, who had just left her cottage on her way to the beach. She spent much of her time in the water since she had acquired finally the art of swimming. As their stay at Grand Isle drew near its close, she felt that she could not give too much time to a diversion which afforded her the only real pleasurable moments that she knew. When Mademoiselle Reisz came and touched her upon the shoulder and spoke to her, the woman seemed to echo the thought which was ever in Edna's mind; or, better, the feeling which constantly possessed her.

Robert's going had some way taken the brightness, the color, the meaning out of everything. The conditions of her

incipiently: in the first stage of existence, just beginning to exist or to come to notice, as in Edna's childhood.

life were in no way changed, but her whole existence was dulled, like a faded garment which seems to be no longer worth wearing. She sought him everywhere—in others whom she induced to talk about him. She went up in the mornings to Madame Lebrun's room, braving the clatter of the old sewing-machine. She sat there and chatted at intervals as Robert had done. She gazed around the room at the pictures and photographs hanging upon the wall, and discovered in some corner an old family album, which she examined with the keenest interest, appealing to Madame Lebrun for enlightenment concerning the many figures and faces which she discovered between its pages.

There was a picture of Madame Lebrun with Robert as a baby, seated in her lap, a round-faced infant with a fist in his mouth. The eyes alone in the baby suggested the man. And that was he also in kilts, at the age of five, wearing long curls and holding a whip in his hand. It made Edna laugh, and she laughed, too, at the portrait in his first long trousers; while another interested her, taken when he left for college, looking thin, long-faced, with eyes full of fire, ambition and great intentions. But there was no recent picture, none which suggested the Robert who had gone away five days ago, leaving a void and wilderness behind him.

"Oh, Robert stopped having his pictures taken when he had to pay for them himself! He found wiser use for his money, he says," explained Madame Lebrun. She had a letter from him, written before he left New Orleans. Edna wished to see the letter, and Madame Lebrun told her to look for it either on the table or the dresser, or perhaps it was on the mantelpiece.

The letter was on the bookshelf. It possessed the greatest interest and attraction for Edna; the envelope, its size and shape, the post-mark, the handwriting. She examined every detail of the outside before opening it. There were only a few lines, setting forth that he would leave the city that afternoon, that he had packed his trunk in good shape, that he was well, and sent her his love and begged to be affectionately remembered to all. There was no special message to Edna except a postscript saying that if Mrs. Pontellier desired to finish the book which he had been reading to her, his mother would find it in his room, among other books there on the table. Edna experienced a pang of jealousy because he had written to his mother rather than to her.

Every one seemed to take for granted that she missed him. Even her husband, when he came down the Saturday following Robert's departure, expressed regret that he had gone.

"How do you get on without him, Edna?" he asked.

"It's very dull without him," she admitted. Mr. Pontellier had seen Robert in the city, and Edna asked him a dozen questions or more. Where had they met? On Carondelet Street, in the morning. They had gone "in" and had a drink and a cigar together. What had they talked about? Chiefly about his prospects in Mexico, which Mr. Pontellier thought were promising. How did he look? How did he seem—grave, or gay, or how? Quite cheerful, and wholly taken up with the idea of his trip, which Mr. Pontellier found altogether natural in a young fellow about to seek fortune and adventure in a strange, queer country.

Edna tapped her foot impatiently, and wondered why the children persisted in playing in the sun when they might be under the trees. She went down and led them out of the sun, scolding the quadroon for not being more attentive.

It did not strike her as in the least grotesque that she should be making of Robert the object of conversation and leading her husband to speak of him. The sentiment which she entertained for Robert in no way resembled that which she felt for her husband, or had ever felt, or ever expected to feel. She had all her life long been accustomed to harbor thoughts and emotions which never voiced themselves. They had never taken the form of struggles. They belonged to her and were her own, and she entertained the conviction that she had a right to them and that they concerned no one but herself. Edna had once told Madame Ratignolle that she would never sacrifice herself for her children, or for any one. Then had followed a rather heated argument; the two women did not appear to understand each other or to be talking the same language. Edna tried to appease her friend, to explain.

"I would give up the unessential; I would give my money, I would give my life for my children; but I wouldn't give myself. I can't make it more clear; it's only something which I am beginning to comprehend, which is revealing itself to me."

"I don't know what you would call the essential, or what you mean by the unessential," said Madame Ratignolle, cheerfully; "but a woman who would give her life for her

children could do no more than that—your Bible tells you
so. I'm sure I couldn't do more than that."

"Oh, yes you could!" laughed Edna.

She was not surprised at Mademoiselle Reisz's question the
morning that lady, following her to the beach, tapped her
on the shoulder and asked if she did not greatly miss her
young friend.

"Oh, good morning, Mademoiselle; is it you? Why, of
course I miss Robert. Are you going down to bathe?"

"Why should I go down to bathe at the very end of the season when I haven't been in the surf all summer," replied the
woman, disagreeably.

"I beg your pardon," offered Edna, in some embarrass-
ment, for she should have remembered that Mademoiselle
Reisz's avoidance of the water had furnished a theme for
much pleasantry. Some among them thought it was on
account of her false hair, or the dread of getting the violets
wet, while others attributed it to the natural aversion for
water sometimes believed to accompany the artistic temperament. Mademoiselle offered Edna some chocolates in a
paper bag, which she took from her pocket, by way of
showing that she bore no ill feeling. She habitually ate
chocolates for their sustaining quality; they contained
much nutriment in small **compass**, she said. They saved
her from starvation, as Madame Lebrun's table was utterly
impossible; and no one save so impertinent a woman as
Madame Lebrun could think of offering such food to people and requiring them to pay for it.

"She must feel very lonely without her son," said Edna,
desiring to change the subject. "Her favorite son, too. It
must have been quite hard to let him go."

Mademoiselle laughed maliciously.

"Her favorite son! Oh, dear! Who could have been imposing such a tale upon you? Aline Lebrun lives for Victor, and
for Victor alone. She has spoiled him into the worthless
creature he is. She worships him and the ground he walks
on. Robert is very well in a way, to give up all the money
he can earn to the family, and keep the barest pittance for
himself. Favorite son, indeed! I miss the poor fellow myself,
my dear. I liked to see him and to hear him about the place
the only Lebrun who is worth a pinch of salt. He comes to
see me often in the city. I like to play to him. That Victor!"

compass: here, amount.

hanging would be too good for him. It's a wonder Robert hasn't beaten him to death long ago."

"I thought he had great patience with his brother," offered Edna, glad to be talking about Robert, no matter what was said.

"Oh! he thrashed him well enough a year or two ago," said Mademoiselle. "It was about a Spanish girl, whom Victor considered that he had some sort of claim upon. He met Robert one day talking to the girl, or walking with her, or bathing with her, or carrying her basket—I don't remember what;—and he became so insulting and abusive that Robert gave him a thrashing on the spot that has kept him comparatively in order for a good while. It's about time he was getting another."

"Was her name Mariequita?" asked Edna.

"Mariequita—yes, that was it; Mariequita. I had forgotten. Oh, she's a sly one, and a bad one, that Mariequita!"

Edna looked down at Mademoiselle Reisz and wondered how she could have listened to her venom so long. For some reason she felt depressed, almost unhappy. She had not intended to go into the water; but she donned her bathing suit, and left Mademoiselle alone, seated under the shade of the children's tent. The water was growing cooler as the season advanced. Edna plunged and swam about with an abandon that thrilled and invigorated her. She remained a long time in the water, half hoping that Mademoiselle Reisz would not wait for her.

But Mademoiselle waited. She was very amiable during the walk back, and raved much over Edna's appearance in her bathing suit. She talked about music. She hoped that Edna would go to see her in the city, and wrote her address with the stub of a pencil on a piece of card which she found in her pocket.

"When do you leave?" asked Edna.

"Next Monday; and you?"

"The following week," answered Edna, adding, "It has been a pleasant summer, hasn't it, Mademoiselle?"

"Well," agreed Mademoiselle Reisz, with a shrug, "rather pleasant, if it hadn't been for the mosquitoes and the Farival twins."

COMMENTARY

This section opens at a dinner party in which Edna receives news that Robert is going to Mexico the same evening. Edna's reflections after the journey to Chênière (in Chapter 14) suggest that the summer is coming to an end, so the dinner scene must not be long after, but the sudden news is completely bewildering for Edna. Chopin offers no concrete indication of how much time has passed since the day on Chênière. Chopin also omits any information about how Robert and Edna have been spending their time since Chênière. On the day that Edna hears about Robert's trip to Mexico, he has spent the morning with her and has said nothing about leaving. His absence in the afternoon seemed unusual, but basking in his presence, Edna had not been concerned. Providing the news at dinner, in front of the whole assembled company, is cowardly, but this character flaw is one that Edna is too distraught to see.

The news that Robert is leaving takes Edna by surprise, and she makes no effort to disguise her bewilderment. Robert's response to Edna's amazement is an "embarrassed and uneasy" silence, one that is made more obvious when others at the table respond to Edna's question, "When is he going?" When Edna's voice begins to rise, Robert finally responds with a matching level of agitation that indicates his own discomfort. Edna could have made this departure easy for him, but it never occurs to her. Robert is running away, and she perhaps senses Robert's escape by his lame efforts to justify his departure.

Edna and Robert's exchange becomes so loud that Madame Lebrun must restore order by knocking on the table with her knife handle, exclaiming that the dinner table is becoming like an insane asylum. For a few moments, the conversation dissolves into petty bickering between Victor and Monsieur Farival. When silence is restored, Robert—looking straight at Edna—addresses his mother and tells her that his sudden departure is an opportunity that he must seize. But as the questioning continues, Robert's replies become increasingly tinged with annoyance. Edna's perception is that Robert appears as if he is "some gentleman on the stage."

While the conversation swirls around her, Edna makes some effort to eat her dinner, but as soon as possible, she leaves the dining room and returns to her room, where she distracts herself with small evening chores. When Edna refuses Madame Lebrun's request that she return, Madame Ratignolle quickly appears at the Pontellier cottage. Adèle Ratignolle obviously suspects the depth of Edna's anguish. Adèle's previous concerns that Edna misread Robert's attentions are confirmed by Edna's behavior at dinner. Moreover, Madame Ratignolle is also concerned about appearances. Adèle tells Edna that her absence from the group wishing Robert good-bye "doesn't look friendly." Adèle is the mother-woman, and her focus is always on doing what is "right" by fulfilling the expectations of society. By refusing to attend, Edna is not playing her role.

Within minutes, Robert appears to say goodbye. He is nervous and unsure of himself and is unable to say how long he will be gone. Edna's anger plainly discomforts him and moves him to sulkily remark, "I never knew you to be out of patience with me before." Edna's response recalls that of a petulant adolescent rather than the response of a married woman who is 28 years old: "Why, I was planning to be together . . . in the city next winter." Her disappointment is unmistakable, and she clings to his hand, pleading with him to write to her.

In the depth of her emotional response to his departure, Edna finally recognizes her infatuation with Robert. She recognizes these symptoms "anew." She has been infatuated before, but she has learned nothing from her past experiences, as she willingly admits. Note that, for Edna, "the future [is] a mystery [that] she never attempted to penetrate." Edna takes no lessons from her past or present experiences to apply to the future. She lives only for the present, focusing only on the momentary pain. After Robert leaves, Edna feels as though she has lost something that she has only recently discovered she needed, and her distress is unmistakable.

The question is always, why does Robert leave? Robert's departure is too hurried, and he is too uncomfortable about the decision for his trip to be the business opportunity that he presents. Robert has made a summer career of languishing over unavailable women. This summer at Grand Isle began in much the same way as the previous summers began. He sets out to devote his attentions to just one woman. He is playing a social game, a summer's entertainment.

COMMENTARY

Edna on porch of summer cottage.
Everett Collection

However, Robert chooses Edna Pontellier, an inflexible Kentucky Presbyterian, a woman out of place and unfamiliar with his Creole world. She does not recognize that he is playing a game, or instead, she refuses to accept it. Nevertheless, she becomes infatuated, and perhaps Robert has also begun to fall in love. The rules of his society limit his quasi-seductions to flirting. No man expects that Robert will move beyond flirting, and consequently, no husband is jealous of Robert's attentions to his wife. Edna can spend many long hours with Robert, and Léonce never considers that Robert may take an inappropriate action.

However, the summer flirtation has changed. Robert is clearly running away from Grand Isle, and more importantly, he is running away from Edna. Robert must abide by the rules of his Creole world. Social order is more important than love, which offers him no social or

economic value. Robert is the son of a woman who rents summer cottages. His summer flirtations increase his worth because he is essentially entertaining the visitors. He is also socializing with the men to whom he needs to cater if he wants to be successful. Robert is 26 years old, and he needs a career opportunity. He knows that he cannot continue indefinitely as a summer flirt, so his decision to go to Mexico is, ostensibly, to find economic opportunity. A social betrayal, especially of a successful New Orleans businessman like Léonce Pontellier, would severely limit Robert's opportunities. However, this kind of business choice is one that Edna cannot understand or accept, so Robert sees little point in explaining to her that their closeness to the precipice, on which they teeter, is endangering their futures.

Edna is at loose ends after Robert's departure. She is initially surprised at the drabness of the days without him, remarking that his absence has "taken the brightness, the color, the meaning out of everything." Like lovers everywhere, she wants to make his absence easier by seeking her own place in his life, so she begins to visit Madame Lebrun in the mornings. On these visits, Edna can talk about Robert and look at photographs of him, memorizing his features and hoping for any word from him. When a letter arrives for his mother, Edna memorizes his handwriting, the feel of the paper, and even the stamp, as well as the words that he has written.

When Léonce tells her that he has seen Robert, Edna sees no awkwardness in asking her husband a dozen questions about Robert. The absence of jealousy on Léonce's part signals how wise Robert's choice to leave has been. Léonce trusts Robert to abide by the rules of social conduct, so he is perfectly comfortable asking Edna, "How do you get on without him?" Edna is so naive that she also sees nothing out of the ordinary in asking her husband about Robert. She reasons that "the sentiment which she entertained for Robert in no way resembled that which she felt for her husband, or had ever felt, or ever expected to feel." Edna has likely never loved Léonce. She admits in Chapter 7 that she once "fancied there was a sympathy of thought and taste between them," but she never acknowledges love. Consequently, Edna sees no conflict between what she feels for Robert and what she feels for Léonce. She is taking nothing away from her husband because she has never given him the essential part of herself.

One area that deserves extra attention is the conversation between Edna and Madame Ratignolle. Edna admits that "[I] would give my life for my children; but I wouldn't give myself." This conversation shocks Adèle, the mother-woman who believes that sacrificing her life—and herself—for her children is part of her obligation as a mother.

Edna is a mother by chance, not by choice. Motherhood is a by-product of her marriage, but she was never gripped by a great desire to be a mother and did not deliberately set out to bear children. She recognizes that the children exist, and she cares for them in sort of a haphazard manner. But when they are not present, she never thinks of them. None of Edna's sentiments can be explained to Madame Ratignolle, who is happily pregnant again and whose life is focused on the well-being of her children.

Edna would sacrifice her life to save her children's lives, but she is not prepared to live a life empty of personal satisfaction, a life devoted only to her children's happiness. Adèle does not understand this distinction, so she happily accepts Edna's promise to die for her children because the Bible asks no more from a woman than such devotion. For Adèle, her world begins and ends with family, and Edna's choices are simply unfathomable.

As the summer comes to an end, Edna distracts herself by spending more time swimming because this activity not only soothes her but also reminds her of Robert. Much of the summer was spent learning to swim, and now this accomplishment is one of which she can be proud. It also reminds her of Robert, who was a part of teaching Edna to swim.

While Edna is on the beach one day, Mademoiselle Reisz appears. Having spent many mornings at Madame Lebrun's talking about Robert, Edna cannot resist the opportunity to speak of him to Mademoiselle Reisz. The pianist mentions that Robert visits her often in the city, and she invites Edna to visit her as well. However, Mademoiselle Reisz's conversation is "full of venom," and her viciousness emphasizes that Mademoiselle Reisz is an odious woman who enjoys little happiness and finds something to criticize in everyone. That she can find so little in life worth celebrating further illustrates the emptiness that a single career woman can expect.

Notes

Chapters 17–19

The Pontelliers have returned to New Orleans after vacationing on Grand Isle, but Edna does not resume her expected duties. Edna ignores the conventions of New Orleans society, and Léonce is concerned that their social position will suffer. When left alone, Edna loses control and throws a vase to the floor. The next morning, Edna is restless and finally decides to gather together some of her drawings and visit Madame Ratignolle. Edna is reassured by Madame Ratignolle's enthusiasm over Edna's art, and Edna gives several drawings to her friend. But the visit to Madame Ratignolle leaves Edna even more dissatisfied with her own life, and she completely abandons the social and domestic duties expected of her.

CHAPTER XVII

The Pontelliers possessed a very charming home on **Esplanade Street** in New Orleans. It was a large, double cottage, with a broad front veranda, whose round, fluted columns supported the sloping roof. The house was painted a dazzling white; the outside shutters, or jalousies, were green. In the yard, which was kept scrupulously neat, were flowers and plants of every description which flourishes in South Louisiana. Within doors the **appointments** were perfect after the conventional type. The softest carpets and rugs covered the floors; rich and tasteful draperies hung at doors and windows. There were paintings, selected with judgment and discrimination, upon the walls. The cut glass, the silver, the heavy damask which daily appeared upon the table were the envy of many women whose husbands were less generous than Mr. Pontellier.

Mr. Pontellier was very fond of walking about his house examining its various appointments and details, to see that nothing was amiss. He greatly valued his possessions, chiefly because they were his, and derived genuine pleasure from contemplating a painting, a statuette, a rare lace curtain—no matter what—after he had bought it and placed it among his household gods.

On Tuesday afternoons—Tuesday being Mrs. Pontellier's **reception day**—there was a constant stream of callers— women who came in carriages or in the street cars, or walked when the air was soft and distance permitted. A light-colored **mulatto** boy, in dress coat and bearing a diminutive silver tray for the reception of cards, admitted them. A maid, in white fluted cap, offered the callers liqueur, coffee, or chocolate, as they might desire.

NOTES

Esplanade Street: a mansion-lined street in New Orleans, populated primarily by upper-class Creoles.

appointments: furniture; equipment.

reception day: one day each week, an upper-class woman was expected to stay home and receive visitors. The day of the week was established when a woman married, and custom demanded she entertain on that day from then on.

mulatto: a person who has one black parent and one white parent.

Mrs. Pontellier, attired in a handsome reception gown, remained in the drawing-room the entire afternoon receiving her visitors. Men sometimes called in the evening with their wives.

This had been the programme which Mrs. Pontellier had religiously followed since her marriage, six years before. Certain evenings during the week she and her husband attended the opera or sometimes the play.

Mr. Pontellier left his home in the mornings between nine and ten o'clock, and rarely returned before half-past six or seven in the evening—dinner being served at half-past seven.

He and his wife seated themselves at table one Tuesday evening, a few weeks after their return from Grand Isle. They were alone together. The boys were being put to bed; the patter of their bare, escaping feet could be heard occasionally, as well as the pursuing voice of the quadroon, lifted in mild protest and entreaty. Mrs. Pontellier did not wear her usual Tuesday reception gown; she was in ordinary house dress. Mr. Pontellier, who was observant about such things, noticed it, as he served the soup and handed it to the boy in waiting.

"Tired out, Edna? Whom did you have? Many callers?" he asked. He tasted his soup and began to season it with pepper, salt, vinegar, mustard—everything within reach.

"There were a good many," replied Edna, who was eating her soup with evident satisfaction. "I found their cards when I got home; I was out."

"Out!" exclaimed her husband, with something like genuine consternation in his voice as he laid down the vinegar cruet and looked at her through his glasses. "Why, what could have taken you out on Tuesday? What did you have to do?"

"Nothing. I simply felt like going out, and I went out."

"Well, I hope you left some suitable excuse," said her husband, somewhat appeased, as he added a dash of cayenne pepper to the soup.

"No, I left no excuse. I told Joe to say I was out, that was all."

"Why, my dear, I should think you'd understand by this time that people don't do such things; we've got to observe **les convenances** if we ever expect to get on and keep up with the procession. If you felt that you had to leave home this afternoon, you should have left some suitable explanation for your absence.

les convenances: social conventions; protocol.

"This soup is really impossible; it's strange that woman hasn't learned yet to make a decent soup. Any free-lunch stand in town serves a better one. Was Mrs. Belthrop here?"

"Bring the tray with the cards, Joe. I don't remember who was here."

The boy retired and returned after a moment, bringing the tiny silver tray, which was covered with ladies' visiting cards. He handed it to Mrs. Pontellier.

"Give it to Mr. Pontellier," she said.

Joe offered the tray to Mr. Pontellier, and removed the soup.

Mr. Pontellier scanned the names of his wife's callers, reading some of them aloud, with comments as he read.

"'The Misses Delasidas.' I worked a big deal in **futures** for their father this morning; nice girls; it's time they were getting married. 'Mrs. Belthrop.' I tell you what it is, Edna; you can't afford to snub Mrs. Belthrop. Why, Belthrop could buy and sell us ten times over. His business is worth a good, round sum to me. You'd better write her a note. 'Mrs. James Highcamp.' Hugh! the less you have to do with Mrs. Highcamp, the better. 'Madame Laforcé.' Came all the way from Carrolton, too, poor old soul. 'Miss Wiggs,' 'Mrs. Eleanor Boltons.'" He pushed the cards aside.

"Mercy!" exclaimed Edna, who had been fuming. "Why are you taking the thing so seriously and making such a fuss over it?"

"I'm not making any fuss over it. But it's just such seeming trifles that we've got to take seriously; such things count."

The fish was scorched. Mr. Pontellier would not touch it. Edna said she did not mind a little scorched taste. The roast was in some way not to his fancy, and he did not like the manner in which the vegetables were served.

"It seems to me," he said, "we spend money enough in this house to procure at least one meal a day which a man could eat and retain his self-respect."

"You used to think the cook was a treasure," returned Edna, indifferently.

"Perhaps she was when she first came; but cooks are only human. They need looking after, like any other class of persons that you employ. Suppose I didn't look after the clerks in my office, just let them run things their own way; they'd soon make a nice mess of me and my business."

futures: a contract for a specific commodity bought or sold for delivery at a later date.

"Where are you going?" asked Edna, seeing that her husband arose from table without having eaten a morsel except a taste of the highly-seasoned soup.

"I'm going to get my dinner at the club. Good night." He went into the hall, took his hat and stick from the stand, and left the house.

She was somewhat familiar with such scenes. They had often made her very unhappy. On a few previous occasions she had been completely deprived of any desire to finish her dinner. Sometimes she had gone into the kitchen to administer a tardy rebuke to the cook. Once she went to her room and studied the cookbook during an entire evening, finally writing out a menu for the week, which left her harassed with a feeling that, after all, she had accomplished no good that was worth the name.

But that evening Edna finished her dinner alone, with forced deliberation. Her face was flushed and her eyes flamed with some inward fire that lighted them. After finishing her dinner she went to her room, having instructed the boy to tell any other callers that she was indisposed.

It was a large, beautiful room, rich and picturesque in the soft, dim light which the maid had turned low. She went and stood at an open window and looked out upon the deep tangle of the garden below. All the mystery and witchery of the night seemed to have gathered there amid the perfumes and the dusky and tortuous outlines of flowers and foliage. She was seeking herself and finding herself in just such sweet, half-darkness which met her moods. But the voices were not soothing that came to her from the darkness and the sky above and the stars. They jeered and sounded mournful notes without promise, devoid even of hope. She turned back into the room and began to walk to and fro down its whole length, without stopping, without resting. She carried in her hands a thin handkerchief, which she tore into ribbons, rolled into a ball, and flung from her. Once she stopped, and taking off her wedding ring, flung it upon the carpet. When she saw it lying there, she stamped her heel upon it, striving to crush it. But her small boot heel did not make an indenture, not a mark upon the little glittering circlet.

In a sweeping passion she seized a glass vase from the table and flung it upon the tiles of the hearth. She wanted to destroy something. The crash and clatter were what she wanted to hear.

A maid, alarmed at the din of breaking glass, entered the room to discover what was the matter.

"A vase fell upon the hearth," said Edna. "Never mind; leave it till morning."

"Oh! you might get some of the glass in your feet, ma'am," insisted the young woman, picking up bits of the broken vase that were scattered upon the carpet. "And here's your ring, ma'am, under the chair."

Edna held out her hand, and taking the ring, slipped it upon her finger.

CHAPTER XVIII

The following morning Mr. Pontellier, upon leaving for his office, asked Edna if she would not meet him in town in order to look at some new fixtures for the library.

"I hardly think we need new fixtures, Léonce. Don't let us get anything new; you are too extravagant. I don't believe you ever think of saving or putting by."

"The way to become rich is to make money, my dear Edna, not to save it," he said. He regretted that she did not feel inclined to go with him and select new fixtures. He kissed her good-by, and told her she was not looking well and must take care of herself. She was unusually pale and very quiet.

She stood on the front **veranda** as he quitted the house, and absently picked a few sprays of **jessamine** that grew upon a trellis near by. She inhaled the odor of the blossoms and thrust them into the bosom of her white morning gown. The boys were dragging along the **banquette** a small "express wagon," which they had filled with blocks and sticks. The quadroon was following them with little quick steps, having assumed a fictitious animation and alacrity for the occasion. A fruit vender was crying his wares in the street.

Edna looked straight before her with a self-absorbed expression upon her face. She felt no interest in anything about her. The street, the children, the fruit vender, the flowers growing there under her eyes, were all part and parcel of an alien world which had suddenly become antagonistic.

She went back into the house. She had thought of speaking to the cook concerning her blunders of the previous night; but Mr. Pontellier had saved her that disagreeable mission,

veranda: a porch, usually roofed or partially enclosed.

jessamine: jasmine, any of a genus (*Jasminum*) of tropical and subtropical plants of the olive family, with fragrant flowers of yellow, red, or white, used in perfumes or for scenting tea.

banquette: a raised way; sidewalk.

for which she was so poorly fitted. Mr. Pontellier's arguments were usually convincing with those whom he employed. He left home feeling quite sure that he and Edna would sit down that evening, and possibly a few subsequent evenings, to a dinner deserving of the name.

Edna spent an hour or two in looking over some of her old sketches. She could see their shortcomings and defects, which were glaring in her eyes. She tried to work a little, but found she was not in the humor. Finally she gathered together a few of the sketches—those which she considered the least discreditable; and she carried them with her when, a little later, she dressed and left the house. She looked handsome and distinguished in her street gown. The tan of the seashore had left her face, and her forehead was smooth, white, and polished beneath her heavy, yellow-brown hair. There were a few freckles on her face, and a small, dark mole near the under lip and one on the temple, half-hidden in her hair.

As Edna walked along the street she was thinking of Robert. She was still under the spell of her infatuation. She had tried to forget him, realizing the inutility of remembering. But the thought of him was like an obsession, ever pressing itself upon her. It was not that she dwelt upon details of their acquaintance, or recalled in any special or peculiar way his personality; it was his being, his existence, which dominated her thought, fading sometimes as if it would melt into the mist of the forgotten, reviving again with an intensity which filled her with an incomprehensible longing.

Edna was on her way to Madame Ratignolle's. Their intimacy, begun at Grand Isle, had not declined, and they had seen each other with some frequency since their return to the city. The Ratignolles lived at no great distance from Edna's home, on the corner of a side street, where Monsieur Ratignolle owned and conducted a drug store which enjoyed a steady and prosperous trade. His father had been in the business before him, and Monsieur Ratignolle stood well in the community and bore an enviable reputation for integrity and clear-headedness. His family lived in commodious apartments over the store, having an entrance on the side within the **porte cochère**. There was something which Edna thought very French, very foreign, about their whole manner of living. In the large and pleasant salon which extended across the width of the house, the Ratignolles entertained their friends once a fortnight with a

porte cochère: a large entrance gateway into a courtyard

soirée musicale, sometimes diversified by card-playing. There was a friend who played upon the 'cello. One brought his flute and another his violin, while there were some who sang and a number who performed upon the piano with various degrees of taste and agility. The Ratignolles' soirées musicales were widely known, and it was considered a privilege to be invited to them.

Edna found her friend engaged in assorting the clothes which had returned that morning from the laundry. She at once abandoned her occupation upon seeing Edna, who had been ushered without ceremony into her presence.

"'Cite can do it as well as I; it is really her business," she explained to Edna, who apologized for interrupting her. And she summoned a young black woman, whom she instructed, in French, to be very careful in checking off the list which she handed her. She told her to notice particularly if a fine linen handkerchief of Monsieur Ratignolle's, which was missing last week, had been returned; and to be sure to set to one side such pieces as required mending and darning.

Then placing an arm around Edna's waist, she led her to the front of the house, to the **salon**, where it was cool and sweet with the odor of great roses that stood upon the hearth in jars.

Madame Ratignolle looked more beautiful than ever there at home, in a negligé which left her arms almost wholly bare and exposed the rich, melting curves of her white throat.

"Perhaps I shall be able to paint your picture some day," said Edna with a smile when they were seated. She produced the roll of sketches and started to unfold them. "I believe I ought to work again. I feel as if I wanted to be doing something. What do you think of them? Do you think it worth while to take it up again and study some more? I might study for a while with Laidpore."

She knew that Madame Ratignolle's opinion in such a matter would be next to valueless, that she herself had not alone decided, but determined; but she sought the words of praise and encouragement that would help her to put heart into her venture.

"Your talent is immense, dear!"

"Nonsense!" protested Edna, well pleased.

"Immense, I tell you," persisted Madame Ratignolle, surveying the sketches one by one, at close range, then holding

soirée musicale: an evening party or gathering featuring music.

salon: drawing room of a private home in French-speaking countries.

them at arm's length, narrowing her eyes, and dropping her head on one side. "Surely, this Bavarian peasant is worthy of framing; and this basket of apples! never have I seen anything more lifelike. One might almost be tempted to reach out a hand and take one."

Edna could not control a feeling which bordered upon complacency at her friend's praise, even realizing, as she did, its true worth. She retained a few of the sketches, and gave all the rest to Madame Ratignolle, who appreciated the gift far beyond its value and proudly exhibited the pictures to her husband when he came up from the store a little later for his midday dinner.

Mr. Ratignolle was one of those men who are called the salt of the earth. His cheerfulness was unbounded, and it was matched by his goodness of heart, his broad charity, and common sense. He and his wife spoke English with an accent which was only discernible through its un-English emphasis and a certain carefulness and deliberation. Edna's husband spoke English with no accent whatever. The Ratignolles understood each other perfectly. If ever the fusion of two human beings into one has been accomplished on this sphere it was surely in their union.

As Edna seated herself at table with them she thought, "**Better a dinner of herbs**," though it did not take her long to discover that it was no dinner of herbs, but a delicious repast, simple, choice, and in every way satisfying.

Better a dinner of herbs: Refers to the biblical passage Proverbs 15:17: Better a dinner of herbs where love is, than a fattened ox and hatred therewith.

Monsieur Ratignolle was delighted to see her, though he found her looking not so well as at Grand Isle, and he advised a tonic. He talked a good deal on various topics, a little politics, some city news and neighborhood gossip. He spoke with an animation and earnestness that gave an exaggerated importance to every syllable he uttered. His wife was keenly interested in everything he said, laying down her fork the better to listen, chiming in, taking the words out of his mouth.

Edna felt depressed rather than soothed after leaving them. The little glimpse of domestic harmony which had been offered her, gave her no regret, no longing. It was not a condition of life which fitted her, and she could see in it but an appalling and hopeless **ennui**. She was moved by a kind of commiseration for Madame Ratignolle—a pity for that colorless existence which never uplifted its possessor beyond the region of blind contentment, in which no moment of anguish ever visited her soul, in which she would never have the taste

ennui: weariness and dissatisfaction resulting from inactivity or lack of interest; boredom.

of life's delirium. Edna vaguely wondered what she meant by "life's delirium." It had crossed her thought like some unsought, extraneous impression.

CHAPTER XIX

Edna could not help but think that it was very foolish, very childish, to have stamped upon her wedding ring and smashed the crystal vase upon the tiles. She was visited by no more outbursts, moving her to such futile expedients. She began to do as she liked and to feel as she liked. She completely abandoned her Tuesdays at home, and did not return the visits of those who had called upon her. She made no ineffectual efforts to conduct her household **en bonne ménagère**, going and coming as it suited her fancy, and, so far as she was able, lending herself to any passing caprice.

en bonne ménagère: in good household management. Edna was not managing her household as was expected.

Mr. Pontellier had been a rather courteous husband so long as he met a certain tacit submissiveness in his wife. But her new and unexpected line of conduct completely bewildered him. It shocked him. Then her absolute disregard for her duties as a wife angered him. When Mr. Pontellier became rude, Edna grew insolent. She had resolved never to take another step backward.

"It seems to me the utmost folly for a woman at the head of a household, and the mother of children, to spend in an atelier days which would be better employed contriving for the comfort of her family."

"I feel like painting," answered Edna. "Perhaps I shan't always feel like it."

"Then in God's name paint! but don't let the family go to the devil. There's Madame Ratignolle; because she keeps up her music, she doesn't let everything else go to chaos. And she's more of a musician than you are a painter."

"She isn't a musician, and I'm not a painter. It isn't on account of painting that I let things go."

"On account of what, then?"

"Oh! I don't know. Let me alone; you bother me."

It sometimes entered Mr. Pontellier's mind to wonder if his wife were not growing a little unbalanced mentally. He could see plainly that she was not herself. That is, he could not see that she was becoming herself and daily casting aside that fictitious self which we assume like a garment with which to appear before the world.

Her husband let her alone as she requested, and went away to his office. Edna went up to her **atelier**—a bright room in the top of the house. She was working with great energy and interest, without accomplishing anything, however, which satisfied her even in the smallest degree. For a time she had the whole household enrolled in the service of art. The boys posed for her. They thought it amusing at first, but the occupation soon lost its attractiveness when they discovered that it was not a game arranged especially for their entertainment. The quadroon sat for hours before Edna's palette, patient as a savage, while the house-maid took charge of the children, and the drawing-room went undusted. But the housemaid, too, served her term as model when Edna perceived that the young woman's back and shoulders were molded on classic lines, and that her hair, loosened from its confining cap, became an inspiration. While Edna worked she sometimes sang low the little air, "Ah! si tu savais!"

It moved her with recollections. She could hear again the ripple of the water, the flapping sail. She could see the glint of the moon upon the bay, and could feel the soft, gusty beating of the hot south wind. A subtle current of desire passed through her body, weakening her hold upon the brushes and making her eyes burn.

There were days when she was very happy without knowing why. She was happy to be alive and breathing, when her whole being seemed to be one with the sunlight, the color, the odors, the luxuriant warmth of some perfect Southern day. She liked then to wander alone into strange and unfamiliar places. She discovered many a sunny, sleepy corner, fashioned to dream in. And she found it good to dream and to be alone and unmolested.

There were days when she was unhappy, she did not know why,—when it did not seem worth while to be glad or sorry, to be alive or dead; when life appeared to her like a grotesque pandemonium and humanity like worms struggling blindly toward inevitable annihilation. She could not work on such a day, nor weave fancies to stir her pulses and warm her blood.

atelier: a studio or workshop, especially one used by an artist.

COMMENTARY

Summer is over, and Edna and her family have returned to their home on Esplanade Street.

The description of their home illustrates Léonce's success as well as the comfort in which the unhappy Edna resides.

The luxurious home is the envy of many other wives and is a home that pleases Léonce, who enjoys inspecting it frequently to ensure its continued perfection. Accordingly, his wife's seeming desertion of responsibilities—for the house and for social conventions—leaves Léonce close to anger. Before her awakening, Edna had always fulfilled her most important social obligation—the exchange of cards and visits on Tuesday afternoons. But now, she refuses to fit into a social plan that is not of her design. Her violation of social customs is a serious problem for Léonce because his business is also affected by Edna's adherence to social conventions. When Edna snubs the wife of Léonce's most important business associate, she is completely unaware and unconcerned at its implications. Edna's question—"Why are you taking this thing so seriously and making such a fuss over it?"—perfectly illustrates how little Edna understands "*les convenances.*" The freedom of summer still lingers in Edna's mind, and she is unwilling to give up her freedom to the conventions of New Orleans society.

Chopin makes clear that Edna has tried to be a "good" wife in the past by studying cookbooks and trying to plan meals. But if Edna found such activities unsatisfactory in the past, she finds them intolerable now. In New Orleans, however, Léonce again speaks to Edna as a disobedient employee because social conventions require that Edna, the wife, is expected to obey as if she is an employee. Unlike Léonce's other employees, she does not collect a salary at the end of the week, but Léonce pays her in other ways. He gives her an impressive house on a fashionable street, and he gives her beautiful clothes and up-to-date furnishings. An important key to Edna's growing awareness is that Léonce gives her only material gifts. He does not share; he does give her equality. However, Edna should not expect equality: Her marriage fulfills the expectations and requirements of the time period. Chopin makes a brave statement about equality in marriage, and she points out that the conventional nineteenth-century marriage is not fulfilling enough for a woman.

Esplande Street.

When Edna goes upstairs later in the evening, she looks out the window. She sees that the whole world exists beyond her window and that she is trapped. She sees, smells, and hears a world of difference outside her window. Her senses are aware of this other world, but she cannot enter it; she cannot experience it. The awareness that she cannot escape from her life leads Edna to throw her wedding ring—the symbolic representation of Léonce—to the floor. She tries to grind it with her shoe, but it easily withstands the onslaught of her attack. Edna cannot cast off her marriage so easily.

The next day, Edna's frustration of the evening before does not dissipate in the morning light, and she is not any more willing to follow her husbands commands. Léonce's concern for his wife is evident because he cautions her to take care of herself, but his concern resembles an owner's concern for one of his prized possessions—he thinks that Edna may be damaging herself. Edna is oblivious to his concern, just as she is oblivious to her children or the world outside her door. She is tormented because she has no right to an awareness of the world beyond the narrow confines of her own space. Just beyond Edna's door is a world that isn't available to her.

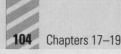

Typical New Orleans mansion.

The night before, Léonce chastised Edna for not receiving her callers, and he was equally dissatisfied with the cooking, a job that Edna was to supervise. However, with little expected of her, Edna turns to her art, but it now fails to satisfy her. All she can see are the flaws in her sketches, and she is unable to concentrate on working. Her restlessness and her inability to focus on any activity reveal a woman at odds with her life, a woman close to exploding. Edna's tension is palpable.

After gathering a few of her better sketches, Edna leaves for Madame Ratignolle's home. Adèle is not only Edna's friend, but she represents the freedom and enjoyment of the past summer. The memories of Robert that consume her during this short walk further point to why Edna seeks solace with Madame Ratignolle. Although Edna cannot speak of her obsession or her unhappiness to Adèle—the mother-woman would be shocked—she is the one person who instinctively understands that Edna needs a friend.

Chopin describes the Ratignolles' home and lifestyle in contrast to that of the Pontelliers'. Monsieur Ratignolle is not as financially successful as Edna's husband, and their home is smaller and above the drug store that

Monsieur Ratignolle owns. Although the store is a long-term family enterprise, it is still a shop; therefore, the Ratignolles have a lower social ranking. Adèle does not receive guests on Tuesdays, but the Ratignolles entertain. Probably, this lifestyle is similar to Edna's own sense of social obligation and is more familiar to her as well. Edna was not born into Léonce's world or into its Creole influence or its social milieu. But even though the more-casual existence of the Ratignolle's is more in keeping with her Kentucky upbringing, their lifestyle is no less stifling.

When Edna arrives at the Ratignolles', she discovers Adèle folding laundry. Although a servant can easily perform this task, the mother-woman worries that her family will suffer without her attention to detail. Her concern serves as quite a contrast to Edna, who cannot and will not supervise her servants. If Léonce's meals are inedible and his home unclean, Edna does not notice or care. But for Madame Ratignolle, everything that her husband or children encounter must be perfect. In short, what is perfect for Adèle is turmoil for Edna. And yet in spite of these differences, Edna needs to hear someone praise her, so she unrolls her sketches and asks Adèle whether she has enough talent to pursue her art.

Art offers Edna the one opportunity that she thinks may be available for individual expression. Edna needs to find her own voice, and her art may offer this option. But regardless of what Adèle may say, Edna decides to continue with additional lessons.

Edna is filled with pity for Adèle, whose marriage is "the fusion of two human beings." Edna, on the other hand, wants to be an individual human being. When Monsieur Ratignolle speaks, Adèle hangs on every word and even completes his thoughts and sentences. Monsieur and Madame Ratignolle are so well matched that an observer cannot distinguish where one ends and the other begins. This life is so horrifying to Edna that she is filled with "pity for that colorless existence." No doubt, Adèle would have been shocked at her friend's thoughts. For the mother-woman, this relationship is the ideal marriage—the meeting of two minds in domestic harmony. And this relationship is the ideal life for Adèle, not for Edna.

When Edna leaves, she is not soothed by the visit; instead, she is nearly filled with despair by Adèle's life of "blind contentment." During the summer, Edna has awakened to the possibilities of something different. Part of her restlessness stems from her inability to know exactly what "something different" involves, and while she walks back to her home, she is sad for Adèle, who will never experience "life's delirium." That Edna does not yet know what her "life's delirium" will be is unimportant—she at least knows of its existence.

In the coming days and weeks, Edna makes no attempt to fulfill her social obligations. She makes no attempt to supervise her home, and she completely abandons her Tuesdays at home. This behavior first bewilders her husband and then angers him. Léonce refers to Edna's behavior, just as he did at Grand Isle, as folly. She spends her days at her studio painting, she ignores her children and husband, and most importantly, she ignores her duties as mistress of the household. Léonce tells Edna to look toward Madame Ratignolle as a model for the ideal wife, but not knowing that she had just determined on an existence that is totally the opposite. Léonce's comparison of Edna to Madame Ratignolle is likely galling to Edna. She pities what Léonce admires, but above all, she wants him to go away and leave her alone. Léonce, of course, wonders whether his wife has lost her mind, and certainly, she is lost to him. Edna resolves never to regress to what she had been in the past, and every day, she moves further away from Léonce.

Although Edna spends her time in her studio, she is not satisfied with her art. One moment, she is happy, and the next, she is not. Sometimes, she is bored and weary, and towards other people, she is manic. Léonce's concern that Edna is becoming "unbalanced mentally" seems especially appropriate in the moments when she cannot work and when she sees life "like a grotesque pandemonium and humanity like worms struggling blindly toward inevitable annihilation." Edna's confusing behavior is not mental illness; instead, her conduct is an attempt to cast aside her "fictitious self" that she has always assumed. Edna does not yet know what she will find under the too-familiar mantle of domesticity. She knows that she will not be a great artist, but she also knows that she is more than a wife and mother.

Notes

Chapters 20–24

Edna decides to visit Mademoiselle Reisz, but when she cannot find her address, she visits Madame Lebrun to get it from her. Robert has sent two letters to his family, but no messages for Edna. A clearly depressed Edna finally learns Mademoiselle Reisz's address and quickly leaves the Lebrun home. Edna arrives at Mademoiselle Reisz's apartment and learns that she, too, has received a letter from Robert. As Mademoiselle plays the piano for Edna, Edna reads the letter and leaves the little apartment in tears. Edna's behavior is an increasing concern for Léonce, who finally asks Doctor Mandelet to pay her a visit. A visit from Edna's father momentary diffuses the tension between Edna and her husband, and when the Colonel leaves to return to Kentucky, Léonce also leaves for an extended business trip. The children have gone to visit their paternal grandmother, and Edna is suddenly alone in the house.

CHAPTER XX

It was during such a mood that Edna hunted up Mademoiselle Reisz. She had not forgotten the rather disagreeable impression left upon her by their last interview; but she nevertheless felt a desire to see her—above all, to listen while she played upon the piano. Quite early in the afternoon she started upon her quest for the pianist. Unfortunately she had mislaid or lost Mademoiselle Reisz's card, and looking up her address in the city directory, she found that the woman lived on Bienville Street, some distance away. The directory which fell into her hands was a year or more old, however, and upon reaching the number indicated, Edna discovered that the house was occupied by a respectable family of mulattoes who had **chambres garnies** to let. They had been living there for six months, and knew absolutely nothing of a Mademoiselle Reisz. In fact, they knew nothing of any of their neighbors; their lodgers were all people of the highest distinction, they assured Edna. She did not linger to discuss class distinctions with Madame Pouponne, but hastened to a neighboring grocery store, feeling sure that Mademoiselle would have left her address with the proprietor.

He knew Mademoiselle Reisz a good deal better than he wanted to know her, he informed his questioner. In truth, he did not want to know her at all, or anything concerning her—the most disagreeable and unpopular woman who ever lived in Bienville Street. He thanked heaven she had left the neighborhood, and was equally thankful that he did not know where she had gone.

NOTES

chambres garnies: furnished rental rooms.

Edna's desire to see Mademoiselle Reisz had increased ten-fold since these unlooked-for obstacles had arisen to thwart it. She was wondering who could give her the information she sought, when it suddenly occurred to her that Madame Lebrun would be the one most likely to do so. She knew it was useless to ask Madame Ratignolle, who was on the most distant terms with the musician, and preferred to know nothing concerning her. She had once been almost as emphatic in expressing herself upon the subject as the corner grocer.

Edna knew that Madame Lebrun had returned to the city, for it was the middle of November. And she also knew where the Lebruns lived, on Chartres Street.

Their home from the outside looked like a prison, with iron bars before the door and lower windows. The iron bars were a relic of the old **régime**, and no one had ever thought of dislodging them. At the side was a high fence enclosing the garden. A gate or door opening upon the street was locked. Edna rang the bell at this side garden gate, and stood upon the banquette, waiting to be admitted.

It was Victor who opened the gate for her. A black woman, wiping her hands upon her apron, was close at his heels. Before she saw them Edna could hear them in altercation, the woman—plainly an anomaly—claiming the right to be allowed to perform her duties, one of which was to answer the bell.

Victor was surprised and delighted to see Mrs. Pontellier, and he made no attempt to conceal either his astonishment or his delight. He was a dark-browed, good-looking young-ster of nineteen, greatly resembling his mother, but with ten times her impetuosity. He instructed the black woman to go at once and inform Madame Lebrun that Mrs. Pontellier desired to see her. The woman grumbled a refusal to do part of her duty when she had not been permitted to do it all, and started back to her interrupted task of weeding the gar-den. Whereupon Victor administered a rebuke in the form of a volley of abuse, which, owing to its rapidity and inco-herence, was all but incomprehensible to Edna. Whatever it was, the rebuke was convincing, for the woman dropped her hoe and went mumbling into the house.

Edna did not wish to enter. It was very pleasant there on the side porch, where there were chairs, a wicker lounge, and a small table. She seated herself, for she was tired from her long tramp; and she began to rock gently and smooth out the folds of her silk parasol. Victor drew up his chair

régime: the period of time (1766–1803) when the Spanish ruled the territory containing New Orleans.

beside her. He at once explained that the black woman's offensive conduct was all due to imperfect training, as he was not there to take her in hand. He had only come up from the island the morning before, and expected to return next day. He stayed all winter at the island; he lived there, and kept the place in order and got things ready for the summer visitors.

But a man needed occasional relaxation, he informed Mrs. Pontellier, and every now and again he drummed up a pretext to bring him to the city. My! but he had had a time of it the evening before! He wouldn't want his mother to know, and he began to talk in a whisper. He was **scintillant** with recollections. Of course, he couldn't think of telling Mrs. Pontellier all about it, she being a woman and not comprehending such things. But it all began with a girl peeping and smiling at him through the shutters as he passed by. Oh! but she was a beauty! Certainly he smiled back, and went up and talked to her. Mrs. Pontellier did not know him if she supposed he was one to let an opportunity like that escape him. Despite herself, the youngster amused her. She must have betrayed in her look some degree of interest or entertainment. The boy grew more daring, and Mrs. Pontellier might have found herself, in a little while, listening to a highly **colored** story but for the timely appearance of Madame Lebrun.

scintillant: give off sparks; flashor sparkle.

colored: altered, influenced, distorted, or exaggerated to some degree.

That lady was still clad in white, according to her custom of the summer. Her eyes beamed an effusive welcome. Would not Mrs. Pontellier go inside? Would she partake of some refreshment? Why had she not been there before? How was that dear Mr. Pontellier and how were those sweet children? Had Mrs. Pontellier ever known such a warm November?

Victor went and reclined on the wicker lounge behind his mother's chair, where he commanded a view of Edna's face. He had taken her parasol from her hands while he spoke to her, and he now lifted it and twirled it above him as he lay on his back. When Madame Lebrun complained that it was so dull coming back to the city; that she saw so few people now; that even Victor, when he came up from the island for a day or two, had so much to occupy him and engage his time; then it was that the youth went into contortions on the lounge and winked mischievously at Edna. She somehow felt like a confederate in crime, and tried to look severe and disapproving.

There had been but two letters from Robert, with little in them, they told her. Victor said it was really not worth while to go inside for the letters, when his mother entreated him to go in search of them. He remembered the contents, which in truth he rattled off very glibly when put to the test.

One letter was written from Vera Cruz and the other from the City of Mexico. He had met Montel, who was doing everything toward his advancement. So far, the financial situation was no improvement over the one he had left in New Orleans, but of course the prospects were vastly better. He wrote of the City of Mexico, the buildings, the people and their habits, the conditions of life which he found there. He sent his love to the family. He inclosed a check to his mother, and hoped she would affectionately remember him to all his friends. That was about the substance of the two letters. Edna felt that if there had been a message for her, she would have received it. The despondent frame of mind in which she had left home began again to overtake her, and she remembered that she wished to find Mademoiselle Reisz.

Madame Lebrun knew where Mademoiselle Reisz lived. She gave Edna the address, regretting that she would not consent to stay and spend the remainder of the afternoon, and pay a visit to Mademoiselle Reisz some other day. The afternoon was already well advanced.

Victor escorted her out upon the banquette, lifted her parasol, and held it over her while he walked to the car with her. He entreated her to bear in mind that the disclosures of the afternoon were strictly confidential. She laughed and bantered him a little, remembering too late that she should have been dignified and reserved.

"How handsome Mrs. Pontellier looked!" said Madame Lebrun to her son.

"Ravishing!" he admitted. "The city atmosphere has improved her. Some way she doesn't seem like the same woman."

CHAPTER XXI

Some people contended that the reason Mademoiselle Reisz always chose apartments up under the roof was to discourage the approach of beggars, peddlars and callers. There were plenty of windows in her little front room. They were for the most part dingy, but as they were nearly always open it did not make so much difference. They often admitted into the room a good deal of smoke and soot; but at the same time all the light and air that there was came through them. From her windows could be seen the crescent of the river, the masts of ships and the big chimneys of the Mississippi steamers. A magnificent piano crowded the apartment. In the next room she slept, and in the third and last she harbored a gasoline stove on which she cooked her meals when disinclined to descend to the neighboring restaurant. It was there also that she ate, keeping her belongings in a rare old buffet, dingy and battered from a hundred years of use.

When Edna knocked at Mademoiselle Reisz's front room door and entered, she discovered that person standing beside the window, engaged in mending or patching an old **prunella gaiter**. The little musician laughed all over when she saw Edna. Her laugh consisted of a contortion of the face and all the muscles of the body. She seemed strikingly homely, standing there in the afternoon light. She still wore the shabby lace and the artificial bunch of violets on the side of her head.

prunella gaiters: shoes with elastic in the sides and no lacing with uppers made of strong worsted twill.

"So you remembered me at last," said Mademoiselle. "I had said to myself, 'Ah, bah! she will never come.'"

"Did you want me to come?" asked Edna with a smile.

"I had not thought much about it," answered Mademoiselle. The two had seated themselves on a little bumpy sofa which stood against the wall. "I am glad, however, that you came. I have the water boiling back there, and was just about to make some coffee. You will drink a cup with me. And how is **la belle dame**? Always handsome! always healthy! always contented!" She took Edna's hand between her strong wiry fingers, holding it loosely without warmth, and executing a sort of double theme upon the back and palm.

la belle dame: beautiful woman.

"Yes," she went on; "I sometimes thought: 'She will never come. She promised as those women in society always do, without meaning it. She will not come.' For I really don't believe you like me, Mrs. Pontellier."

"I don't know whether I like you or not," replied Edna, gazing down at the little woman with a quizzical look.

The candor of Mrs. Pontellier's admission greatly pleased Mademoiselle Reisz. She expressed her gratification by repairing forthwith to the region of the gasoline stove and rewarding her guest with the promised cup of coffee. The coffee and the biscuit accompanying it proved very acceptable to Edna, who had declined refreshment at Madame

Letter from Robert lying on the table.

Lebrun's and was now beginning to feel hungry. Mademoiselle set the tray which she brought in upon a small table near at hand, and seated herself once again on the lumpy sofa.

"I have had a letter from your friend," she remarked, as she poured a little cream into Edna's cup and handed it to her.

"My friend?"

"Yes, your friend Robert. He wrote to me from the City of Mexico."

"Wrote to you?" repeated Edna in amazement, stirring her coffee absently.

"Yes, to me. Why not? Don't stir all the warmth out of your coffee; drink it. Though the letter might as well have been sent to you; it was nothing but Mrs. Pontellier from beginning to end."

"Let me see it," requested the young woman, entreatingly.

"No; a letter concerns no one but the person who writes it and the one to whom it is written."

"Haven't you just said it concerned me from beginning to end?"

"It was written about you, not to you. 'Have you seen Mrs. Pontellier? How is she looking?' he asks. 'As Mrs. Pontellier says,' or 'as Mrs. Pontellier once said.' 'If Mrs. Pontellier should call upon you, play for her that Impromptu of Chopin's, my favorite. I heard it here a day or two ago, but not as you play it. I should like to know how it affects her,' and so on, as if he supposed we were constantly in each other's society."

"Let me see the letter."

"Oh, no."

"Have you answered it?"

"No."

"Let me see the letter."

"No, and again, no."

"Then play the Impromptu for me."

"It is growing late; what time do you have to be home?"

"Time doesn't concern me. Your question seems a little rude. Play the Impromptu."

"But you have told me nothing of yourself. What are you doing?"

"Painting!" laughed Edna. "I am becoming an artist. Think of it!"

"Ah! an artist! You have pretensions, Madame."

"Why pretensions? Do you think I could not become an artist?"

"I do not know you well enough to say. I do not know your talent or your temperament. To be an artist includes much; one must possess many gifts—absolute gifts—which have not been acquired by one's own effort. And, moreover, to succeed, the artist must possess the courageous soul."

"What do you mean by the courageous soul?"

"Courageous, ma foi! The brave soul. The soul that dares and defies."

"Show me the letter and play for me the Impromptu. You see that I have persistence. Does that quality count for anything in art?"

"It counts with a foolish old woman whom you have captivated," replied Mademoiselle, with her wriggling laugh.

The letter was right there at hand in the drawer of the little table upon which Edna had just placed her coffee cup. Mademoiselle opened the drawer and drew forth the letter, the topmost one. She placed it in Edna's hands, and without further comment arose and went to the piano.

Mademoiselle played a soft interlude. It was an improvisation. She sat low at the instrument, and the lines of her body settled into ungraceful curves and angles that gave it an appearance of deformity. Gradually and imperceptibly the interlude melted into the soft opening minor chords of the Chopin Impromptu.

Edna did not know when the Impromptu began or ended. She sat in the sofa corner reading Robert's letter by the fading light. Mademoiselle had glided from the Chopin into the quivering love-notes of **Isolde**'s song, and back again to the Impromptu with its soulful and poignant longing.

The shadows deepened in the little room. The music grew strange and fantastic—turbulent, insistent, plaintive and soft with entreaty. The shadows grew deeper. The music filled the room. It floated out upon the night, over the housetops, the crescent of the river, losing itself in the silence of the upper air.

Edna was sobbing, just as she had wept one midnight at Grand Isle when strange, new voices awoke in her. She arose in some agitation to take her departure. "May I come again, Mademoiselle?" she asked at the threshold.

"Come whenever you feel like it. Be careful; the stairs and landings are dark; don't stumble."

Isolde: the Irish princess of medieval legend who was betrothed to King Mark of Cornwall and loved by Tristram, the king's nephew. The legend was made into a famous opera by Richard Wagner.

Mademoiselle reentered and lit a candle. Robert's letter was on the floor. She stooped and picked it up. It was crumpled and damp with tears. Mademoiselle smoothed the letter out, restored it to the envelope, and replaced it in the table drawer.

CHAPTER XXII

One morning on his way into town Mr. Pontellier stopped at the house of his old friend and family physician, Doctor Mandelet. The Doctor was a semi-retired physician, resting, as the saying is, upon his laurels. He bore a reputation for wisdom rather than skill—leaving the active practice of medicine to his assistants and younger contemporaries—and was much sought for in matters of consultation. A few families, united to him by bonds of friendship, he still attended when they required the services of a physician. The Pontelliers were among these.

Mr. Pontellier found the Doctor reading at the open window of his study. His house stood rather far back from the street, in the center of a delightful garden, so that it was quiet and peaceful at the old gentleman's study window. He was a great reader. He stared up disapprovingly over his eye-glasses as Mr. Pontellier entered, wondering who had the temerity to disturb him at that hour of the morning.

"Ah, Pontellier! Not sick, I hope. Come and have a seat. What news do you bring this morning?" He was quite portly, with a profusion of gray hair, and small blue eyes which age had robbed of much of their brightness but none of their penetration.

"Oh! I'm never sick, Doctor. You know that I come of tough fiber—of that old Creole race of Pontelliers that dry up and finally blow away. I came to consult—no, not precisely to consult—to talk to you about Edna. I don't know what ails her."

"Madame Pontellier not well," marveled the Doctor. "Why, I saw her—I think it was a week ago—walking along Canal Street, the picture of health, it seemed to me."

"Yes, yes; she seems quite well," said Mr. Pontellier, leaning forward and whirling his stick between his two hands; "but she doesn't act well. She's odd, she's not like herself. I can't make her out, and I thought perhaps you'd help me."

"How does she act?" inquired the Doctor.

"Well, it isn't easy to explain," said Mr. Pontellier, throwing himself back in his chair. "She lets the housekeeping go to the dickens."

"Well, well; women are not all alike, my dear Pontellier. We've got to consider—"

"I know that; I told you I couldn't explain. Her whole attitude—toward me and everybody and everything—has changed. You know I have a quick temper, but I don't want to quarrel or be rude to a woman, especially my wife; yet I'm driven to it, and feel like ten thousand devils after I've made a fool of myself. She's making it devilishly uncomfortable for me," he went on nervously. "She's got some sort of notion in her head concerning the eternal rights of women; and—you understand—we meet in the morning at the breakfast table."

The old gentleman lifted his shaggy eyebrows, protruded his thick nether lip, and tapped the arms of his chair with his cushioned fingertips.

"What have you been doing to her, Pontellier?"

"Doing! **Parbleu**!"

"Has she," asked the Doctor, with a smile, "has she been associating of late with a circle of pseudo-intellectual women—super-spiritual superior beings? My wife has been telling me about them."

"That's the trouble," broke in Mr. Pontellier, "she hasn't been associating with any one. She has abandoned her Tuesdays at home, has thrown over all her acquaintances, and goes tramping about by herself, moping in the streetcars, getting after dark. I tell you she's peculiar. I don't like it; I feel a little worried over it."

This was a new aspect for the Doctor. "Nothing hereditary?" he asked, seriously. "Nothing peculiar about her family antecedents, is there?"

"Oh, no, indeed! She comes of sound old Presbyterian Kentucky stock. The old gentleman, her father, I have heard, used to atone for his weekday sins with his Sunday devotions. I know for a fact, that his race horses literally ran away with the prettiest bit of Kentucky farming land I ever laid eyes upon. Margaret—you know Margaret—she has all the Presbyterianism undiluted. And the youngest is something of a vixen. By the way, she gets married in a couple of weeks from now."

"Send your wife up to the wedding," exclaimed the Doctor, foreseeing a happy solution. "Let her stay among her own people for a while; it will do her good."

Parbleu: a mild oath, meaning "my God"

"That's what I want her to do. She won't go to the marriage. She says a wedding is one of the most lamentable spectacles on earth. Nice thing for a woman to say to her husband!" exclaimed Mr. Pontellier, fuming anew at the recollection.

"Pontellier," said the Doctor, after a moment's reflection, "let your wife alone for a while. Don't bother her, and don't let her bother you. Woman, my dear friend, is a very peculiar and delicate organism—a sensitive and highly organized woman, such as I know Mrs. Pontellier to be, is especially peculiar. It would require an inspired psychologist to deal successfully with them. And when ordinary fellows like you and me attempt to cope with their idiosyncrasies the result is bungling. Most women are moody and whimsical. This is some passing whim of your wife, due to some cause or causes which you and I needn't try to fathom. But it will pass happily over, especially if you let her alone. Send her around to see me."

"Oh! I couldn't do that; there'd be no reason for it," objected Mr. Pontellier.

"Then I'll go around and see her," said the Doctor. "I'll drop in to dinner some evening **en bon ami**."

en bon ami: as a friend.

"Do! by all means," urged Mr. Pontellier. "What evening will you come? Say Thursday. Will you come Thursday?" he asked, rising to take his leave.

"Very well; Thursday. My wife may possibly have some engagement for me Thursday. In case she has, I shall let you know. Otherwise, you may expect me."

Mr. Pontellier turned before leaving to say:

"I am going to New York on business very soon. I have a big scheme on hand, and want to be on the field proper to pull the ropes and handle the ribbons. We'll let you in on the inside if you say so, Doctor," he laughed.

"No, I thank you, my dear sir," returned the Doctor. "I leave such ventures to you younger men with the fever of life still in your blood."

"What I wanted to say," continued Mr. Pontellier, with his hand on the knob; "I may have to be absent a good while. Would you advise me to take Edna along?"

"By all means, if she wishes to go. If not, leave her here. Don't contradict her. The mood will pass, I assure you. It may take a month, two, three months—possibly longer, but it will pass; have patience."

"Well, good-by, **à jeudi**," said Mr. Pontellier, as he let himself out.

à jeudi: until Thursday.

The Doctor would have liked during the course of conversation to ask, "Is there any man in the case?" but he knew his Creole too well to make such a blunder as that.

He did not resume his book immediately, but sat for a while meditatively looking out into the garden.

CHAPTER XXIII

Edna's father was in the city, and had been with them several days. She was not very warmly or deeply attached to him, but they had certain tastes in common, and when together they were companionable. His coming was in the nature of a welcome disturbance; it seemed to furnish a new direction for her emotions.

He had come to purchase a wedding gift for his daughter, Janet, and an outfit for himself in which he might make a creditable appearance at her marriage. Mr. Pontellier had selected the bridal gift, as every one immediately connected with him always deferred to his taste in such matters. And his suggestions on the question of dress—which too often assumes the nature of a problem were of inestimable value to his father-in-law. But for the past few days the old gentleman had been upon Edna's hands, and in his society she was becoming acquainted with a new set of sensations. He had been a colonel in the Confederate army, and still maintained, with the title, the military bearing which had always accompanied it. His hair and mustache were white and silky, emphasizing the rugged bronze of his face. He was tall and thin, and wore his coats padded, which gave a fictitious breadth and depth to his shoulders and chest. Edna and her father looked very distinguished together, and excited a good deal of notice during their **perambulations**. Upon his arrival she began by introducing him to her atelier and making a sketch of him. He took the whole matter very seriously. If her talent had been ten-fold greater than it was, it would not have surprised him, convinced as he was that he had bequeathed to all of his daughters the germs of a masterful capability, which only depended upon their own efforts to be directed toward successful achievement.

Before her pencil he sat rigid and unflinching, as he had faced the cannon's mouth in days gone by. He resented the intrusion of the children, who gaped with wondering eyes at him, sitting so stiff up there in their mother's bright atelier. When they drew near he motioned them away with an expressive action of the foot, loath to disturb the fixed lines of his countenance, his arms, or his rigid shoulders.

perambulation: a walk; a stroll.

Edna, anxious to entertain him, invited Mademoiselle Reisz to meet him, having promised him a treat in her piano playing; but Mademoiselle declined the invitation. So together they attended a soirée musicale at the Ratignolles'. Monsieur and Madame Ratignolle made much of the Colonel, installing him as the guest of honor and engaging him at once to dine with them the following Sunday, or any day which he might select. Madame coquetted with him in the most captivating and naive manner, with eyes, gestures, and a profusion of compliments, till the Colonel's old head felt thirty years younger on his padded shoulders. Edna marveled, not comprehending. She herself was almost devoid of **coquetry**.

coquetry: the behavior or act of a coquette; flirting.

There were one or two men whom she observed at the soirée musicale; but she would never have felt moved to any kittenish display to attract their notice—to any feline or feminine wiles to express herself toward them. Their personality attracted her in an agreeable way. Her fancy selected them, and she was glad when a lull in the music gave them an opportunity to meet her and talk with her. Often on the street the glance of strange eyes had lingered in her memory, and sometimes had disturbed her.

Mr. Pontellier did not attend these soirées musicales. He considered them **bourgeois**, and found more diversion at the club. To Madame Ratignolle he said the music dispensed at her soirées was too "heavy," too far beyond his untrained comprehension. His excuse flattered her. But she disapproved of Mr. Pontellier's club, and she was frank enough to tell Edna so.

bourgeois: middle-class; also used variously to mean conventional, smug, materialistic, etc.

"It's a pity Mr. Pontellier doesn't stay home more in the evenings. I think you would be more—well, if you don't mind my saying it—more united, if he did."

"Oh! dear no!" said Edna, with a blank look in her eyes. "What should I do if he stayed home? We wouldn't have anything to say to each other."

She had not much of anything to say to her father, for that matter; but he did not antagonize her. She discovered that he interested her, though she realized that he might not interest her long; and for the first time in her life she felt as if she were thoroughly acquainted with him. He kept her busy serving him and ministering to his wants. It amused her to do so. She would not permit a servant or one of the children to do anything for him which she might do herself. Her husband noticed, and thought it was the expression of a deep filial attachment which he had never suspected.

The Colonel drank numerous "toddies" during the course of the day, which left him, however, imperturbed. He was an expert at concocting strong drinks. He had even invented some, to which he had given fantastic names, and for whose manufacture he required diverse ingredients that it devolved upon Edna to procure for him.

When Doctor Mandelet dined with the Pontelliers on Thursday he could discern in Mrs. Pontellier no trace of that morbid condition which her husband had reported to him. She was excited and in a manner radiant. She and her father had been to the race course, and their thoughts when they seated themselves at table were still occupied with the events of the afternoon, and their talk was still of the track. The Doctor had not kept pace with turf affairs. He had certain recollections of racing in what he called "the good old times" when the Lecompte stables flourished, and he drew upon this fund of memories so that he might not be left out and seem wholly devoid of the modern spirit. But he failed to impose upon the Colonel, and was even far from impressing him with this trumped-up knowledge of bygone days. Edna had staked her father on his last venture, with the most gratifying results to both of them. Besides, they had met some very charming people, according to the Colonel's impressions. Mrs. Mortimer Merriman and Mrs. James Highcamp, who were there with Alcée Arobin, had joined them and had enlivened the hours in a fashion that warmed him to think of.

Mr. Pontellier himself had no particular leaning toward horseracing, and was even rather inclined to discourage it as a pastime, especially when he considered the fate of that blue-grass farm in Kentucky. He endeavored, in a general way, to express a particular disapproval, and only succeeded in arousing the ire and opposition of his father-in-law. A pretty dispute followed, in which Edna warmly espoused her father's cause and the Doctor remained neutral.

He observed his hostess attentively from under his shaggy brows, and noted a subtle change which had transformed her from the listless woman he had known into a being who, for the moment, seemed **palpitant** with the forces of life. Her speech was warm and energetic. There was no repression in her glance or gesture. She reminded him of some beautiful, sleek animal waking up in the sun.

The dinner was excellent. The claret was warm and the champagne was cold, and under their beneficent influence

palpitant: trembling

the threatened unpleasantness melted and vanished with the fumes of the wine.

Mr. Pontellier warmed up and grew reminiscent. He told some amusing plantation experiences, recollections of old Iberville and his youth, when he hunted 'possum in company with some friendly **darky**; thrashed the pecan trees, shot the **grosbec**, and roamed the woods and fields in mischievous idleness.

The Colonel, with little sense of humor and of the fitness of things, related a somber episode of those dark and bitter days, in which he had acted a conspicuous part and always formed a central figure. Nor was the Doctor happier in his selection, when he told the old, ever new and curious story of the waning of a woman's love, seeking strange, new channels, only to return to its legitimate source after days of fierce unrest. It was one of the many little human documents which had been unfolded to him during his long career as a physician. The story did not seem especially to impress Edna. She had one of her own to tell, of a woman who paddled away with her lover one night in a pirogue and never came back. They were lost amid the **Baratarian Islands**, and no one ever heard of them or found trace of them from that day to this. It was a pure invention. She said that Madame Antoine had related it to her. That, also, was an invention. Perhaps it was a dream she had had. But every glowing word seemed real to those who listened. They could feel the hot breath of the Southern night; they could hear the long sweep of the pirogue through the glistening moonlit water, the beating of birds' wings, rising startled from among the reeds in the salt-water pools; they could see the faces of the lovers, pale, close together, rapt in oblivious forgetfulness, drifting into the unknown.

The champagne was cold, and its subtle fumes played fantastic tricks with Edna's memory that night.

Outside, away from the glow of the fire and the soft lamplight, the night was chill and murky. The Doctor doubled his old-fashioned cloak across his breast as he strode home through the darkness. He knew his fellow-creatures better than most men; knew that inner life which so seldom unfolds itself to unanointed eyes. He was sorry he had accepted Pontellier's invitation. He was growing old, and beginning to need rest and an imperturbed spirit. He did not want the secrets of other lives thrust upon him.

"I hope it isn't Arobin," he muttered to himself as he walked. "I hope to heaven it isn't Alcée Arobin."

darky: a racist term used for black people in the turn-of-the-century South.

grosbec: any of various passerine birds with a thick, strong, conical bill. Usually spelled grosbeak.

Baratarian Islands: islands located in Barataria Bay, just off the coast of Louisiana in the Gulf of Mexico.

CHAPTER XXIV

Edna and her father had a warm, and almost violent dispute upon the subject of her refusal to attend her sister's wedding. Mr. Pontellier declined to interfere, to interpose either his influence or his authority. He was following Doctor Mandelet's advice, and letting her do as she liked. The Colonel reproached his daughter for her lack of filial kindness and respect, her want of sisterly affection and womanly consideration. His arguments were labored and unconvincing. He doubted if Janet would accept any excuse—forgetting that Edna had offered none. He doubted if Janet would ever speak to her again, and he was sure Margaret would not.

Edna was glad to be rid of her father when he finally took himself off with his wedding garments and his bridal gifts, with his padded shoulders, his Bible reading, his "toddies" and ponderous oaths.

Mr. Pontellier followed him closely. He meant to stop at the wedding on his way to New York and endeavor by every means which money and love could devise to atone somewhat for Edna's incomprehensible action.

"You are too lenient, too lenient by far, Léonce," asserted the Colonel. "Authority, coercion are what is needed. Put your foot down good and hard; the only way to manage a wife. Take my word for it."

The Colonel was perhaps unaware that he had coerced his own wife into her grave. Mr. Pontellier had a vague suspicion of it which he thought it needless to mention at that late day.

Edna was not so consciously gratified at her husband's leaving home as she had been over the departure of her father. As the day approached when he was to leave her for a comparatively long stay, she grew melting and affectionate, remembering his many acts of consideration and his repeated expressions of an ardent attachment. She was solicitous about his health and his welfare. She bustled around, looking after his clothing, thinking about heavy underwear, quite as Madame Ratignolle would have done under similar circumstances. She cried when he went away, calling him her dear, good friend, and she was quite certain she would grow lonely before very long and go to join him in New York.

But after all, a radiant peace settled upon her when she at last found herself alone. Even the children were gone. Old Madame Pontellier had come herself and carried them off to

Iberville with their quadroon. The old madame did not venture to say she was afraid they would be neglected during Léonce's absence; she hardly ventured to think so. She was hungry for them—even a little fierce in her attachment. She did not want them to be wholly "children of the pavement," she always said when begging to have them for a space. She wished them to know the country, with its streams, its fields, its woods, its freedom, so delicious to the young. She wished them to taste something of the life their father had lived and known and loved when he, too, was a little child.

When Edna was at last alone, she breathed a big, genuine sigh of relief. A feeling that was unfamiliar but very delicious came over her. She walked all through the house, from one room to another, as if inspecting it for the first time. She tried the various chairs and lounges, as if she had never sat and reclined upon them before. And she perambulated around the outside of the house, investigating, looking to see if windows and shutters were secure and in order. The flowers were like new acquaintances; she approached them in a familiar spirit, and made herself at home among them. The garden walks were damp, and Edna called to the maid to bring out her rubber sandals. And there she stayed, and stooped, digging around the plants, trimming, picking dead, dry leaves. The children's little dog came out, interfering, getting in her way. She scolded him, laughed at him, played with him. The garden smelled so good and looked so pretty in the afternoon sunlight. Edna plucked all the bright flowers she could find, and went into the house with them, she and the little dog.

Even the kitchen assumed a sudden interesting character which she had never before perceived. She went in to give directions to the cook, to say that the butcher would have to bring much less meat, that they would require only half their usual quantity of bread, of milk and groceries. She told the cook that she herself would be greatly occupied during Mr. Pontellier's absence, and she begged her to take all thought and responsibility of the **larder** upon her own shoulders.

That night Edna dined alone. The candelabra, with a few candies in the center of the table, gave all the light she needed. Outside the circle of light in which she sat, the large dining-room looked solemn and shadowy. The cook, placed **upon her mettle**, served a delicious repast—a luscious tenderloin broiled a point. The wine tasted good; the **marron glacé** seemed to be just what she wanted. It was so pleasant, too, to dine in a comfortable peignoir.

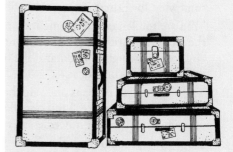

Traveling trunk and luggage.

larder: a supply of food; provisions.

upon her mettle: roused or prepared to do her best.

marron glacé: marrons in syrup or glazed with sugar; candied chestnuts.

She thought a little sentimentally about Léonce and the children, and wondered what they were doing. As she gave a dainty scrap or two to the doggie, she talked intimately to him about Etienne and Raoul. He was beside himself with astonishment and delight over these companionable advances, and showed his appreciation by his little quick, snappy barks and a lively agitation.

Then Edna sat in the library after dinner and read **Emerson** until she grew sleepy. She realized that she had neglected her reading, and determined to start anew upon a course of improving studies, now that her time was completely her own to do with as she liked.

Emerson: Ralph Waldo Emerson (1803–82); U.S. essayist, philosopher, and poet.

After a refreshing bath, Edna went to bed. And as she snuggled comfortably beneath the **eiderdown** a sense of restfulness invaded her, such as she had not known before.

eiderdown: a quilt stuffed with the soft, fine breast feathers, or down, of the eider duck.

COMMENTARY

During one of her moods of discontent, Edna decides to visit Mademoiselle Reisz. This decision creates a considerable adventure for Edna, who has lost the pianist's address. Her search for the older woman creates a necessary diversion for Edna, who encounters several different people along her journey. She finds out from a former grocer that the summer visitors at Grand Isle are not alone in finding Mademoiselle Reisz disagreeable. And although he is happy to tell Edna all he knows of the pianist, what he does not know is her address. As any thwarted child knows, not succeeding only inspires a greater desire to succeed, and Edna is not about to give up on her search so easily.

In many ways, Edna has become the child that Léonce accuses her of being. She is impetuous and is determined to do what she wants, regardless of the cost to herself or anyone else. She does not throw her wedding ring anymore or throw vases. But although she has achieved some control—at least on the surface—she still determines to obey no one but herself. Suddenly, the search for Mademoiselle Reisz is very important to Edna, even though she is still not sure that she likes the woman. In the past weeks, Edna has struggled to find some direction. She is not certain where the direction will take her, but the pianist may provide some answers. Despite her disagreeable nature, she is an artist, and she also answers to no one but herself.

Edna finally realizes that Madame Lebrun knows Mademoiselle Reisz's address. The Lebrun home is drastically different from the Pontellier's home. Chopin describes it as looking like a prison, with bars on the windows and door. Before Victor answers the door, Edna hears him arguing with the servant, who insists that opening the door is her job. Edna may not be the only woman wondering about her place in the world. Victor is astonished by Edna's visit, which is most unusual: The fashionable, wealthy Madame Pontellier should not be calling on the plebian Lebruns, but Edna cares little for propriety. Her whole journey has been one of impropriety. She refuses to enter the house and, instead, sits on the porch talking to Victor. While they wait for Madame Lebrun to appear, Victor tells Edna about his conquest of a young woman the previous evening—a completely inappropriate conversation for a man to be having with a married woman. Victor is too ill-bred to realize his rudeness, but most likely, he sees Edna as the kind of woman who won't be offended. This perception indicates how far beyond the pale Edna has slipped. Victor should not have even considered such a conversation, and he is prevented from providing the raciest details only by the timely arrival of his mother.

Edna does learn Mademoiselle Reisz's address, but she also discovers more important information: Robert sent the family two letters. Victor refuses to retrieve them, instead reciting their contents. Robert wants his mother to "remember him to all his friends." The lack of a personal message once again depresses Edna, but this reaction only indicates how little she understands New Orleans society. She is a married woman, and Robert cannot write to her, nor send her a special remembrance without compromising her reputation. He is now protecting Edna.

A despondent Edna soon leaves with Mademoiselle Reisz's address, but Victor's familiarity continues even as she is leaving. Edna matches his behavior with her own, "remembering too late that she should have been dignified and reserved." This acknowledgement suggests that she knows what is proper, but she chooses not to obey the rules.

After she leaves, Victor and Madame Lebrun remark at how handsome Edna looks; she looks "ravishing" according to Victor. Although she is still despondent, the changes of the past weeks have changed Edna in visible ways. The freedom that she is seeking has made her more beautiful, and readers should note that although she's not happy yet, Edna seems to feel that life holds more.

Edna finally arrives at Mademoiselle Reisz's apartment. Chopin describes the small apartment in some detail, as she has with the other homes. Homes are important because they help define their occupants. Madame Ratignolle's home is like its occupant—comfortable and homey and filled with children and love. Edna's home is like her husband—formal and filled with wealth, but the essential elements that bring satisfaction in life are missing. Mademoiselle Reisz's apartment is small and dingy, but she always insists on an apartment on the top floor so she has a commanding view of the world. Her apartment is decorated to reflect her needs and personality, and at its center is her piano— the one possession that truly defines her.

Mademoiselle Reisz also notices that Edna looks beautiful, although the comment seems more automatic and less genuine than it does when Victor Lebrun remarks on Edna's appearance. Because Edna no longer plays the socially correct role, she bluntly admits to the pianist that she is not sure whether she likes her. Edna's willingness to tell the truth immediately sets her apart from other society women, none of whom bother to visit Mademoiselle Reisz. The pianist immediately tells Edna that Robert has written to her, although he writes only of

Madame Pontellier. Expectedly, Edna demands to see the letter, a request that Mademoiselle Reisz refuses.

Obviously, Mademoiselle Reisz knows how badly Edna longs for word from Robert, and her delay in letting Edna read the letter seems like cruel teasing. Of course, Mademoiselle Reisz's behavior is consistently rude and disagreeable, and Edna does not appear surprised at the pianist's refusal. The news that Edna has become an artist is met with derision by Mademoiselle Reisz, who says "you have pretensions . . . the artist must possess the courageous soul." The implication is clear: Edna may not be brave enough or daring enough to be an artist.

Eventually, Mademoiselle Reisz surrenders the letter from Robert and begins to play Chopin's "Impromptu." Whether the music or the letter or both affect her, Edna soon dissolves into tears. Robert has written a love letter for Edna—the letter she has been longing to receive—though he sends it to Mademoiselle Reisz. He cannot address words of love to Edna—she is another man's wife, but he fills the letter with questions about Edna and with reminisces of Edna. When she leaves, the old woman invites her back. She does not discourage Edna's passions for Robert; she realizes that Edna is different from other society women and that her affection for Robert is genuine.

In the space of an afternoon, Edna has moved throughout New Orleans and has visited neighborhoods in which she has never before been. In Mademoiselle Reisz's apartment, Edna mentally moves beyond her marriage and even farther from her house on Esplanade Street. In fact, she has gone much farther than her own neighborhood and society have gone.

The visit from Doctor Mandelet illustrates how concerned Léonce is with the disruption in his marriage. Chopin indicates that the physician is not capable of dealing with Edna's changes. Chopin mentions that he is "resting upon his laurels." In other words, he is old, and the problems of the "new woman" are well beyond his experience. Indeed, one of his first questions concerns what he labels the "pseudo-intellectual woman— super-spiritual superior beings." The use of this label indicates that Doctor Mandelet treats what he does not understand with sarcasm and derision. He worries that Edna has fallen in with the pseudo-intellectual women, and he refuses to treat these women with respect.

The doctor's next question concerns her family antecedents—are any of Edna's family peculiar? His inquiry pertains to naturalism, a literary movement of the late nineteenth century arguing that people should take no real responsibility for their actions because their behavior is predetermined by their environment or their family's genetic heritage. When Léonce responds that none of these factors are a reasonable source for Edna's behavior, the doctor falls back on the traditional idea that "[m]ost women are moody and whimsical"; thus, he diminishes and negates Edna's problems as "idiosyncrasies."

One point that Léonce makes clear is that he and Edna are no longer sleeping together. He tells Doctor Mandelet that "we meet in the morning at the breakfast table." And then he explains Edna's refusal to attend her sister's wedding. Indeed, she points out that such an event is "one of the most lamentable spectacles on earth." The doctor expresses the opinion that Edna's mood will pass, but privately, he wonders, "Is there any man in the case?" According to Doctor Mandelet, Edna can be unhappy only if she has fallen under the influence of intellectual women, if her family is peculiar, or if there is another man besides her husband. These men don't realize that Edna may have awakened to something more important—her individuality.

In this scene, the doctor sees the deterioration of the Pontellier household from Léonce's perspective. His frustration, which mirrors Edna's frustration in Chapter 18, forces him to seek help from the only source he dares to approach—an old family doctor who will keep his confidences. Léonce is always concerned with appearances, and whatever solution he takes to resolve the problems in his home will satisfy his desire to maintain "*les convenances,*" the conventions.

The visit from Edna's father provides a crucial turn of events. In an effort to entertain the Colonel, Edna takes him to one of Madame Ratignolle's *soirée musicale* evenings. Madame Ratignolle entertains Edna's father with all the coquetry that Edna herself lacks. This scene further illustrates the basic differences between the two women. Edna has no feminine wiles with which to express herself, nor does she see any man at the performance whom she wants to attract. But attraction is not the point; the charming flirting of the Creole woman is habitual, and no one takes it seriously except, perhaps, Edna.

Madame Ratignolle's flirting recalls her flirting with Robert at Grand Isle, the flirting that Edna perceived as serious. Madame Ratignolle takes a few moments during the course of the evening to suggest that perhaps Edna should encourage Léonce to spend more time with her. She has noticed the distance between the Pontelliers, and the happiness of her own marriage validates her solution—more time spent together strengthens the marriage. Edna, of course, is aghast at the suggestion because she wants more time away from Léonce.

For Chopin's audience, the notion that husband and wives may have little to say to one another is not so unusual, nor does it provide sufficient cause for Edna's unhappiness. In the late nineteenth century, husbands and wives were not expected to be giddily in love after years of marriage. And although women readers may have understood Edna's complaints, men were shocked that Edna's response, "We wouldn't have anything to say to each other," was considered a defect in the marriage.

One of the activities that Edna uses to distract her father is a trip to the racetrack.

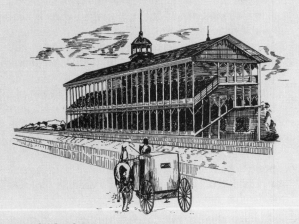

Jockey Club Race Course.

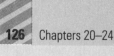

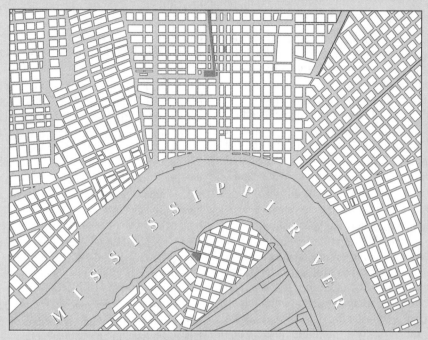
New Orleans in 1872.

Their trip provides a pivotal moment for Edna, who meets Alcée Arobin at the races. Edna's husband does not approve of the races; he sees them as a degenerate way of life. But the Colonel, who drinks far too much, enjoys the races, and so does Edna, who is quite knowledgeable about the horses. At dinner the same evening, Doctor Mandelet notices that Edna has indeed changed. Instead of the "listless woman" that he remembers, Edna has become a "beautiful, sleek animal waking up in the sun." The sensuality of Edna is unmistakable, and Doctor Mandelet's words suggest that even he recognizes her awakening—one wonders why Léonce does not. Moreover, Doctor Mandelet's last thoughts suggest that he is aware of the next stage of Edna's awakening: "I hope to heaven it isn't Alcée Arobin." The racetrack has provided the opening of another window for Edna and another, although different, awakening.

At the end of the evening, each visitor tells a story, revealing much about the speaker. Léonce tells a story about his plantation experiences at his family home in Iberville. The stories reveal a mischievous youth. Like the teller, the stories are ordinary and not particularly memorable, though told with humor. The colonel's story is a "somber episode" from his past; he plays the heroic figure—the way in which he sees himself. The doctor's

story is interesting and directed toward Edna: He tells the story of a woman who momentary loses her way but who finally returns to the love of her husband. This story is the best that he can do to provide hope for Léonce and a model of happiness for Edna, who remains unimpressed with the doctor's tale. Edna's story is a fantasy in which a young woman runs away with her lover never to return. She dreams of escape, and she relates it so well that her audience senses the truth in the story.

The Colonel's departure is marred by an argument when Edna refuses to attend her sister's wedding. He suggests that no excuse can possibly justify her sisterly slight. But Edna offers no excuse, just as she offered no excuse for the neglect of her household, the cessation of her social Tuesdays at home, or any other action she has lately taken. To avoid taking a step back, Edna refuses to be put in a position of explaining herself.

The Colonel's departure is followed closely by Léonce's departure. Edna's reaction to the latter departure points out how conflicted she feels. She does genuinely care for Léonce, and her affection is evident now that he leaves for a lengthy trip. Furthermore, Edna is momentarily afraid of being alone. Even the children are gone; their grandmother has taken them to the plantation in Iberville.

When finally left alone in the large house, Edna is relieved. Her "big, genuine sigh of relief" is akin to breathing after a long period of holding one's breath. The house feels and looks different to Edna, and her happiness in this new solitude is palpable. The flowers smell differently, the dog is more playful, and as a result, her existence is more enjoyable. Without Léonce to chide her, the cook finally performs at her best, creating the delicious meals Léonce had always wanted. To achieve this success, Edna tells the cook that she has control over the kitchen. In contrast, Léonce assumes that, to achieve success, people must be browbeaten into obedience. He assumes that the cook's poor repasts were the result of Edna's neglect, but in fact, they may have been the result of Léonce's demands. This realization suggests that Edna may have been happier and more creative if Léonce given her more freedom.

Edna waving good-bye to her children.

Notes

Notes

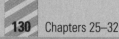

Chapters 25–32

Now that she is alone, Edna spends an increasing amount of time at the horse races, in the company of Alcée Arobin. Arobin increases his efforts to seduce Edna, recognizing her awakening vulnerability and determined to take advantage of it. When Edna becomes frightened and rebuffs his advances, Arobin carefully manipulates her into moving forward. Even though Arobin's seduction is clearly effective, Edna still thinks of Robert. She escapes Arobin to visit Mademoiselle Reisz and read Robert's letters to the pianist.

Although Edna is living alone, she does not feel completely free. She wants to escape her husband's control by escaping his house and possessions. Edna decides to move from her husband's house, rent a small house nearby, and invite her closest friends to a farewell dinner party at her old home.

When Edna learns that Robert is returning to New Orleans, she's ecstatic. Despite her longing to see Robert, she finally succumbs to Arobin's advances later that evening. Within days, Edna begins planning for her move as well as her final dinner party in her husband's house. Within a short time, all these plans come to fruition; the dinner party Edna hosts is a success, her move is completed, and Arobin is more firmly entrenched as Edna's lover. Although he has not returned from his business trip, Léonce concentrates on saving face with an announcement that the Pontelliers' home is being extensively remodeled—thus accounting for Edna's move out of the family home.

CHAPTER XXV

NOTES

When the weather was dark and cloudy Edna could not work. She needed the sun to mellow and temper her mood to the sticking point. She had reached a stage when she seemed to be no longer feeling her way, working, when in the humor, with sureness and ease. And being devoid of ambition, and striving not toward accomplishment, she drew satisfaction from the work in itself.

On rainy or melancholy days Edna went out and sought the society of the friends she had made at Grand Isle. Or else she stayed indoors and nursed a mood with which she was becoming too familiar for her own comfort and peace of mind. It was not despair; but it seemed to her as if life were passing by, leaving its promise broken and unfulfilled. Yet there were other days when she listened, was led on and deceived by fresh promises which her youth held out to her.

She went again to the races, and again. Alcée Arobin and Mrs. Highcamp called for her one bright afternoon in Arobin's **drag**. Mrs. Highcamp was a worldly but unaffected, intelligent, slim, tall blonde woman in the forties, with an indifferent manner and blue eyes that stared. She had a daughter who served her as a pretext for cultivating the society of young men of fashion. Alcée Arobin was one of them. He was a familiar figure at the race course, the opera, the fashionable clubs. There was a perpetual smile in his eyes, which seldom failed to awaken a corresponding cheerfulness in any one who looked into them and listened to his good-humored voice. His manner was quiet, and at times a little insolent. He possessed a good figure, a pleasing face, not overburdened with depth of thought or feeling; and his dress was that of the conventional man of fashion.

He admired Edna extravagantly, after meeting her at the races with her father. He had met her before on other occasions, but she had seemed to him unapproachable until that day. It was at his instigation that Mrs. Highcamp called to ask her to go with them to the **Jockey Club** to witness the turf event of the season.

There were possibly a few track men out there who knew the race horse as well as Edna, but there was certainly none who knew it better. She sat between her two companions as one having authority to speak. She laughed at Arobin's pretensions, and deplored Mrs. Highcamp's ignorance. The race horse was a friend and intimate associate of her childhood. The atmosphere of the stables and the breath of the blue grass paddock revived in her memory and lingered in her nostrils. She did not perceive that she was talking like her father as the sleek **geldings** ambled in review before them. She played for very high stakes, and fortune favored her. The fever of the game flamed in her cheeks and eyes, and it got into her blood and into her brain like an intoxicant. People turned their heads to look at her, and more than one lent an attentive ear to her utterances, hoping thereby to secure the elusive but ever-desired "tip." Arobin caught the contagion of excitement which drew him to Edna like a magnet. Mrs. Highcamp remained, as usual, unmoved, with her indifferent stare and uplifted eyebrows.

Edna stayed and dined with Mrs. Highcamp upon being urged to do so. Arobin also remained and sent away his drag.

The dinner was quiet and uninteresting, save for the cheerful efforts of Arobin to enliven things. Mrs. Highcamp deplored the absence of her daughter from the races, and

drag: a type of private stagecoach of the nineteenth century, with seats inside and on top, drawn by four horses.

Jockey Club: a luxurious social club limited to a select group of the New Orleans upper class.

geldings: castrated male horses.

tried to convey to her what she had missed by going to the "**Dante** reading" instead of joining them. The girl held a geranium leaf up to her nose and said nothing, but looked knowing and noncommittal. Mr. Highcamp was a plain, bald-headed man, who only talked under compulsion. He was unresponsive. Mrs. Highcamp was full of delicate courtesy and consideration toward her husband. She addressed most of her conversation to him at table. They sat in the library after dinner and read the evening papers together under the drop-light; while the younger people went into the drawing-room near by and talked. Miss Highcamp played some selections from **Grieg** upon the piano. She seemed to have apprehended all of the composer's coldness and none of his poetry. While Edna listened she could not help wondering if she had lost her taste for music.

When the time came for her to go home, Mr. Highcamp grunted a lame offer to escort her, looking down at his slippered feet with tactless concern. It was Arobin who took her home. The **car** ride was long, and it was late when they reached Esplanade Street. Arobin asked permission to enter for a second to light his cigarette—his match safe was empty. He filled his match safe, but did not light his cigarette until he left her, after she had expressed her willingness to go to the races with him again.

Edna was neither tired nor sleepy. She was hungry again, for the Highcamp dinner, though of excellent quality, had lacked abundance. She rummaged in the larder and brought forth a slice of Gruyere and some crackers. She opened a bottle of beer which she found in the icebox. Edna felt extremely restless and excited. She vacantly hummed a fantastic tune as she poked at the wood embers on the hearth and munched a cracker.

She wanted something to happen—something, anything; she did not know what. She regretted that she had not made Arobin stay a half hour to talk over the horses with her. She counted the money she had won. But there was nothing else to do, so she went to bed, and tossed there for hours in a sort of monotonous agitation.

In the middle of the night she remembered that she had forgotten to write her regular letter to her husband; and she decided to do so next day and tell him about her afternoon at the Jockey Club. She lay wide awake composing a letter which was nothing like the one which she wrote next day. When the maid awoke her in the morning Edna was dreaming of Mr. Highcamp playing the piano at the entrance of a

Dante: Dante Alighieri (1265–1321); Italian poet who wrote *The Divine Comedy.*

Grieg: Edvard Grieg (1843–1907); Norwegian composer.

car: here, streetcar.

music store on Canal Street, while his wife was saying to Alcée Arobin, as they boarded an Esplanade Street car:

"What a pity that so much talent has been neglected! but I must go."

When, a few days later, Alcée Arobin again called for Edna in his drag, Mrs. Highcamp was not with him. He said they would pick her up. But as that lady had not been apprised of his intention of picking her up, she was not at home. The daughter was just leaving the house to attend the meeting of a branch Folk Lore Society, and regretted that she could not accompany them. Arobin appeared nonplused, and asked Edna if there were any one else she cared to ask.

She did not deem it worth while to go in search of any of the fashionable acquaintances from whom she had withdrawn herself. She thought of Madame Ratignolle, but knew that her fair friend did not leave the house, except to take a languid walk around the block with her husband after nightfall. Mademoiselle Reisz would have laughed at such a request from Edna. Madame Lebrun might have enjoyed the outing, but for some reason Edna did not want her. So they went alone, she and Arobin.

The afternoon was intensely interesting to her. The excitement came back upon her like a remittent fever. Her talk grew familiar and confidential. It was no labor to become intimate with Arobin. His manner invited easy confidence. The preliminary stage of becoming acquainted was one which he always endeavored to ignore when a pretty and engaging woman was concerned.

He stayed and dined with Edna. He stayed and sat beside the wood fire. They laughed and talked; and before it was time to go he was telling her how different life might have been if he had known her years before. With ingenuous frankness he spoke of what a wicked, ill-disciplined boy he had been, and impulsively drew up his cuff to exhibit upon his wrist the scar from a saber cut which he had received in a duel outside of Paris when he was nineteen. She touched his hand as she scanned the red **cicatrice** on the inside of his white wrist. A quick impulse that was somewhat spasmodic impelled her fingers to close in a sort of clutch upon his hand. He felt the pressure of her pointed nails in the flesh of his palm.

She arose hastily and walked toward the mantel.

"The sight of a wound or scar always agitates and sickens me," she said. "I shouldn't have looked at it."

cicatrice: scar.

"I beg your pardon," he entreated, following her; "it never occurred to me that it might be repulsive."

He stood close to her, and the effrontery in his eyes repelled the old, vanishing self in her, yet drew all her awakening sensuousness. He saw enough in her face to impel him to take her hand and hold it while he said his lingering good night.

"Will you go to the races again?" he asked.

"No," she said. "I've had enough of the races. I don't want to lose all the money I've won, and I've got to work when the weather is bright, instead of—"

"Yes; work; to be sure. You promised to show me your work. What morning may I come up to your atelier? To-morrow?"

"No!"

"Day after?"

"No, no."

"Oh, please don't refuse me! I know something of such things. I might help you with a stray suggestion or two."

"No. Good night. Why don't you go after you have said good night? I don't like you," she went on in a high, excited pitch, attempting to draw away her hand. She felt that her words lacked dignity and sincerity, and she knew that he felt it.

"I'm sorry you don't like me. I'm sorry I offended you. How have I offended you? What have I done? Can't you forgive me?" And he bent and pressed his lips upon her hand as if he wished never more to withdraw them.

"Mr. Arobin," she complained, "I'm greatly upset by the excitement of the afternoon; I'm not myself. My manner must have misled you in some way. I wish you to go, please." She spoke in a monotonous, dull tone. He took his hat from the table, and stood with eyes turned from her, looking into the dying fire. For a moment or two he kept an impressive silence.

"Your manner has not misled me, Mrs. Pontellier," he said finally. "My own emotions have done that. I couldn't help it. When I'm near you, how could I help it? Don't think anything of it, don't bother, please. You see, I go when you command me. If you wish me to stay away, I shall do so. If you let me come back, I—oh! you will let me come back?"

He cast one appealing glance at her, to which she made no response. Alcée Arobin's manner was so genuine that it often deceived even himself.

Edna did not care or think whether it were genuine or not. When she was alone she looked mechanically at the back of her hand which he had kissed so warmly. Then she leaned her head down on the mantelpiece. She felt somewhat like a woman who in a moment of passion is betrayed into an act of infidelity, and realizes the significance of the act without being wholly awakened from its glamour. The thought was passing vaguely through her mind, "What would he think?"

She did not mean her husband; she was thinking of Robert Lebrun. Her husband seemed to her now like a person whom she had married without love as an excuse.

She lit a candle and went up to her room. Alcée Arobin was absolutely nothing to her. Yet his presence, his manners, the warmth of his glances, and above all the touch of his lips upon her hand had acted like a narcotic upon her.

She slept a languorous sleep, interwoven with vanishing dreams.

CHAPTER XXVI

Alcée Arobin wrote Edna an elaborate note of apology, palpitant with sincerity. It embarrassed her; for in a cooler, quieter moment it appeared to her, absurd that she should have taken his action so seriously, so dramatically. She felt sure that the significance of the whole occurrence had lain in her own self-consciousness. If she ignored his note it would give undue importance to a trivial affair. If she replied to it in a serious spirit it would still leave in his mind the impression that she had in a susceptible moment yielded to his influence. After all, it was no great matter to have one's hand kissed. She was provoked at his having written the apology. She answered in as light and bantering a spirit as she fancied it deserved, and said she would be glad to have him look in upon her at work whenever he felt the inclination and his business gave him the opportunity.

He responded at once by presenting himself at her home with all his disarming naivete. And then there was scarcely a day which followed that she did not see him or was not reminded of him. He was prolific in pretexts. His attitude became one of good-humored subservience and tacit adoration. He was ready at all times to submit to her moods, which were as often kind as they were cold. She grew accustomed to him. They became intimate and friendly by imperceptible degrees, and then by leaps. He sometimes talked in a way that astonished her at first and brought the crimson into her face; in a way that pleased her at last, appealing to the animalism that stirred impatiently within her.

There was nothing which so quieted the turmoil of Edna's senses as a visit to Mademoiselle Reisz. It was then, in the presence of that personality which was offensive to her, that the woman, by her divine art, seemed to reach Edna's spirit and set it free.

It was misty, with heavy, lowering atmosphere, one afternoon, when Edna climbed the stairs to the pianist's apartments under the roof. Her clothes were dripping with moisture. She felt chilled and pinched as she entered the room. Mademoiselle was poking at a rusty stove that smoked a little and warmed the room indifferently. She was endeavoring to heat a pot of chocolate on the stove. The room looked cheerless and dingy to Edna as she entered. A bust of Beethoven, covered with a hood of dust, scowled at her from the mantelpiece.

"Ah! here comes the sunlight!" exclaimed Mademoiselle, rising from her knees before the stove. "Now it will be warm and bright enough; I can let the fire alone."

She closed the stove door with a bang, and approaching, assisted in removing Edna's dripping **mackintosh**.

mackintosh: a waterproof outer coat, a raincoat.

"You are cold; you look miserable. The chocolate will soon be hot. But would you rather have a taste of brandy? I have scarcely touched the bottle which you brought me for my cold." A piece of red flannel was wrapped around Mademoiselle's throat; a stiff neck compelled her to hold her head on one side.

"I will take some brandy," said Edna, shivering as she removed her gloves and overshoes. She drank the liquor from the glass as a man would have done. Then flinging herself upon the uncomfortable sofa she said, "Mademoiselle, I am going to move away from my house on Esplanade Street."

"Ah!" ejaculated the musician, neither surprised nor especially interested. Nothing ever seemed to astonish her very much. She was endeavoring to adjust the bunch of violets which had become loose from its fastening in her hair. Edna drew her down upon the sofa, and taking a pin from her own hair, secured the shabby artificial flowers in their accustomed place.

"Aren't you astonished?"

"Passably. Where are you going? to New York? to Iberville? to your father in Mississippi? where?"

"Just two steps away," laughed Edna, "in a little four-room house around the corner. It looks so cozy, so inviting and restful, whenever I pass by; and it's for rent. I'm tired looking after that big house. It never seemed like mine, anyway—like home. It's too much trouble. I have to keep too many servants. I am tired bothering with them."

"That is not your true reason, ma belle. There is no use in telling me lies. I don't know your reason, but you have not told me the truth." Edna did not protest or endeavor to justify herself.

"The house, the money that provides for it, are not mine. Isn't that enough reason?"

"They are your husband's," returned Mademoiselle, with a shrug and a malicious elevation of the eyebrows.

"Oh! I see there is no deceiving you. Then let me tell you: It is a caprice. I have a little money of my own from my mother's estate, which my father sends me by driblets. I won a large sum this winter on the races, and I am beginning to sell my sketches. Laidpore is more and more pleased with my work; he says it grows in force and individuality. I cannot judge of that myself, but I feel that I have gained in ease and confidence. However, as I said, I have sold a good many through Laidpore. I can live in the tiny house for little or nothing, with one servant. Old Celestine, who works occasionally for me, says she will come stay with me and do my work. I know I shall like it, like the feeling of freedom and independence."

"What does your husband say?"

"I have not told him yet. I only thought of it this morning. He will think I am demented, no doubt. Perhaps you think so."

Mademoiselle shook her head slowly. "Your reason is not yet clear to me," she said.

Neither was it quite clear to Edna herself; but it unfolded itself as she sat for a while in silence. Instinct had prompted her to put away her husband's bounty in casting off her allegiance. She did not know how it would be when he returned. There would have to be an understanding, an explanation. Conditions would some way adjust themselves, she felt; but whatever came, she had resolved never again to belong to another than herself.

"I shall give a grand dinner before I leave the old house!" Edna exclaimed. "You will have to come to it, Mademoiselle. I will give you everything that you like to eat and to drink. We shall sing and laugh and be merry for once." And she uttered a sigh that came from the very depths of her being.

If Mademoiselle happened to have received a letter from Robert during the interval of Edna's visits, she would give her the letter unsolicited. And she would seat herself at the piano and play as her humor prompted her while the young woman read the letter.

The little stove was roaring; it was red-hot, and the chocolate in the tin sizzled and sputtered. Edna went forward and opened the stove door, and Mademoiselle rising, took a letter from under the bust of Beethoven and handed it to Edna.

"Another! so soon!" she exclaimed, her eyes filled with delight. "Tell me, Mademoiselle, does he know that I see his letters?"

"Never in the world! He would be angry and would never write to me again if he thought so. Does he write to you? Never a line. Does he send you a message? Never a word. It is because he loves you, poor fool, and is trying to forget you, since you are not free to listen to him or to belong to him."

"Why do you show me his letters, then?"

"Haven't you begged for them? Can I refuse you anything? Oh! you cannot deceive me," and Mademoiselle approached her beloved instrument and began to play. Edna did not at once read the letter. She sat holding it in her hand, while the music penetrated her whole being like an effulgence, warming and brightening the dark places of her soul. It prepared her for joy and exultation.

"Oh!" she exclaimed, letting the letter fall to the floor. "Why did you not tell me?" She went and grasped Mademoiselle's hands up from the keys. "Oh! unkind! malicious! Why did you not tell me?"

"That he was coming back? No great news, ma foi. I wonder he did not come long ago."

"But when, when?" cried Edna, impatiently. "He does not say when."

"He says 'very soon.' You know as much about it as I do; it is all in the letter."

"But why? Why is he coming? Oh, if I thought—" and she snatched the letter from the floor and turned the pages this way and that way, looking for the reason, which was left untold.

"If I were young and in love with a man," said Mademoiselle, turning on the stool and pressing her wiry hands between her knees as she looked down at Edna, who sat on the floor holding the letter, "it seems to me he would have to be some **grand esprit**; a man with lofty aims and ability to reach them; one who stood high enough to attract the notice of his fellow-men. It seems to me if I were young and in love I should never deem a man of ordinary caliber worthy of my devotion."

grand esprit: great spirit.

"Now it is you who are telling lies and seeking to deceive me, Mademoiselle; or else you have never been in love, and know nothing about it. Why," went on Edna, clasping her knees and looking up into Mademoiselle's twisted face, "do you suppose a woman knows why she loves? Does she select? Does she say to herself: 'Go to! Here is a distinguished statesman with presidential possibilities; I shall proceed to fall in love with him.' Or, 'I shall set my heart upon this musician, whose fame is on every tongue?' Or, 'This financier, who controls the world's money markets?'"

"You are purposely misunderstanding me, **ma reine**. Are you in love with Robert?"

ma reine: my queen (or my love).

"Yes," said Edna. It was the first time she had admitted it, and a glow overspread her face, blotching it with red spots.

"Why?" asked her companion. "Why do you love him when you ought not to?"

Edna, with a motion or two, dragged herself on her knees before Mademoiselle Reisz, who took the glowing face between her two hands.

"Why? Because his hair is brown and grows away from his temples; because he opens and shuts his eyes, and his nose is a little out of drawing; because he has two lips and a square chin, and a little finger which he can't straighten from having played baseball too energetically in his youth. Because—"

"Because you do, in short," laughed Mademoiselle. "What will you do when he comes back?" she asked.

"Do? Nothing, except feel glad and happy to be alive."

She was already glad and happy to be alive at the mere thought of his return. The murky, lowering sky, which had depressed her a few hours before, seemed bracing and invigorating as she splashed through the streets on her way home.

She stopped at a confectioner's and ordered a huge box of bonbons for the children in Iberville. She slipped a card in the box, on which she scribbled a tender message and sent an abundance of kisses.

Before dinner in the evening Edna wrote a charming letter to her husband, telling him of her intention to move for a while into the little house around the block, and to give a farewell dinner before leaving, regretting that he was not there to share it, to help out with the menu and assist her in entertaining the guests. Her letter was brilliant and brimming with cheerfulness.

CHAPTER XXVII

"What is the matter with you?" asked Arobin that evening. "I never found you in such a happy mood." Edna was tired by that time, and was reclining on the lounge before the fire.

"Don't you know the weather prophet has told us we shall see the sun pretty soon?"

"Well, that ought to be reason enough," he acquiesced. "You wouldn't give me another if I sat here all night imploring you." He sat close to her on a low **tabouret**, and as he spoke his fingers lightly touched the hair that fell a little over her forehead. She liked the touch of his fingers through her hair, and closed her eyes sensitively.

"One of these days," she said, "I'm going to pull myself together for a while and think—try to determine what character of a woman I am; for, candidly, I don't know. By all the codes which I am acquainted with, I am a devilishly wicked specimen of the sex. But some way I can't convince myself that I am. I must think about it."

"Don't. What's the use? Why should you bother thinking about it when I can tell you what manner of woman you are." His fingers strayed occasionally down to her warm, smooth cheeks and firm chin, which was growing a little full and double.

"Oh, yes! You will tell me that I am adorable; everything that is captivating. Spare yourself the effort."

"No; I shan't tell you anything of the sort, though I shouldn't be lying if I did."

"Do you know Mademoiselle Reisz?" she asked irrelevantly.

"The pianist? I know her by sight. I've heard her play."

"She says queer things sometimes in a bantering way that you don't notice at the time and you find yourself thinking about afterward."

"For instance?"

"Well, for instance, when I left her to-day, she put her arms around me and felt my shoulder blades, to see if my wings were strong, she said. 'The bird that would soar above the

tabouret: a low, upholstered footstool. Also spelled taboret.

level plain of tradition and prejudice must have strong wings. It is a sad spectacle to see the weaklings bruised, exhausted, fluttering back to earth.'

"Whither would you soar?"

"I'm not thinking of any extraordinary flights. I only half comprehend her."

"I've heard she's partially demented," said Arobin.

"She seems to me wonderfully sane," Edna replied.

"I'm told she's extremely disagreeable and unpleasant. Why have you introduced her at a moment when I desired to talk of you?"

"Oh! talk of me if you like," cried Edna, clasping her hands beneath her head; "but let me think of something else while you do."

"I'm jealous of your thoughts tonight. They're making you a little kinder than usual; but some way I feel as if they were wandering, as if they were not here with me." She only looked at him and smiled. His eyes were very near. He leaned upon the lounge with an arm extended across her, while the other hand still rested upon her hair. They continued silently to look into each other's eyes. When he leaned forward and kissed her, she clasped his head, holding his lips to hers.

It was the first kiss of her life to which her nature had really responded. It was a flaming torch that kindled desire.

CHAPTER XXVIII

Edna cried a little that night after Arobin left her. It was only one phase of the **multitudinous** emotions which had assailed her. There was with her an overwhelming feeling of irresponsibility. There was the shock of the unexpected and the unaccustomed. There was her husband's reproach looking at her from the external things around her which he had provided for her external existence. There was Robert's reproach making itself felt by a quicker, fiercer, more overpowering love, which had awakened within her toward him. Above all, there was understanding. She felt as if a mist had been lifted from her eyes, enabling her to took upon and comprehend the significance of life, that monster made up of beauty and brutality. But among the conflicting sensations which **assailed** her, there was neither shame nor remorse. There was a dull pang of regret because it was not the kiss of love which had inflamed her, because it was not love which had held this cup of life to her lips.

multitudinous: very numerous; many.

assailed: attacked physically and violently; assaulted.

CHAPTER XXIX

Without even waiting for an answer from her husband regarding his opinion or wishes in the matter, Edna hastened her preparations for quitting her home on Esplanade Street and moving into the little house around the block. A feverish anxiety attended her every action in that direction. There was no moment of deliberation, no interval of repose between the thought and its fulfillment. Early upon the morning following those hours passed in Arobin's society, Edna set about securing her new abode and hurrying her arrangements for occupying it. Within the precincts of her home she felt like one who has entered and lingered within the portals of some forbidden temple in which a thousand muffled voices bade her begone.

Whatever was her own in the house, everything which she had acquired aside from her husband's bounty, she caused to be transported to the other house, supplying simple and meager deficiencies from her own resources.

Arobin found her with rolled sleeves, working in company with the house-maid when he looked in during the afternoon. She was splendid and robust, and had never appeared handsomer than in the old blue gown, with a red silk handkerchief knotted at random around her head to protect her hair from the dust. She was mounted upon a high stepladder, unhooking a picture from the wall when he entered. He had found the front door open, and had followed his ring by walking in unceremoniously.

"Come down!" he said. "Do you want to kill yourself?" She greeted him with affected carelessness, and appeared absorbed in her occupation.

If he had expected to find her languishing, reproachful, or indulging in sentimental tears, he must have been greatly surprised.

He was no doubt prepared for any emergency, ready for any one of the foregoing attitudes, just as he bent himself easily and naturally to the situation which confronted him.

"Please come down," he insisted, holding the ladder and looking up at her.

"No," she answered; "Ellen is afraid to mount the ladder. Joe is working over at the '**pigeon house**'—that's the name Ellen gives it, because it's so small and looks like a pigeon house—and some one has to do this."

Arobin pulled off his coat, and expressed himself ready and willing to tempt fate in her place. Ellen brought him one of

pigeon house: small bird house for domesticated pigeons.

her dust-caps, and went into contortions of mirth, which she found it impossible to control, when she saw him put it on before the mirror as grotesquely as he could. Edna herself could not refrain from smiling when she fastened it at his request. So it was he who in turn mounted the ladder, unhooking pictures and curtains, and dislodging ornaments as Edna directed. When he had finished he took off his dust-cap and went out to wash his hands.

Edna was sitting on the tabouret, idly brushing the tips of a feather duster along the carpet when he came in again.

"Is there anything more you will let me do?" he asked.

"That is all," she answered. "Ellen can manage the rest." She kept the young woman occupied in the drawing-room, unwilling to be left alone with Arobin.

"What about the dinner?" he asked; "the grand event, the **coup d'état**?"

"It will be day after to-morrow. Why do you call it the 'coup d'état?' Oh! it will be very fine; all my best of everything—crystal, silver and gold, Sèvres, flowers, music, and champagne to swim in. I'll let Léonce pay the bills. I wonder what he'll say when he sees the bills.

"And you ask me why I call it a coup d'état?" Arobin had put on his coat, and he stood before her and asked if his **cravat** was **plumb**. She told him it was, looking no higher than the tip of his collar.

"When do you go to the 'pigeon house?'—with all due acknowledgment to Ellen."

"Day after to-morrow, after the dinner. I shall sleep there."

"Ellen, will you very kindly get me a glass of water?" asked Arobin. "The dust in the curtains, if you will pardon me for hinting such a thing, has parched my throat to a crisp."

"While Ellen gets the water," said Edna, rising, "I will say good-by and let you go. I must get rid of this grime, and I have a million things to do and think of."

"When shall I see you?" asked Arobin, seeking to detain her, the maid having left the room.

"At the dinner, of course. You are invited."

"Not before?—not to-night or to-morrow morning or tomorrow noon or night? or the day after morning or noon? Can't you see yourself, without my telling you, what an eternity it is?"

coup d'état: the sudden, forcible overthrow of a ruler, government, etc., sometimes with violence, by a small group of people already having some political or military authority.

cravat: a necktie.

plumb: perfectly vertical; straight down.

He had followed her into the hall and to the foot of the stairway, looking up at her as she mounted with her face half turned to him.

"Not an instant sooner," she said. But she laughed and looked at him with eyes that at once gave him courage to wait and made it torture to wait.

CHAPTER XXX

Though Edna had spoken of the dinner as a very grand affair, it was in truth a very small affair and very select, in so much as the guests invited were few and were selected with discrimination. She had counted upon an even dozen seating themselves at her round mahogany board, forgetting for the moment that Madame Ratignolle was to the last degree **souffrante** and unpresentable, and not foreseeing that Madame Lebrun would send a thousand regrets at the last moment. So there were only ten, after all, which made a cozy, comfortable number.

souffrante: suffering or ill; here, a reference to the late stage of pregnancy.

There were Mr. and Mrs. Merriman, a pretty, vivacious little woman in the thirties; her husband, a jovial fellow, something of a **shallow-pate**, who laughed a good deal at other people's witticisms, and had thereby made himself extremely popular. Mrs. Highcamp had accompanied them. Of course, there was Alcée Arobin; and Mademoiselle Reisz had consented to come. Edna had sent her a fresh bunch of violets with black lace trimmings for her hair. Monsieur Ratignolle brought himself and his wife's excuses. Victor Lebrun, who happened to be in the city, bent upon relaxation, had accepted with **alacrity**. There was a Miss Mayblunt, no longer in her teens, who looked at the world through **lorgnettes** and with the keenest interest. It was thought and said that she was intellectual; it was suspected of her that she wrote under a **nom de guerre**. She had come with a gentleman by the name of Gouvernail, connected with one of the daily papers, of whom nothing special could be said, except that he was observant and seemed quiet and inoffensive. Edna herself made the tenth, and at half-past eight they seated themselves at table, Arobin and Monsieur Ratignolle on either side of their hostess.

shallow-pate: a person lacking depth or intelligence.

alacrity: eager willingness or readiness, often manifested by quick, lively action.

lorgnettes: a pair of eyeglasses attached to a handle.

nom de guerre: a pseudonym.

Mrs. Highcamp sat between Arobin and Victor Lebrun. Then came Mrs. Merriman, Mr. Gouvernail, Miss Mayblunt, Mr. Merriman, and Mademoiselle Reisz next to Monsieur Ratignolle.

There was something extremely gorgeous about the appearance of the table, an effect of splendor conveyed by a cover of pale yellow satin under strips of lace-work. There were wax candles, in massive brass candelabra, burning softly under yellow silk shades; full, fragrant roses, yellow and red, abounded. There were silver and gold, as she had said there would be, and crystal which glittered like the gems which the women wore.

The ordinary stiff dining chairs had been discarded for the occasion and replaced by the most commodious and luxurious which could be collected throughout the house. Mademoiselle Reisz, being exceedingly diminutive, was elevated upon cushions, as small children are sometimes hoisted at table upon bulky volumes.

"Something new, Edna?" exclaimed Miss Mayblunt, with lorgnette directed toward a magnificent cluster of diamonds that sparkled, that almost sputtered, in Edna's hair, just over the center of her forehead.

"Quite new; 'brand' new, in fact; a present from my husband. It arrived this morning from New York. I may as well admit that this is my birthday, and that I am twenty-nine. In good time I expect you to drink my health. Meanwhile, I shall ask you to begin with this cocktail, composed—would you say 'composed?'" with an appeal to Miss Mayblunt— "composed by my father in honor of Sister Janet's wedding."

Before each guest stood a tiny glass that looked and sparkled like a garnet gem.

"Then, all things considered," spoke Arobin, "it might not be amiss to start out by drinking the Colonel's health in the cocktail which he composed, on the birthday of the most charming of women—the daughter whom he invented."

Mr. Merriman's laugh at this sally was such a genuine outburst and so contagious that it started the dinner with an agreeable swing that never slackened.

Miss Mayblunt begged to be allowed to keep her cocktail untouched before her, just to look at. The color was marvelous! She could compare it to nothing she had ever seen, and the garnet lights which it emitted were unspeakably rare. She pronounced the Colonel an artist, and stuck to it.

Monsieur Ratignolle was prepared to take things seriously; the **mets**, the **entre-mets**, the service, the decorations, even the people. He looked up from his **pompano** and inquired of Arobin if he were related to the gentleman of that name who formed one of the firm of Laitner and Arobin,

mets: main dish or main course.

entre-mets: a dish served between the main courses or as a side dish.

pompano: any of various edible, marine North American and West Indian jack fishes.

lawyers. The young man admitted that Laitner was a warm personal friend, who permitted Arobin's name to decorate the firm's letterheads and to appear upon a shingle that graced Perdido Street.

"There are so many inquisitive people and institutions abounding," said Arobin, "that one is really forced as a matter of convenience these days to assume the virtue of an occupation if he has it not."

Monsieur Ratignolle stared a little, and turned to ask Mademoiselle Reisz if she considered the symphony concerts up to the standard which had been set the previous winter. Mademoiselle Reisz answered Monsieur Ratignolle in French, which Edna thought a little rude, under the circumstances, but characteristic. Mademoiselle had only disagreeable things to say of the symphony concerts, and insulting remarks to make of all the musicians of New Orleans, singly and collectively. All her interest seemed to be centered upon the delicacies placed before her.

Mr. Merriman said that Mr. Arobin's remark about inquisitive people reminded him of a man from Waco the other day at the St. Charles Hotel—but as Mr. Merriman's stories were always lame and lacking point, his wife seldom permitted him to complete them. She interrupted him to ask if he remembered the name of the author whose book she had bought the week before to send to a friend in Geneva. She was talking "books" with Mr. Gouvernail and trying to draw from him his opinion upon current literary topics. Her husband told the story of the Waco man privately to Miss Mayblunt, who pretended to be greatly amused and to think it extremely clever.

Mrs. Highcamp hung with languid but unaffected interest upon the warm and impetuous volubility of her left-hand neighbor, Victor Lebrun. Her attention was never for a moment withdrawn from him after seating herself at table; and when he turned to Mrs. Merriman, who was prettier and more vivacious than Mrs. Highcamp, she waited with easy indifference for an opportunity to reclaim his attention. There was the occasional sound of music, of mandolins, sufficiently removed to be an agreeable accompaniment rather than an interruption to the conversation. Outside the soft, monotonous splash of a fountain could be heard; the sound penetrated into the room with the heavy odor of jessamine that came through the open windows.

The golden shimmer of Edna's satin gown spread in rich folds on either side of her. There was a soft fall of lace encircling her shoulders. It was the color of her skin, without the glow, the myriad living tints that one may sometimes discover in vibrant flesh. There was something in her attitude, in her whole appearance when she leaned her head against the high-backed chair and spread her arms, which suggested the regal woman, the one who rules, who looks on, who stands alone.

But as she sat there amid her guests, she felt the old ennui overtaking her; the hopelessness which so often assailed her, which came upon her like an obsession, like something extraneous, independent of volition. It was something which announced itself; a chill breath that seemed to issue from some vast cavern wherein discords waited. There came over her the acute longing which always summoned into her spiritual vision the presence of the beloved one, overpowering her at once with a sense of the unattainable.

The moments glided on, while a feeling of good fellowship passed around the circle like a mystic cord, holding and binding these people together with jest and laughter. Monsieur Ratignolle was the first to break the pleasant charm. At ten o'clock he excused himself. Madame Ratignolle was waiting for him at home. She was bien souffrante, and she was filled with vague dread, which only her husband's presence could allay.

Mademoiselle Reisz arose with Monsieur Ratignolle, who offered to escort her to the car. She had eaten well; she had tasted the good, rich wines, and they must have turned her head, for she bowed pleasantly to all as she withdrew from table. She kissed Edna upon the shoulder, and whispered: **"Bonne nuit, ma reine; soyez sage."** She had been a little bewildered upon rising, or rather, descending from her cushions, and Monsieur Ratignolle gallantly took her arm and led her away.

Mrs. Highcamp was weaving a garland of roses, yellow and red. When she had finished the garland, she laid it lightly upon Victor's black curls. He was reclining far back in the luxurious chair, holding a glass of champagne to the light.

As if a magician's wand had touched him, the garland of roses transformed him into a vision of Oriental beauty. His cheeks were the color of crushed grapes, and his dusky eyes glowed with a languishing fire.

"Sapristi!" exclaimed Arobin.

But Mrs. Highcamp had one more touch to add to the picture. She took from the back of her chair a white silken

Bonne nuit, ma reine, soyez sage: Good night, my queen, behave well.

scarf, with which she had covered her shoulders in the early part of the evening. She draped it across the boy in graceful folds, and in a way to conceal his black, conventional evening dress. He did not seem to mind what she did to him, only smiled, showing a faint gleam of white teeth, while he continued to gaze with narrowing eyes at the light through his glass of champagne.

"Oh! to be able to paint in color rather than in words!" exclaimed Miss Mayblunt, losing herself in a rhapsodic dream as she looked at him.

"'There was a graven image of Desire
Painted with red blood on a ground of gold.'"
murmured Gouvernail, under his breath.

The effect of the wine upon Victor was to change his accustomed volubility into silence. He seemed to have abandoned himself to a reverie, and to be seeing pleasing visions in the amber bead.

"Sing," entreated Mrs. Highcamp. "Won't you sing to us?"

"Let him alone," said Arobin.

"He's posing," offered Mr. Merriman; "let him have it out."

"I believe he's paralyzed," laughed Mrs. Merriman. And leaning over the youth's chair, she took the glass from his hand and held it to his lips. He sipped the wine slowly, and when he had drained the glass she laid it upon the table and wiped his lips with her little filmy handkerchief.

"Yes, I'll sing for you," he said, turning in his chair toward Mrs. Highcamp. He clasped his hands behind his head, and looking up at the ceiling began to hum a little, trying his voice like a musician tuning an instrument. Then, looking at Edna, he began to sing:

"Ah! si tu savais!"

"Stop!" she cried, "don't sing that. I don't want you to sing it," and she laid her glass so impetuously and blindly upon the table as to shatter it against a carafe. The wine spilled over Arobin's legs and some of it trickled down upon Mrs. Highcamp's black gauze gown. Victor had lost all idea of courtesy, or else he thought his hostess was not in earnest, for he laughed and went on:

"Ah! si tu savais

Ce que tes yeux me disent"—

"Oh! you mustn't! you mustn't," exclaimed Edna, and pushing back her chair she got up, and going behind him placed her hand over his mouth. He kissed the soft palm that pressed upon his lips.

Ce que tes yeux me disent: What your eyes are saying to me.

"No, no, I won't, Mrs. Pontellier. I didn't know you meant it," looking up at her with caressing eyes. The touch of his lips was like a pleasing sting to her hand. She lifted the garland of roses from his head and flung it across the room.

"Come, Victor; you've posed long enough. Give Mrs. Highcamp her scarf."

Mrs. Highcamp undraped the scarf from about him with her own hands. Miss Mayblunt and Mr. Gouvernail suddenly conceived the notion that it was time to say good night. And Mr. and Mrs. Merriman wondered how it could be so late.

Before parting from Victor, Mrs. Highcamp invited him to call upon her daughter, who she knew would be charmed to meet him and talk French and sing French songs with him. Victor expressed his desire and intention to call upon Miss Highcamp at the first opportunity which presented itself. He asked if Arobin were going his way. Arobin was not.

The mandolin players had long since stolen away. A profound stillness had fallen upon the broad, beautiful street. The voices of Edna's disbanding guests jarred like a discordant note upon the quiet harmony of the night.

CHAPTER XXXI

"Well?" questioned Arobin, who had remained with Edna after the others had departed.

"Well," she reiterated, and stood up, stretching her arms, and feeling the need to relax her muscles after having been so long seated.

"What next?" he asked.

"The servants are all gone. They left when the musicians did. I have dismissed them. The house has to be closed and locked, and I shall trot around to the pigeon house, and shall send Celestine over in the morning to straighten things up."

He looked around, and began to turn out some of the lights.

"What about upstairs?" he inquired.

"I think it is all right; but there may be a window or two unlatched. We had better look; you might take a candle and see. And bring me my wrap and hat on the foot of the bed in the middle room."

He went up with the light, and Edna began closing doors and windows. She hated to shut in the smoke and the fumes of the wine. Arobin found her cape and hat, which he brought down and helped her to put on.

When everything was secured and the lights put out, they
left through the front door, Arobin locking it and taking
the key, which he carried for Edna. He helped her down
the steps.

"Will you have a spray of jessamine?" he asked, breaking
off a few blossoms as he passed.

"No; I don't want anything."

She seemed disheartened, and had nothing to say. She took
his arm, which he offered her, holding up the weight of her
satin train with the other hand. She looked down, noticing
the black line of his leg moving in and out so close to her
against the yellow shimmer of her gown. There was the
whistle of a railway train somewhere in the distance, and
the midnight bells were ringing. They met no one in their
short walk.

The "pigeon house" stood behind a locked gate, and a shallow **parterre** that had been somewhat neglected. There was
a small front porch, upon which a long window and the
front door opened. The door opened directly into the parlor; there was no side entry. Back in the yard was a room
for servants, in which old Celestine had been ensconced.

Edna had left a lamp burning low upon the table. She had
succeeded in making the room look habitable and home-
like. There were some books on the table and a lounge near
at hand. On the floor was a fresh **matting**, covered with a
rug or two; and on the walls hung a few tasteful pictures.
But the room was filled with flowers. These were a surprise
to her. Arobin had sent them, and had had Celestine
distribute them during Edna's absence. Her bedroom was
adjoining, and across a small passage were the dining room
and kitchen.

Edna seated herself with every appearance of discomfort.

"Are you tired?" he asked.

"Yes, and chilled, and miserable. I feel as if I had been
wound up to a certain pitch—too tight—and something
inside of me had snapped." She rested her head against the
table upon her bare arm.

"You want to rest," he said, "and to be quiet. I'll go; I'll
leave you and let you rest."

"Yes," she replied.

He stood up beside her and smoothed her hair with his
soft, magnetic hand. His touch conveyed to her a certain
physical comfort. She could have fallen quietly asleep there

parterre: an ornamental garden area in which the flower
beds and path form a pattern.

matting: a woven fabric of fiber, as straw or hemp, for
mats, floor covering, wrapping, etc.

if he had continued to pass his hand over her hair. He brushed the hair upward from the nape of her neck.

"I hope you will feel better and happier in the morning," he said. "You have tried to do too much in the past few days. The dinner was the last straw; you might have dispensed with it."

"Yes," she admitted; "it was stupid."

"No, it was delightful; but it has worn you out." His hand had strayed to her beautiful shoulders, and he could feel the response of her flesh to his touch. He seated himself beside her and kissed her lightly upon the shoulder.

"I thought you were going away," she said, in an uneven voice.

"I am, after I have said good night."

"Good night," she murmured.

He did not answer, except to continue to caress her. He did not say good night until she had become supple to his gentle, seductive entreaties.

CHAPTER XXXII

When Mr. Pontellier learned of his wife's intention to abandon her home and take up her residence elsewhere, he immediately wrote her a letter of unqualified disapproval and remonstrance. She had given reasons which he was unwilling to acknowledge as adequate. He hoped she had not acted upon her rash impulse; and he begged her to consider first, foremost, and above all else, what people would say. He was not dreaming of scandal when he uttered this warning; that was a thing which would never have entered into his mind to consider in connection with his wife's name or his own. He was simply thinking of his financial integrity. It might get noised about that the Pontelliers had met with reverses, and were forced to conduct their **ménage** on a humbler scale than heretofore. It might do incalculable mischief to his business prospects.

ménage: a household; domestic establishment .

But remembering Edna's whimsical turn of mind of late, and foreseeing that she had immediately acted upon her impetuous determination, he grasped the situation with his usual promptness and handled it with his well-known business tact and cleverness.

The same mail which brought to Edna his letter of disapproval carried instructions—the most minute instructions—to a well-known architect concerning the remodeling of his home, changes which he had long contemplated, and which he desired carried forward during his temporary absence.

Expert and reliable packers and movers were engaged to convey the furniture, carpets, pictures—everything movable, in short—to places of security. And in an incredibly short time the Pontellier house was turned over to the artisans. There was to be an addition—a small **snuggery**; there was to be **frescoing**, and hardwood flooring was to be put into such rooms as had not yet been subjected to this improvement.

Furthermore, in one of the daily papers appeared a brief notice to the effect that Mr. and Mrs. Pontellier were contemplating a summer sojourn abroad, and that their handsome residence on Esplanade Street was undergoing sumptuous alterations, and would not be ready for occupancy until their return. Mr. Pontellier had saved appearances!

Edna admired the skill of his maneuver, and avoided any occasion to balk his intentions. When the situation as set forth by Mr. Pontellier was accepted and taken for granted, she was apparently satisfied that it should be so.

The pigeon house pleased her. It at once assumed the intimate character of a home, while she herself invested it with a charm which it reflected like a warm glow. There was with her a feeling of having descended in the social scale, with a corresponding sense of having risen in the spiritual. Every step which she took toward relieving herself from obligations added to her strength and expansion as an individual. She began to look with her own eyes; to see and to apprehend the deeper undercurrents of life. No longer was she content to "feed upon opinion" when her own soul had invited her.

After a little while, a few days, in fact, Edna went up and spent a week with her children in Iberville. They were delicious February days, with all the summer's promise hovering in the air.

How glad she was to see the children! She wept for very pleasure when she felt their little arms clasping her; their hard, ruddy cheeks pressed against her own glowing cheeks. She looked into their faces with hungry eyes that could not be satisfied with looking. And what stories they had to tell their mother! About the pigs, the cows, the mules! About riding to the mill behind Gluglu; fishing

snuggery: a snug or comfortable place, room, etc., especially a small private room or booth in a public house.

frescoing: the art or technique of painting with watercolors on wet plaster.

back in the lake with their Uncle Jasper; picking pecans with Lidie's little black brood, and hauling chips in their express wagon. It was a thousand times more fun to haul real chips for old lame Susie's real fire than to drag painted blocks along the banquette on Esplanade Street!

She went with them herself to see the pigs and the cows, to look at the darkies laying the cane, to thrash the pecan trees, and catch fish in the back lake. She lived with them a whole week long, giving them all of herself, and gathering and filling herself with their young existence. They listened, breathless, when she told them the house in Esplanade Street was crowded with workmen, hammering, nailing, sawing, and filling the place with clatter. They wanted to know where their bed was; what had been done with their rocking-horse; and where did Joe sleep, and where had Ellen gone, and the cook? But, above all, they were fired with a desire to see the little house around the block. Was there any place to play? Were there any boys next door? Raoul, with pessimistic foreboding, was convinced that there were only girls next door. Where would they sleep, and where would papa sleep? She told them the fairies would fix it all right.

The old Madame was charmed with Edna's visit, and showered all manner of delicate attentions upon her. She was delighted to know that the Esplanade Street house was in a dismantled condition. It gave her the promise and pretext to keep the children indefinitely.

It was with a wrench and a pang that Edna left her children. She carried away with her the sound of their voices and the touch of their cheeks. All along the journey homeward their presence lingered with her like the memory of a delicious song. But by the time she had regained the city the song no longer echoed in her soul. She was again alone.

COMMENTARY

Now that she is living alone, Edna spends much of her time working on her art. However, on days when she cannot focus on her drawing, she looks elsewhere for diversion. Edna is recently on an emotional roller coaster. Her awakening has left her aware of the opportunities, but these opportunities have not yet materialized. Edna is often bored and restless; she is waiting for something to happen, the "promise broken and unfulfilled." Edna is aware of a world that exists beyond the life she has known with Léonce, and she has awakened to the many possibilities of living a life according to her own expectations. With Léonce gone and the children away, Edna can freely experience a new life, but thus far, little has happened. Edna seems to be waiting for all these new opportunities to come to her. Edna's restlessness in the beginning of Chapter 25 reflects her uncertainty about how to take advantage of this time on her own. All her life, Edna has belonged to men—first to her father and then to Léonce and even to her sons. Now Edna has no responsibilities or demands, and she can decide for herself how to fill her days. She can paint, go to the races, and visit friends. The time alone, though ripe with possibilities, lacks the structure she has always known. And so far, Edna is unsure how to proceed. In her desire to escape her husband's control, Edna has never really planned for what she will do when she finally escapes. The possibilities of a new life exist, but Edna is not yet sure what these possibilities entail; she just needs for them to exist.

Alcée Arobin appears to distract Edna; initially, he seems to provide an innocent digression from her boredom and uncertainty. Edna, who enjoyed going to the races with her father when he was in town, starts going to them frequently. Edna knows horses and finds excitement at the track, which is an arena of alcohol, men, and gambling that she understands and recognizes from her childhood in Kentucky. Edna feels at home at the races—a feeling she enjoys in very few places in New Orleans.

Alcée Arobin also attends the races frequently, and he is able to insinuate himself into Edna's company more often. Finally, Arobin calls upon Edna to take her to the races. He is accompanied by Mrs. Highcamp; she provides the chaperone necessary to adhere to society's standards and excuses Edna's appearance in public in the company of a single man.

After an evening at the Highcamp home, Arobin offers to escort Edna home. He initiates the seduction process at which he excels. After Arobin's departure, Edna is unsettled and unusually hungry, just as she was on the day in which she and Robert journeyed to the Chênière Caminada. Furthermore, Edna is again awakened to her own sexuality, feeling "restless and excited." A few days later, Arobin arrives to escort Edna without Mrs. Highcamp—a deliberate attempt to get Edna alone—and Edna does not "deem it worth while" to find a suitable chaperone to accompany them. Although being alone with Arobin compromises Edna's reputation, she is willing to defy convention. For Edna, the conventions of society are artificial constructs that limit her potential and enclose her in pointless rules.

At the races, Edna is once again excited by the day's events and by Arobin's presence, which invites "an easy confidence." Within hours, she feels a growing intimacy, especially after he stays for dinner and spends the evening with her. His frankness in describing his faults disarms Edna, but Arobin uses his confidences in a measured manner, designed to entice his prey. From tenderly holding Edna's hand to allowing his eyes to linger on her face, Arobin reveals that he is a master at seduction. Moreover, Edna's reaction increases his awareness of her vulnerability and her interest as an object for his intentions.

After Arobin departs, Edna is left to consider the evening. She knows how nearly she has slipped toward infidelity, yet she never for a moment considers Léonce or her marriage. When Edna thinks about infidelity, she thinks about Robert. She has almost been unfaithful to Robert, but when she retires to her bed, she thinks of Arobin—not Robert.

Soon, Edna's days are filled with Alcée Arobin, who seeks any excuse to see her. As the days pass, Arobin becomes more daring, more intimate in both his language and his actions. Edna finds that he appeals to "the animalism that stirred impatiently within her." Edna thinks that she can control Arobin, but she underestimates his experience as well as her own inexperience. That he creates a "turmoil within her" is clear when she returns to Mademoiselle Reisz's apartment for a visit. Edna needs to talk to someone, and she cannot confide in anyone else. She can hardly talk to Madame Ratignolle about the turmoil in her life. The happy mother-woman wouldn't understand any of Edna's actions—spending time with Arobin, or her newly formed plan to find a place of her own.

The atmosphere at Mademoiselle Reisz's is vastly different from the environment at Edna's home. Edna can be completely honest, and she does not waste any time on empty pleasantries. Edna immediately tells the old pianist that she is going to move into her own house. Edna wants to move from the Pontellier home for many reasons. The large house is Léonce's, as well as the furnishings and the money used to pay for the items within the house—which clearly reflects Léonce's personality, not Edna's. More importantly, Edna has decided "never again to belong to another than herself." In Léonce's house, Edna can only be his possession and never her own person. She has not yet articulated this point, but it is there, at the core of her decision. Her growing relationship with Arobin also affects her decision. Eventually, Léonce will return, and certainly Edna cannot continue to see Arobin—or any other man— while she remains under her husband's roof. She has already moved away from Léonce in spirit; now she needs to move away physically as well.

Edna continues to visit Mademoiselle Reisz and read more letters from Robert. Mademoiselle Reisz insists that Robert is not aware that Edna reads the letters he writes to the old woman. While she listens to Mademoiselle Reisz's playing, Edna reads the most recent letter, which includes some shocking news: Robert is returning soon.

Robert ran away in an effort to forget Edna, says Mademoiselle Reisz, who suggests that Robert is in love with Edna. Thus, she finally forces Edna to admit that she is in love with Robert. The knowledge of Robert's return and her own public avowal of love leave Edna radiant with happiness.

Mademoiselle Reisz has played a large role in the events of the past months. Her initial role was unintentional: Her music stirred in Edna an awakening to the passions that were missing in her life. As a result, the pianist became a sort of confidante to the troubled Edna by encouraging her visits and endorsing a level of behavior that was outside the expected and accepted behavior of ladies in Edna's social circle. She plainly encourages Edna's infatuation, first by providing the letters, and later by suggesting that Robert loves Edna,

thereby eliciting Edna's declaration of love for Robert. Mademoiselle Reisz is a lonely, often disagreeable, old spinster. Chopin suggests that Mademoiselle Reisz has few friends and few opportunities for happiness. She may be trying to live vicariously through Edna, and if she is doing so, she is encouraging Edna to reject everything in her life for the love of a penniless young man.

The problem for Edna is not whether she is strong enough to leave her husband and children and all the wealth and social position her marriage offers. The real issue is whether Robert is brave enough to match Edna's courage. Edna has much to lose, and Mademoiselle Reisz admits this when she asks whether Edna's "wings are strong." If she is to survive, she will have to be very strong.

Later in the evening, Edna's happiness is apparent to Arobin, who takes advantage of her obvious good mood to stroke her hair in an obvious caress. Edna asks whether she is wicked, and Arobin's fingers continue to move down her face and neck as his caresses continue. He recognizes that her mind is elsewhere, but does not mind, because her whole mood is one of detached welcome. He thinks that he is in control, but when he leans forward to kiss Edna for the first time, she pulls him down, and Edna kisses him. Edna is not only the recipient of Arobin's kiss, but an equal partner. Arobin does not leave until Edna has submitted totally.

Chopin intends for her readers to understand that the evening ends in a sexual culmination of their relationship. Edna describes the "shock of the unexpected and unaccustomed . . . [and of] understanding." Edna also "felt as if a mist had been lifted from her eyes." This sexual encounter is vastly different than the ones with her husband, and Edna is filled with a new awareness of herself. She feels uncomfortable about her husband as well as Robert, but she sees no intrinsic sin in her actions and feels no remorse. She has not betrayed Robert, because her act with Arobin was one of passion and not love. As for Léonce, Edna feels that she no longer belongs to him in any way. Their union was an external union of property, and she is no longer his property.

While Edna prepares to move out of her husband's house, she separates the possessions that she owns from the ones that she sees as solely her husband's. The new house has been labeled the "pigeon house," and indeed, it appears that Edna is about to "fly the coop." When Arobin arrives he is surprised at what he finds. Edna is not sad or morose at leaving; instead, he finds her upon a high ladder moving a picture. Of course, Arobin is resourceful and always prepared for any eventuality. When he finds that he does not have to console Edna, he offers to help her. The scene is one of happiness, as Arobin dons one of Edna's dust-caps as "grotesquely as he could." Laughter is an effective ploy of Arobin's, who is always happy and smiling. His silliness is a marked contrast to the seriousness of Léonce, who would never do the work of servants or make himself ridiculous to entertain Edna.

Chopin teases the readers with the preparation for Edna's dinner party. Readers cannot help but anticipate that this party signals a momentous event. Edna plans to use the best china and glassware in the Pontellier home. She orders elaborate flowers and arranges for champagne and music. The dinner is intended to be a celebration—a celebration of Edna's independence.

Of course, she lets Léonce pay for her independence and sees no contradiction in doing so. But moving to the pigeon house is meant to signal an end to Léonce's ownership of Edna, and making him pay for her celebration appears as a final insult to hurl at her marriage. Edna's action is a thoughtless appropriation of Léonce that, on the surface at least, appears to contradict all that she is trying to accomplish. But another consideration is that, in this one instance, Edna is using her husband in much the same way as he has used her throughout their marriage. She is acting like a man by giving orders and using all the resources available to her.

The party is a small one, with only her closest friends present. Edna has long since abandoned her husband's social contacts and there is no reason now for including them in her life. The grouping is an eclectic one of guests who seem to have little in common. Most of the guests are new to readers, who are not familiar with the Merrimans, Miss Mayblunt, and Mr. Governail. Moreover, Mademoiselle Reisz is an odd choice for a party that includes Arobin and Mrs. Highcamp—just as Monsieur Ratignolle seems an even odder choice for this group. Edna's invitation to Victor Lebrun is especially strange, except that he reminds her of Robert. The luxuriousness of the table and its setting point to the wealth of the Pontelliers and makes clear just what Edna is giving up by moving from her husband's house. Edna is wearing a

magnificent cluster of diamonds, a birthday gift from Léonce. Nonetheless, the setting and Edna's dress express of a measure of sensuality.

Monsieur Ratignolle does not know Arobin's reputation, and he is obviously disconcerted to learn that Arobin has no employment. Monsieur Ratignolle is the first to leave, offering the excuse that his wife is awaiting him at home. Mademoiselle Reisz also leaves, taking advantage of Monsieur Ratignolle's offer to escort her home. As the remaining group continues to consume wine, the congenial atmosphere seems to dissolve. Victor brings the evening to an end in a drunken rendition of the song that Robert used to sing to Edna. She considers it their song, and Victor's drunken singing provokes an emotional outburst from Edna that brings the party to an end.

Edna is recently on an emotional roller coaster. Robert has been on Edna's mind ever since she learned that he is returning. Her relationship with Arobin has been little more than a surrogate romance intended to pass Edna's time. While she waits for Robert to return, she plays over in her mind possible scenarios of their reunion. But she is also moving from her husband's house and into her own, and she continues her affair with Arobin. Moreover, the gala evening could not possibly live up to its preparation. Thus, Edna is tired and depressed, and her emotional outburst is understandable. After everyone else has left the party, only Arobin remains behind; he is certain that he holds the key to Edna's emotional response.

Directly after the party ends, Edna leaves her husband's house for the last time. Her exhaustion is the culmination of weeks and months of stress. When she says that, "something inside me had snapped," Edna is reacting to all the events and changes in her life. She has fallen in love with one man, begun an affair with another, and left her husband's home without telling her husband that she is leaving him—all within a few short months.

Although Arobin seems sympathetic to Edna's fatigue and emotional turmoil, he lingers even after promising to leave. He is convinced that he is the cause of her emotional state, so instead of leaving, he begins caressing Edna until she finally succumbs. Any illusion that he cares about Edna should be dispelled. He cares about his own sexual conquest and so he stays to collect his reward.

To cover for Edna's move from their home, Léonce creates a fiction in which he is remodeling their home. Within days, movers are dispatched to remove all the furnishings.

Movers removing furniture from the Pontellier house.

Although he manages to save face, Léonce also takes the opportunity to chastise Edna. She is happy that he has found a way to save his own reputation. Although Edna cares little for appearances, she does not hate Léonce, and his ability to protect himself is something that she can even admire.

Meanwhile, Edna is happy in her little house. Her past social obligations are replaced with a greater satisfaction in her own growth as an individual. Edna visits her children, and she enjoys their stories and the time she spends with them. Enjoying the touch and smell of her children, Edna is now at her most maternal. Motherhood is easier for Edna when it occurs infrequently and at a distance: She is a better mother when she need not be one all the time. When Edna leaves her children, they no longer exist for her, and she forgets them before she arrives back in New Orleans.

Her ability to forget her children easily reminds readers that Edna is not the mother-woman so cherished in New Orleans society. Edna's children exist in another part of her life, a part so incidental to her life that she can easily set her family aside. The children are content with their grandmother, and Edna is content to have them there. When they are out of her sight, she rarely thinks of them or concerns herself with their well-being.

Lest readers think of Edna merely as a selfish woman, poorly suited to motherhood, it is important to note that not all women want to be mothers and not all women should be mothers. In Chopin's era, most women had little choice in the matter and were often forced into motherhood by social convention. That is certainly the case with Edna.

Notes

Chapters 33–39

On a visit to Mademoiselle Reisz, Edna encounters Robert, who has returned from abroad. Their reunion is awkward, and they do not resume their relationship. Edna continues to meet Arobin, until she unexpectedly encounters Robert again. After declaring their love for one another, they are interrupted by the news that Madame Ratignolle is about to give birth, and Edna's presence is requested. The labor is difficult, but eventually, Edna is free to leave and return home, where Robert is no longer waiting. In the morning, Edna returns to Grand Isle. She returns to the water and the solace that she found while swimming last summer. Edna swims far out from the beach, too far to be able to return.

CHAPTER XXXIII

It happened sometimes when Edna went to see Mademoiselle Reisz that the little musician was absent, giving a lesson or making some small necessary household purchase. The key was always left in a secret hiding-place in the entry, which Edna knew. If Mademoiselle happened to be away, Edna would usually enter and wait for her return.

When she knocked at Mademoiselle Reisz's door one afternoon there was no response; so unlocking the door, as usual, she entered and found the apartment deserted, as she had expected. Her day had been quite filled up, and it was for a rest, for a refuge, and to talk about Robert, that she sought out her friend.

She had worked at her canvas—a young Italian character study—all the morning, completing the work without the model; but there had been many interruptions, some incident to her modest housekeeping, and others of a social nature.

Madame Ratignolle had dragged herself over, avoiding the too public thoroughfares, she said. She complained that Edna had neglected her much of late. Besides, she was consumed with curiosity to see the little house and the manner in which it was conducted. She wanted to hear all about the dinner party; Monsieur Ratignolle had left so early. What had happened after he left? The champagne and grapes which Edna sent over were too delicious. She had so little appetite; they had refreshed and toned her stomach. Where on earth was she going to put Mr. Pontellier in that little house, and the boys? And then she made Edna promise to go to her when her hour of trial overtook her.

NOTES

"At any time—any time of the day or night, dear," Edna assured her.

Before leaving Madame Ratignolle said:

"In some way you seem to me like a child, Edna. You seem to act without a certain amount of reflection which is necessary in this life. That is the reason I want to say you mustn't mind if I advise you to be a little careful while you are living here alone. Why don't you have some one come and stay with you? Wouldn't Mademoiselle Reisz come?"

"No; she wouldn't wish to come, and I shouldn't want her always with me."

"Well, the reason—you know how evil-minded the world is—some one was talking of Alcée Arobin visiting you. Of course, it wouldn't matter if Mr. Arobin had not such a dreadful reputation. Monsieur Ratignolle was telling me that his attentions alone are considered enough to ruin a womans name."

"Does he boast of his successes?" asked Edna, indifferently, squinting at her picture.

"No, I think not. I believe he is a decent fellow as far as that goes. But his character is so well known among the men. I shan't be able to come back and see you; it was very, very imprudent to-day."

"Mind the step!" cried Edna.

"Don't neglect me," entreated Madame Ratignolle; "and don't mind what I said about Arobin, or having some one to stay with you."

"Of course not," Edna laughed. "You may say anything you like to me." They kissed each other good-by. Madame Ratignolle had not far to go, and Edna stood on the porch a while watching her walk down the street.

Then in the afternoon Mrs. Merriman and Mrs. Highcamp had made their "**party call**." Edna felt that they might have dispensed with the formality. They had also come to invite her to play **vingt-et-un** one evening at Mrs. Merriman's. She was asked to go early, to dinner, and Mr. Merriman or Mr. Arobin would take her home. Edna accepted in a half-hearted way. She sometimes felt very tired of Mrs. Highcamp and Mrs. Merriman.

Late in the afternoon she sought refuge with Mademoiselle Reisz, and stayed there alone, waiting for her, feeling a kind of repose invade her with the very atmosphere of the shabby, unpretentious little room.

party call: a thank-you visit to a hostess that women were expected to make within a week of a party if they had not attended one of the hostess' parties before.

vingt-et-un: a card game called "twenty-one" or "blackjack."

Edna sat at the window, which looked out over the housetops and across the river. The window frame was filled with
pots of flowers, and she sat and picked the dry leaves from
a rose geranium. The day was warm, and the breeze which
blew from the river was very pleasant. She removed her hat
and laid it on the piano. She went on picking the leaves
and digging around the plants with her hat pin. Once she
thought she heard Mademoiselle Reisz approaching. But it
was a young black girl, who came in, bringing a small bun-
dle of laundry, which she deposited in the adjoining room,
and went away.

Edna seated herself at the piano, and softly picked out with
one hand the bars of a piece of music which lay open
before her. A half-hour went by. There was the occasional
sound of people going and coming in the lower hall. She
was growing interested in her occupation of picking out
the aria, when there was a second rap at the door. She
vaguely wondered what these people did when they found
Mademoiselle's door locked.

"Come in," she called, turning her face toward the door.
And this time it was Robert Lebrun who presented himself.
She attempted to rise; she could not have done so without
betraying the agitation which mastered her at sight of him,
so she fell back upon the stool, only exclaiming, "Why,
Robert!"

He came and clasped her hand, seemingly without knowing what he was saying or doing.

"Mrs. Pontellier! How do you happen—oh! how well you
look! Is Mademoiselle Reisz not here? I never expected to
see you."

"When did you come back?" asked Edna in an unsteady
voice, wiping her face with her handkerchief. She seemed
ill at ease on the piano stool, and he begged her to take the
chair by the window.

She did so, mechanically, while he seated himself on the
stool.

"I returned day before yesterday," he answered, while he
leaned his arm on the keys, bringing forth a crash of discordant sound.

"Day before yesterday!" she repeated, aloud; and went on
thinking to herself, "day before yesterday," in a sort of an
uncomprehending way. She had pictured him seeking her
at the very first hour, and he had lived under the same sky
since day before yesterday; while only by accident had he

stumbled upon her. Mademoiselle must have lied when she said, "Poor fool, he loves you."

"Day before yesterday," she repeated, breaking off a spray of Mademoiselle's geranium; "then if you had not met me here to-day you wouldn't—when—that is, didn't you mean to come and see me?"

"Of course, I should have gone to see you. There have been so many things—" he turned the leaves of Mademoiselle's music nervously. "I started in at once yesterday with the old firm. After all there is as much chance for me here as there was there—that is, I might find it profitable some day. The Mexicans were not very congenial."

So he had come back because the Mexicans were not congenial; because business was as profitable here as there; because of any reason, and not because he cared to be near her. She remembered the day she sat on the floor, turning the pages of his letter, seeking the reason which was left untold.

She had not noticed how he looked—only feeling his presence; but she turned deliberately and observed him. After all, he had been absent but a few months, and was not changed. His hair—the color of hers—waved back from his temples in the same way as before. His skin was not more burned than it had been at Grand Isle. She found in his eyes, when he looked at her for one silent moment, the same tender caress, with an added warmth and entreaty which had not been there before the same glance which had penetrated to the sleeping places of her soul and awakened them.

A hundred times Edna had pictured Robert's return, and imagined their first meeting. It was usually at her home, whither he had sought her out at once. She always fancied him expressing or betraying in some way his love for her. And here, the reality was that they sat ten feet apart, she at the window, crushing geranium leaves in her hand and smelling them, he twirling around on the piano stool, saying:

"I was very much surprised to hear of Mr. Pontellier's absence; it's a wonder Mademoiselle Reisz did not tell me; and your moving—mother told me yesterday. I should think you would have gone to New York with him, or to Iberville with the children, rather than be bothered here with housekeeping. And you are going abroad, too, I hear. We shan't have you at Grand Isle next summer; it won't seem—do you see much of Mademoiselle Reisz? She often spoke of you in the few letters she wrote."

"Do you remember that you promised to write to me when you went away?" A flush overspread his whole face.

"I couldn't believe that my letters would be of any interest to you."

"That is an excuse; it isn't the truth." Edna reached for her hat on the piano. She adjusted it, sticking the hat pin through the heavy coil of hair with some deliberation.

"Are you not going to wait for Mademoiselle Reisz?" asked Robert.

"No; I have found when she is absent this long, she is liable not to come back till late." She drew on her gloves, and Robert picked up his hat.

"Won't you wait for her?" asked Edna.

"Not if you think she will not be back till late," adding, as if suddenly aware of some discourtesy in his speech, "and I should miss the pleasure of walking home with you." Edna locked the door and put the key back in its hiding-place.

They went together, picking their way across muddy streets and sidewalks encumbered with the cheap display of small tradesmen. Part of the distance they rode in the car, and after disembarking, passed the Pontellier mansion, which looked broken and half torn asunder. Robert had never known the house, and looked at it with interest.

"I never knew you in your home," he remarked.

"I am glad you did not."

"Why?" She did not answer. They went on around the corner, and it seemed as if her dreams were coming true after all, when he followed her into the little house.

"You must stay and dine with me, Robert. You see I am all alone, and it is so long since I have seen you. There is so much I want to ask you."

She took off her hat and gloves. He stood irresolute, making some excuse about his mother who expected him; he even muttered something about an engagement. She struck a match and lit the lamp on the table; it was growing dusk. When he saw her face in the lamp-light, looking pained, with all the soft lines gone out of it, he threw his hat aside and seated himself.

"Oh! you know I want to stay if you will let me!" he exclaimed. All the softness came back. She laughed, and went and put her hand on his shoulder.

"This is the first moment you have seemed like the old Robert. I'll go tell Celestine." She hurried away to tell Celestine to set an extra place. She even sent her off in search of some added delicacy which she had not thought of for herself. And she recommended great care in dripping the coffee and having the omelet done to a proper turn.

When she reentered, Robert was turning over magazines, sketches, and things that lay upon the table in great disorder. He picked up a photograph, and exclaimed:

"Alcée Arobin! What on earth is his picture doing here?"

"I tried to make a sketch of his head one day," answered Edna, "and he thought the photograph might help me. It was at the other house. I thought it had been left there. I must have packed it up with my drawing materials."

"I should think you would give it back to him if you have finished with it."

"Oh! I have a great many such photographs. I never think of returning them. They don't amount to anything."
Robert kept on looking at the picture.

"It seems to me—do you think his head worth drawing? Is he a friend of Mr. Pontellier's? You never said you knew him."

"He isn't a friend of Mr. Pontellier's; he's a friend of mine. I always knew him—that is, it is only of late that I know him pretty well. But I'd rather talk about you, and know what you have been seeing and doing and feeling out there in Mexico." Robert threw aside the picture.

"I've been seeing the waves and the white beach of Grand Isle; the quiet, grassy street of the Chênière; the old fort at Grande Terre. I've been working like a machine, and feeling like a lost soul. There was nothing interesting."

She leaned her head upon her hand to shade her eyes from the light.

"And what have you been seeing and doing and feeling all these days?" he asked.

"I've been seeing the waves and the white beach of Grand Isle; the quiet, grassy street of the Chênière Caminada; the old sunny fort at Grande Terre. I've been working with a little more comprehension than a machine, and still feeling like a lost soul. There was nothing interesting."

"Mrs. Pontellier, you are cruel," he said, with feeling, closing his eyes and resting his head back in his chair. They remained in silence till old Celestine announced dinner.

CHAPTER XXXIV

The dining-room was very small. Edna's round mahogany would have almost filled it. As it was there was but a step or two from the little table to the kitchen, to the mantel, the small buffet, and the side door that opened out on the narrow brick-paved yard.

A certain degree of ceremony settled upon them with the announcement of dinner. There was no return to **personalities**. Robert related incidents of his sojourn in Mexico, and Edna talked of events likely to interest him, which had occurred during his absence. The dinner was of ordinary quality, except for the few delicacies which she had sent out to purchase. Old Celestine, with a bandana **tignon** twisted about her head, hobbled in and out, taking a personal interest in everything; and she lingered occasionally to talk **patois** with Robert, whom she had known as a boy.

He went out to a neighboring cigar stand to purchase cigarette papers, and when he came back he found that Celestine had served the black coffee in the parlor.

"Perhaps I shouldn't have come back," he said. "When you are tired of me, tell me to go."

"You never tire me. You must have forgotten the hours and hours at Grand Isle in which we grew accustomed to each other and used to being together."

"I have forgotten nothing at Grand Isle," he said, not looking at her, but rolling a cigarette. His tobacco pouch, which he laid upon the table, was a fantastic embroidered silk affair, evidently the handiwork of a woman.

"You used to carry your tobacco in a rubber pouch," said Edna, picking up the pouch and examining the needlework.

"Yes; it was lost."

"Where did you buy this one? In Mexico?"

"It was given to me by a Vera Cruz girl; they are very generous," he replied, striking a match and lighting his cigarette.

"They are very handsome, I suppose, those Mexican women; very picturesque, with their black eyes and their lace scarfs."

"Some are; others are hideous just as you find women everywhere."

"What was she like—the one who gave you the pouch? You must have known her very well."

personalities: here, personal matters.

tignon: a Creole word for bun: the hair is wrapped in a scarf and the scarf is wrapped around the head.

patois: a form of a language differing generally from the accepted standard, as a provincial or local dialect.

"She was very ordinary. She wasn't of the slightest importance. I knew her well enough."

"Did you visit at her house? Was it interesting? I should like to know and hear about the people you met, and the impressions they made on you."

"There are some people who leave impressions not so lasting as the imprint of an oar upon the water."

"Was she such a one?"

"It would be ungenerous for me to admit that she was of that order and kind." He thrust the pouch back in his pocket, as if to put away the subject with the trifle which had brought it up.

Arobin dropped in with a message from Mrs. Merriman, to say that the card party was postponed on account of the illness of one of her children.

"How do you do, Arobin?" said Robert, rising from the obscurity.

"Oh! Lebrun. To be sure! I heard yesterday you were back. How did they treat you down in Mexique?"

"Fairly well."

"But not well enough to keep you there. Stunning girls, though, in Mexico. I thought I should never get away from Vera Cruz when I was down there a couple of years ago."

"Did they embroider slippers and tobacco pouches and hat-bands and things for you?" asked Edna.

"Oh! my! no! I didn't get so deep in their regard. I fear they made more impression on me than I made on them."

"You were less fortunate than Robert, then."

"I am always less fortunate than Robert. Has he been imparting tender confidences?"

"I've been imposing myself long enough," said Robert, rising, and shaking hands with Edna. "Please convey my regards to Mr. Pontellier when you write."

He shook hands with Arobin and went away.

"Fine fellow, that Lebrun," said Arobin when Robert had gone. "I never heard you speak of him."

"I knew him last summer at Grand Isle," she replied.

"Here is that photograph of yours. Don't you want it?"

"What do I want with it? Throw it away." She threw it back on the table.

"I'm not going to Mrs. Merriman's," she said. "If you see her, tell her so. But perhaps I had better write. I think I shall write now, and say that I am sorry her child is sick, and tell her not to count on me."

"It would be a good scheme," acquiesced Arobin. "I don't blame you; stupid lot!"

Edna opened the blotter, and having procured paper and pen, began to write the note. Arobin lit a cigar and read the evening paper, which he had in his pocket.

"What is the date?" she asked. He told her.

"Will you mail this for me when you go out?"

"Certainly." He read to her little bits out of the newspaper, while she straightened things on the table.

"What do you want to do?" he asked, throwing aside the paper. "Do you want to go out for a walk or a drive or anything? It would be a fine night to drive."

"No; I don't want to do anything but just be quiet. You go away and amuse yourself. Don't stay."

"I'll go away if I must; but I shan't amuse myself. You know that I only live when I am near you."

He stood up to bid her good night.

"Is that one of the things you always say to women?"

"I have said it before, but I don't think I ever came so near meaning it," he answered with a smile. There were no warm lights in her eyes; only a dreamy, absent look.

"Good night. I adore you. Sleep well," he said, and he kissed her hand and went away.

She stayed alone in a kind of reverie—a sort of stupor. Step by step she lived over every instant of the time she had been with Robert after he had entered Mademoiselle Reisz's door. She recalled his words, his looks. How few and meager they had been for her hungry heart! A vision—a transcendently seductive vision of a Mexican girl arose before her. She writhed with a jealous pang. She wondered when he would come back. He had not said he would come back. She had been with him, had heard his voice and touched his hand. But some way he had seemed nearer to her off there in Mexico.

CHAPTER XXXV

The morning was full of sunlight and hope. Edna could see before her no denial—only the promise of excessive joy. She lay in bed awake, with bright eyes full of speculation. "He loves you, poor fool." If she could but get that conviction firmly fixed in her mind, what mattered about the rest? She felt she had been childish and unwise the night before in giving herself over to despondency. She **recapitulated** the motives which no doubt explained Robert's reserve. They were not insurmountable; they would not hold if he really loved her; they could not hold against her own passion, which he must come to realize in time. She pictured him going to his business that morning. She even saw how he was dressed; how he walked down one street, and turned the corner of another; saw him bending over his desk, talking to people who entered the office, going to his lunch, and perhaps watching for her on the street. He would come to her in the afternoon or evening, sit and roll his cigarette, talk a little, and go away as he had done the night before. But how delicious it would be to have him there with her! She would have no regrets, nor seek to penetrate his reserve if he still chose to wear it.

Edna ate her breakfast only half dressed. The maid brought her a delicious printed scrawl from Raoul, expressing his love, asking her to send him some bonbons, and telling her they had found that morning ten tiny white pigs all lying in a row beside Lidie's big white pig.

A letter also came from her husband, saying he hoped to be back early in March, and then they would get ready for that journey abroad which he had promised her so long, which he felt now fully able to afford; he felt able to travel as people should, without any thought of small economies—thanks to his recent speculations in Wall Street.

Much to her surprise she received a note from Arobin, written at midnight from the club. It was to say good morning to her, to hope she had slept well, to assure her of his devotion, which he trusted she in some faintest manner returned.

All these letters were pleasing to her. She answered the children in a cheerful frame of mind, promising them bonbons, and congratulating them upon their happy find of the little pigs.

She answered her husband with friendly evasiveness,—not with any fixed design to mislead him, only because all sense of reality had gone out of her life; she had abandoned herself to Fate, and awaited the consequences with indifference.

To Arobin's note she made no reply. She put it under Celestine's stove-lid.

Edna worked several hours with much spirit. She saw no one but a picture dealer, who asked her if it were true that she was going abroad to study in Paris.

recapitulated: repeated briefly, as in an outline; summarized.

She said possibly she might, and he negotiated with her for some Parisian studies to reach him in time for the holiday trade in December.

Robert did not come that day. She was keenly disappointed. He did not come the following day, nor the next. Each morning she awoke with hope, and each night she was a prey to despondency. She was tempted to seek him out. But far from yielding to the impulse, she avoided any occasion which might throw her in his way. She did not go to Mademoiselle Reisz's nor pass by Madame Lebrun's, as she might have done if he had still been in Mexico.

When Arobin, one night, urged her to drive with him, she went—out to the lake, on the Shell Road. His horses were full of mettle, and even a little unmanageable. She liked the rapid gait at which they spun along, and the quick, sharp sound of the horses' hoofs on the hard road. They did not stop anywhere to eat or to drink. Arobin was not needlessly imprudent. But they ate and they drank when they regained Edna's little dining-room—which was comparatively early in the evening.

It was late when he left her. It was getting to be more than a passing whim with Arobin to see her and be with her. He had detected the latent sensuality, which unfolded under his delicate sense of her nature's requirements like a torpid, torrid, sensitive blossom.

There was no despondency when she fell asleep that night; nor was there hope when she awoke in the morning.

An old, sleeping cat.

CHAPTER XXXVI

There was a garden out in the suburbs; a small, leafy corner, with a few green tables under the orange trees. An old cat slept all day on the stone step in the sun, and an old **mulatresse** slept her idle hours away in her chair at the open window, till, some one happened to knock on one of the green tables. She had milk and cream cheese to sell, and bread and butter. There was no one who could make such excellent coffee or fry a chicken so golden brown as she.

mulatresse: female mulatto.

The place was too modest to attract the attention of people of fashion, and so quiet as to have escaped the notice of those in search of pleasure and dissipation. Edna had discovered it accidentally one day when the high-board gate stood ajar. She caught sight of a little green table, blotched with the checkered sunlight that filtered through the quivering leaves overhead. Within she had found the

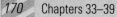

slumbering mulatresse, the drowsy cat, and a glass of milk which reminded her of the milk she had tasted in Iberville.

She often stopped there during her perambulations; sometimes taking a book with her, and sitting an hour or two under the trees when she found the place deserted. Once or twice she took a quiet dinner there alone, having instructed Celestine beforehand to prepare no dinner at home. It was the last place in the city where she would have expected to meet any one she knew.

Still she was not astonished when, as she was partaking of a modest dinner late in the afternoon, looking into an open book, stroking the cat, which had made friends with her— she was not greatly astonished to see Robert come in at the tall garden gate.

"I am destined to see you only by accident," she said, shoving the cat off the chair beside her. He was surprised, ill at ease, almost embarrassed at meeting her thus so unexpectedly.

"Do you come here often?" he asked.

"I almost live here," she said.

"I used to drop in very often for a cup of Catiche's good coffee. This is the first time since I came back."

"She'll bring you a plate, and you will share my dinner. There's always enough for two—even three." Edna had intended to be indifferent and as reserved as he when she met him; she had reached the determination by a laborious train of reasoning, incident to one of her despondent moods. But her resolve melted when she saw him before designing Providence had led him into her path.

"Why have you kept away from me, Robert?" she asked, closing the book that lay open upon the table.

"Why are you so personal, Mrs. Pontellier? Why do you force me to idiotic subterfuges?" he exclaimed with sudden warmth. "I suppose there's no use telling you I've been very busy, or that I've been sick, or that I've been to see you and not found you at home. Please let me off with any one of these excuses."

"You are the embodiment of selfishness," she said. "You save yourself something—I don't know what—but there is some selfish motive, and in sparing yourself you never consider for a moment what I think, or how I feel your neglect and indifference. I suppose this is what you would call unwomanly; but I have got into a habit of expressing myself. It doesn't matter to me, and you may think me unwomanly if you like."

"No; I only think you cruel, as I said the other day. Maybe not intentionally cruel; but you seem to be forcing me into disclosures which can result in nothing; as if you would have me bare a wound for the pleasure of looking at it, without the intention or power of healing it."

"I'm spoiling your dinner, Robert; never mind what I say. You haven't eaten a morsel."

"I only came in for a cup of coffee." His sensitive face was all disfigured with excitement.

"Isn't this a delightful place?" she remarked. "I am so glad it has never actually been discovered. It is so quiet, so sweet, here. Do you notice there is scarcely a sound to be heard? It's so out of the way; and a good walk from the car. However, I don't mind walking. I always feel so sorry for women who don't like to walk; they miss so much—so many rare little glimpses of life; and we women learn so little of life on the whole.

"Catiche's coffee is always hot. I don't know how she manages it, here in the open air. Celestine's coffee gets cold bringing it from the kitchen to the dining-room. Three lumps! How can you drink it so sweet? Take some of the cress with your chop; it's so biting and crisp. Then there's the advantage of being able to smoke with your coffee out here. Now, in the city—aren't you going to smoke?"

"After a while," he said, laying a cigar on the table.

"Who gave it to you?" she laughed.

"I bought it. I suppose I'm getting reckless; I bought a whole box." She was determined not to be personal again and make him uncomfortable.

The cat made friends with him, and climbed into his lap when he smoked his cigar. He stroked her silky fur, and talked a little about her. He looked at Edna's book, which he had read; and he told her the end, to save her the trouble of wading through it, he said.

Again he accompanied her back to her home; and it was after dusk when they reached the little "pigeon-house." She did not ask him to remain, which he was grateful for, as it permitted him to stay without the discomfort of blundering through an excuse which he had no intention of considering. He helped her to light the lamp; then she went into her room to take off her hat and to bathe her face and hands.

When she came back Robert was not examining the pictures and magazines as before; he sat off in the shadow, leaning his head back on the chair as if in a reverie. Edna lingered a moment beside the table, arranging the books there. Then she went across the room to where he sat. She bent over the arm of his chair and called his name.

"Robert," she said, "are you asleep?"

"No," he answered, looking up at her.

She leaned over and kissed him—a soft, cool, delicate kiss, whose voluptuous sting penetrated his whole being—then she moved away from him. He followed, and took her in his arms, just holding her close to him. She put her hand up to his face and pressed his cheek against her own. The action was full of love and tenderness. He sought her lips again. Then he drew her down upon the sofa beside him and held her hand in both of his.

"Now you know," he said, "now you know what I have been fighting against since last summer at Grand Isle; what drove me away and drove me back again."

"Why have you been fighting against it?" she asked. Her face glowed with soft lights.

"Why? Because you were not free; you were Léonce Pontellier's wife. I couldn't help loving you if you were ten times his wife; but so long as I went away from you and kept away I could help telling you so." She put her free hand up to his shoulder, and then against his cheek, rubbing it softly. He kissed her again. His face was warm and flushed.

"There in Mexico I was thinking of you all the time, and longing for you."

"But not writing to me," she interrupted.

"Something put into my head that you cared for me; and I lost my senses. I forgot everything but a wild dream of your some way becoming my wife."

"Your wife!"

"Religion, loyalty, everything would give way if only you cared."

"Then you must have forgotten that I was Léonce Pontellier's wife."

"Oh! I was demented, dreaming of wild, impossible things, recalling men who had set their wives free, we have heard of such things."

"Yes, we have heard of such things."

"I came back full of vague, mad intentions. And when I got here—"

"When you got here you never came near me!" She was still caressing his cheek.

"I realized what a cur I was to dream of such a thing, even if you had been willing."

She took his face between her hands and looked into it as if she would never withdraw her eyes more. She kissed him on the forehead, the eyes, the cheeks, and the lips.

"You have been a very, very foolish boy, wasting your time dreaming of impossible things when you speak of Mr. Pontellier setting me free! I am no longer one of Mr. Pontellier's possessions to dispose of or not. I give myself where I choose. If he were to say, 'Here, Robert, take her and be happy; she is yours,' I should laugh at you both."

His face grew a little white. "What do you mean?" he asked.

There was a knock at the door. Old Celestine came in to say that Madame Ratignolle's servant had come around the back way with a message that Madame had been taken sick and begged Mrs. Pontellier to go to her immediately.

"Yes, yes," said Edna, rising; "I promised. Tell her yes—to wait for me. I'll go back with her."

"Let me walk over with you," offered Robert.

"No," she said; "I will go with the servant. She went into her room to put on her hat, and when she came in again she sat once more upon the sofa beside him. He had not stirred. She put her arms about his neck.

"Good-by, my sweet Robert. Tell me good-by." He kissed her with a degree of passion which had not before entered into his caress, and strained her to him.

"I love you," she whispered, "only you; no one but you. It was you who awoke me last summer out of a life-long, stupid dream. Oh! you have made me so unhappy with your indifference. Oh! I have suffered, suffered! Now you are here we shall love each other, my Robert. We shall be everything to each other. Nothing else in the world is of any consequence. I must go to my friend; but you will wait for me? No matter how late; you will wait for me, Robert?"

"Don't go; don't go! Oh! Edna, stay with me," he pleaded. "Why should you go? Stay with me, stay with me."

"I shall come back as soon as I can; I shall find you here." She buried her face in his neck, and said good-by again. Her seductive voice, together with his great love for her, had enthralled his senses, had deprived him of every impulse but the longing to hold her and keep her.

CHAPTER XXXVII

Edna looked in at the drug store. Monsieur Ratignolle was putting up a mixture himself, very carefully, dropping a red liquid into a tiny glass. He was grateful to Edna for having come; her presence would be a comfort to his wife. Madame Ratignolle's sister, who had always been with her at such trying times, had not been able to come up from the plantation, and Adèle had been inconsolable until Mrs. Pontellier so kindly promised to come to her. The nurse had been with them at night for the past week, as she lived a great distance away. And Dr. Mandelet had been coming and going all the afternoon. They were then looking for him any moment.

Edna hastened upstairs by a private stairway that led from the rear of the store to the apartments above. The children were all sleeping in a back room. Madame Ratignolle was in the salon, whither she had strayed in her suffering impatience. She sat on the sofa, clad in an ample white peignoir, holding a handkerchief tight in her hand with a nervous clutch. Her face was drawn and pinched, her sweet blue eyes haggard and unnatural. All her beautiful hair had been drawn back and plaited. It lay in a long braid on the sofa pillow, coiled like a golden serpent. The nurse, a comfortable looking **Griffe** woman in white apron and cap, was urging her to return to her bedroom.

Griffe: person with one mulatto parent and one black parent.

"There is no use, there is no use," she said at once to Edna. "We must get rid of Mandelet; he is getting too old and careless. He said he would be here at half-past seven; now it must be eight. See what time it is, Josephine."

The woman was possessed of a cheerful nature, and refused to take any situation too seriously, especially a situation with which she was so familiar. She urged Madame to have courage and patience. But Madame only set her teeth hard into her under lip, and Edna saw the sweat gather in beads on her white forehead. After a moment or two she uttered a profound sigh and wiped her face with the handkerchief rolled in a ball. She appeared exhausted. The nurse gave her a fresh handkerchief, sprinkled with cologne water.

"This is too much!" she cried. "Mandelet ought to be killed! Where is Alphonse? Is it possible I am to be abandoned like this—neglected by every one?"

"Neglected, indeed!" exclaimed the nurse. Wasn't she there? And here was Mrs. Pontellier leaving, no doubt, a pleasant evening at home to devote to her? And wasn't Monsieur

Ratignolle coming that very instant through the hall? And Josephine was quite sure she had heard Doctor Mandelet's **coupé**. Yes, there it was, down at the door.

Adèle consented to go back to her room. She sat on the edge of a little low couch next to her bed.

coupé: a closed carriage seating two passengers, with a seat outside for the driver.

Doctor Mandelet paid no attention to Madame Ratignolle's upbraidings. He was accustomed to them at such times, and was too well convinced of her loyalty to doubt it.

He was glad to see Edna, and wanted her to go with him into the salon and entertain him. But Madame Ratignolle would not consent that Edna should leave her for an instant. Between agonizing moments, she chatted a little, and said it took her mind off her sufferings.

Edna began to feel uneasy. She was seized with a vague dread. Her own like experiences seemed far away, unreal, and only half remembered. She recalled faintly an ecstasy of pain, the heavy odor of chloroform, a stupor which had deadened sensation, and an awakening to find a little new life to which she had given being, added to the great unnumbered multitude of souls that come and go.

She began to wish she had not come; her presence was not necessary. She might have invented a pretext for staying away; she might even invent a pretext now for going. But Edna did not go. With an inward agony, with a flaming, outspoken revolt against the ways of Nature, she witnessed the scene of torture.

She was still stunned and speechless with emotion when later she leaned over her friend to kiss her and softly say good-by. Adèle, pressing her cheek, whispered in an exhausted voice: "Think of the children, Edna. Oh think of the children! Remember them!"

CHAPTER XXXVIII

Edna still felt dazed when she got outside in the open air. The Doctor's coupé had returned for him and stood before the porte cochère. She did not wish to enter the coupé, and told Doctor Mandelet she would walk; she was not afraid, and would go alone. He directed his carriage to meet him at Mrs. Pontellier's, and he started to walk home with her.

Up—away up, over the narrow street between the tall houses, the stars were blazing. The air was mild and caressing, but cool with the breath of spring and the night. They walked slowly, the Doctor with a heavy, measured tread and his hands behind him; Edna, in an absent-minded way, as she had walked one night at Grand Isle, as if her thoughts had gone ahead of her and she was striving to overtake them.

"You shouldn't have been there, Mrs. Pontellier," he said. "That was no place for you. Adèle is full of whims at such times. There were a dozen women she might have had with her, unimpressionable women. I felt that it was cruel, cruel. You shouldn't have gone."

"Oh, well!" she answered, indifferently. "I don't know that it matters after all. One has to think of the children some time or other; the sooner the better."

"When is Léonce coming back?"

"Quite soon. Some time in March."

"And you are going abroad?"

"Perhaps—no, I am not going. I'm not going to be forced into doing things. I don't want to go abroad. I want to be let alone. Nobody has any right—except children, per-haps—and even then, it seems to me—or it did seem—" She felt that her speech was voicing the incoherency of her thoughts, and stopped abruptly.

"The trouble is," sighed the Doctor, grasping her meaning intuitively, "that youth is given up to illusions. It seems to be a provision of Nature; a decoy to secure mothers for the race. And Nature takes no account of moral consequences, of **arbitrary** conditions which we create, and which we feel obliged to maintain at any cost."

"Yes," she said. "The years that are gone seem like dreams—if one might go on sleeping and dreaming—but to wake up and find—oh! well! perhaps it is better to wake up after all, even to suffer, rather than to remain a dupe to illusions all one's life."

"It seems to me, my dear child," said the Doctor at parting, holding her hand, "you seem to me to be in trouble. I am not going to ask for your confidence. I will only say that if ever you feel moved to give it to me, perhaps I might help you. I know I would understand, and I tell you there are not many who would—not many, my dear."

"Some way I don't feel moved to speak of things that trou-ble me. Don't think I am ungrateful or that I don't appreci-ate your sympathy. There are periods of despondency and suffering which take possession of me. But I don't want

arbitrary: not fixed by rules, but left to one's judgment or choice; discretionary.

anything but my own way. That is wanting a good deal, of course, when you have to trample upon the lives, the hearts, the prejudices of others—but no matter-still, I shouldn't want to trample upon the little lives. Oh! I don't know what I'm saying, Doctor. Good night. Don't blame me for anything."

"Yes, I will blame you if you don't come and see me soon. We will talk of things you never have dreamt of talking about before. It will do us both good. I don't want you to blame yourself, whatever comes. Good night, my child."

She let herself in at the gate, but instead of entering she sat upon the step of the porch. The night was quiet and soothing. All the tearing emotion of the last few hours seemed to fall away from her like a somber, uncomfortable garment, which she had but to loosen to be rid of. She went back to that hour before Adèle had sent for her; and her senses kindled afresh in thinking of Robert's words, the pressure of his arms, and the feeling of his lips upon her own. She could picture at that moment no greater bliss on earth than possession of the beloved one. His expression of love had already given him to her in part. When she thought that he was there at hand, waiting for her, she grew numb with the intoxication of expectancy. It was so late; he would be asleep perhaps. She would awaken him with a kiss. She hoped he would be asleep that she might arouse him with her caresses.

Still, she remembered Adèle's voice whispering, "Think of the children; think of them." She meant to think of them; that determination had driven into her soul like a death wound—but not to-night. To-morrow would be time to think of everything.

Robert was not waiting for her in the little parlor. He was nowhere at hand. The house was empty. But he had scrawled on a piece of paper that lay in the lamplight:

"I love you. Good-by—because I love you."

Edna grew faint when she read the words. She went and sat on the sofa. Then she stretched herself out there, never uttering a sound. She did not sleep. She did not go to bed. The lamp sputtered and went out. She was still awake in the morning, when Celestine unlocked the kitchen door and came in to light the fire.

CHAPTER XXXIX

Victor, with hammer and nails and scraps of **scantling**, was patching a corner of one of the galleries. Mariequita sat near by, dangling her legs, watching him work, and handing him nails from the tool-box. The sun was beating down upon them. The girl had covered her head with her apron folded into a square pad. They had been talking for an hour or more. She was never tired of hearing Victor describe the dinner at Mrs. Pontellier's. He exaggerated every detail, making it appear a veritable **Lucullean** feast. The flowers were in tubs, he said. The champagne was quaffed from huge golden goblets. Venus rising from the foam could have presented no more entrancing a spectacle than Mrs. Pontellier, blazing with beauty and diamonds at the head of the board, while the other women were all of them youthful **houris**, possessed of incomparable charms.

She got it into her head that Victor was in love with Mrs. Pontellier, and he gave her evasive answers, framed so as to confirm her belief. She grew sullen and cried a little, threatening to go off and leave him to his fine ladies. There were a dozen men crazy about her at the Chênière; and since it was the fashion to be in love with married people, why, she could run away any time she liked to New Orleans with Celina's husband.

Celina's husband was a fool, a coward, and a pig, and to prove it to her, Victor intended to hammer his head into a jelly the next time he encountered him. This assurance was very consoling to Mariequita. She dried her eyes, and grew cheerful at the prospect.

They were still talking of the dinner and the allurements of city life when Mrs. Pontellier herself slipped around the corner of the house. The two youngsters stayed dumb with amazement before what they considered to be an apparition. But it was really she in flesh and blood, looking tired and a little travel-stained.

"I walked up from the wharf," she said, "and heard the hammering. I supposed it was you, mending the porch. It's a good thing. I was always tripping over those loose planks last summer. How dreary and deserted everything looks!"

It took Victor some little time to comprehend that she had come in Beaudelet's lugger, that she had come alone, and for no purpose but to rest.

"There's nothing fixed up yet, you see. I'll give you my room; it's the only place."

scantling: a small beam or timber, especially one of small cross section, as a two-by-four.

Lucullean: as in the banquets of Lucius Lucinius Lucullus (c.110–c.57 B.C.); Roman general and consul: proverbial for his wealth and luxurious banquets.

houris: seductively beautiful women.

"Any corner will do," she assured him.

"And if you can stand Philomel's cooking," he went on, "though I might try to get her mother while you are here. Do you think she would come?" turning to Mariequita.

Mariequita thought that perhaps Philomel's mother might come for a few days, and money enough.

Beholding Mrs. Pontellier make her appearance, the girl had at once suspected a lovers' rendezvous. But Victor's astonishment was so genuine, and Mrs. Pontellier's indifference so apparent, that the disturbing notion did not lodge long in her brain. She contemplated with the greatest interest this woman who gave the most sumptuous dinners in America, and who had all the men in New Orleans at her feet.

"What time will you have dinner?" asked Edna. "I'm very hungry; but don't get anything extra."

"I'll have it ready in little or no time," he said, bustling and packing away his tools. "You may go to my room to brush up and rest yourself. Mariequita will show you."

"Thank you," said Edna. "But, do you know, I have a notion to go down to the beach and take a good wash and even a little swim, before dinner?"

"The water is too cold!" they both exclaimed. "Don't think of it."

"Well, I might go down and try—dip my toes in. Why, it seems to me the sun is hot enough to have warmed the very depths of the ocean. Could you get me a couple of towels? I'd better go right away, so as to be back in time. It would be a little too chilly if I waited till this afternoon."

Mariequita ran over to Victor's room, and returned with some towels, which she gave to Edna.

"I hope you have fish for dinner," said Edna, as she started to walk away; "but don't do anything extra if you haven't."

"Run and find Philomel's mother," Victor instructed the girl. "I'll go to the kitchen and see what I can do. By Gimminy! Women have no consideration! She might have sent me word."

Edna walked on down to the beach rather mechanically, not noticing anything special except that the sun was hot. She was not dwelling upon any particular train of thought. She had done all the thinking which was necessary after Robert went away, when she lay awake upon the sofa till morning.

She had said over and over to herself: "To-day it is Arobin; to-morrow it will be some one else. It makes no difference to me, it doesn't matter about Léonce Pontellier—but Raoul and Etienne!" She understood now clearly what she had meant long ago when she said to Adèle Ratignolle that she would give up the unessential, but she would never sacrifice herself for her children.

Despondency had come upon her there in the wakeful night, and had never lifted. There was no one thing in the world that she desired. There was no human being whom she wanted near her except Robert; and she even realized that the day would come when he, too, and the thought of him would melt out of her existence, leaving her alone. The children appeared before her like antagonists who had overcome her; who had overpowered and sought to drag her into the soul's slavery for the rest of her days. But she knew a way to elude them. She was not thinking of these things when she walked down to the beach.

The water of the Gulf stretched out before her, gleaming with the million lights of the sun. The voice of the sea is seductive, never ceasing, whispering, clamoring, murmuring, inviting the soul to wander in abysses of solitude. All along the white beach, up and down, there was no living thing in sight. A bird with a broken wing was beating the air above, reeling, fluttering, circling disabled down, down to the water.

Edna had found her old bathing suit still hanging, faded, upon its accustomed peg.

She put it on, leaving her clothing in the bath-house. But when she was there beside the sea, absolutely alone, she cast the unpleasant, pricking garments from her, and for the first time in her life she stood naked in the open air, at the mercy of the sun, the breeze that beat upon her, and the waves that invited her.

How strange and awful it seemed to stand naked under the sky! how delicious! She felt like some new-born creature, opening its eyes in a familiar world that it had never known.

The foamy wavelets curled up to her white feet, and coiled like serpents about her ankles. She walked out. The water was chill, but she walked on. The water was deep, but she lifted her white body and reached out with a long, sweeping stroke. The touch of the sea is sensuous, enfolding the body in its soft, close embrace.

She went on and on. She remembered the night she swam far out, and recalled the terror that seized her at the fear of being unable to regain the shore. She did not look back now, but went on and on, thinking of the blue-grass meadow that she had traversed when a little child, believing that it had no beginning and no end.

Her arms and legs were growing tired.

She thought of Léonce and the children. They were a part of her life. But they need not have thought that they could possess her, body and soul. How Mademoiselle Reisz would have laughed, perhaps sneered, if she knew! "And you call yourself an artist! What pretensions, Madame! The artist must possess the courageous soul that dares and defies."

Exhaustion was pressing upon and overpowering her.

"Good-by—because I love you." He did not know; he did not understand. He would never understand. Perhaps Doctor Mandelet would have understood if she had seen him—but it was too late; the shore was far behind her, and her strength was gone.

She looked into the distance, and the old terror flamed up for an instant, then sank again. Edna heard her father's voice and her sister Margaret's. She heard the barking of an old dog that was chained to the sycamore tree. The spurs of the cavalry officer clanged as he walked across the porch. There was the hum of bees, and the musky odor of pinks filled the air.

COMMENTARY

Edna's relationship with Arobin has become the object of gossip. Ostensibly, the purpose of Madame Ratignolle's visit is to hear all about the dinner party, which she was unable to attend. But in reality, Madame Ratignolle wants to caution Edna about this gossip as well as the danger inherent in her actions—clearly a warning from a friend.

Madame Ratignolle understands the conventions of New Orleans society; she says that Edna acts "without a certain amount of reflection which is necessary in this life." Madame Ratignolle goes so far as to suggest that Edna find a chaperone to live with her and protect her reputation, but the last thing Edna wants is another keeper.

Edna is so unconcerned with this gossip that when Madame Ratignolle suggests that Arobin's own reputation is enough to ruin a woman, Edna is indifferent even to the notion that he may be bragging about her as a conquest. Edna's reputation has become so compromised that Madame Ratignolle is unable to visit her again.

Madame Ratignolle's accusation that Edna is "like a child" contains a strong element of truth. If a child is willful and selfish, intent on taking whatever she wishes, Edna is like a child. But Edna is not concerned with her behavior; her focus is on her own happiness. She has had enough of being the obedient wife, and as a reaction to being imprisoned in the past, she becomes just the opposite of what she had been. She had been obedient, but now she is willful; she had been chaste and even prudish, but now she is involved in an affair with a notorious rake. Thus, she is reminiscent of a child.

Later, Edna again seeks refuge at Mademoiselle Reisz's apartment. Edna has spent many hours imaging a romantic reunion with Robert. In the months since his departure, less than nine months to judge by Madame Ratignolle's pregnancy, Robert has become a fantasy lover for Edna. He has been gone longer than he was actually a presence in her life. During his absence, he has achieved an almost surreal quality, and, of course, in person he cannot achieve the reality with which Edna has endowed him. When Robert appears at Mademoiselle Reisz's apartment, Edna is crushed to find out that he has been in New Orleans for two days and hasn't yet come to see her. Even this meeting is only by accident—he was unaware that she would be visiting on this day.

Unfortunately, Edna still does not understand Robert's adherence to Creole social conventions. She expected him to visit her immediately when he returned, but he cannot, because she lives alone. Unlike Edna, Robert cannot reject social conventions. How little Edna understands of this aspect of Robert's life is evident in her questioning him about why he did not write to her. Edna is always honest now, and her pain at Robert's neglect is an honest reaction to her disappointment. For Edna, all her dreams of Robert, which had sustained her these past months, have blown up.

Her dreams, of course, were just dreams. Edna has never understood the impossibility of her dreams, and she has never understood that Robert lacks her strength. Edna has accomplished many brave deeds in recent months. She has forged a life separate from the life with her husband by moving out of his home. Edna has rejected the conventional role of the obedient wife and has found that she is strong enough to be her own woman.

Conversely, Robert ran away rather than confront his growing involvement with Edna. He even lacked the courage to write to her; instead, he directed his letters to Mademoiselle Reisz, letters in which he persistently asked about the woman from whom he was fleeing. Rather than seek out Edna upon his return, Robert has again proved himself a coward by not letting her know of his arrival. One can hardly believe that Mademoiselle

Reisz, who was corresponding with Robert, never mentioned Edna's visits or that she read Robert's letters. He would certainly have known of Edna's continued interest. But because Robert is a dreamer who lacks Edna's convictions and strength, he will not pursue his own happiness.

Although Edna is hurt by Robert's betrayal, she cannot completely give up on her dream, and when he offers to walk her home, she is too happy to be in his presence to pretend otherwise. Edna could have left Robert at Mademoiselle Reisz's apartment, but she would not have reflected her true desire—to be with him. When they arrive at her home, Edna again acknowledges how important her dreams of happiness with Robert have become. To Edna, "it seem[s] as if her dreams [are] coming true after all." In her fantasies, Robert has always been in the house with her, and now he is actually present. For a few moments, he seems like the Robert she knew the previous summer.

But this reality is very different from her dreams. Robert finds the picture of Alcée Arobin and becomes jealous. As she had with her children, Edna is able to carefully separate the different segments of her life; she catalogues people into their own special niches and easily puts them away when she no longer needs them. Likewise, she dismisses Arobin, who has been little more than a distraction for Edna while she waited for her real love to reappear. He no longer matters to her.

Edna has awakened to many things—namely, the truth of her own life. Robert, though, has yet to make this journey, so the atmosphere during their dinner holds "a certain degree of ceremony." This artifice is due largely to Robert's nervous reserve and to Edna's uncertainty and confusion about what should happen next. Robert's admission, that he has "forgotten nothing at Grand Isle," is a cautious declaration that gives away little of his feelings. Edna simply cannot penetrate Robert's careful demeanor to find the man she fell in love with the previous summer. And when Robert pulls out a tobacco pouch given to him by a Vera Cruz girl, it is Edna's turn to be jealous.

In the midst of this tension-filled moment, Arobin arrives. Edna allows herself to mock Robert as she trades witticisms with Arobin at Robert's expense. Edna reveals the depth of her disappointment and the pain that Robert's behavior has caused. Robert's final admonition, that Edna remember him to her husband, is designed to remind Edna that she does still have a husband.

After Robert's departure, Arobin is unable to break Edna's reverie, so he finally departs. Edna scarcely notices because she is so involved in going over every moment of the evening. She finally realizes that her fantasy of Robert holds no more reality than it did in Vera Cruz.

With the coming of morning, Edna is again hopeful. She is certain that Robert loves her and that he will not be able to resist being with her. She is also certain that he will be unable to resist the force of her passion.

Edna receives three letters in the morning mail. The first is from one of her sons, Raoul, telling her of the birth of ten little piglets. The birth of these small animals helps remind readers that another, more important birth is also imminent: Madame Ratignolle is also expecting to deliver her child at any moment.

Edna also receives a letter from her husband, whom Chopin does not mention by name. He ceased to be Léonce when he left for New York, and he was referred to only as Mr. Pontellier in recent chapters. Now he is merely Edna's husband. With each move away from his first name, he becomes a bit less real to Edna. The note from Léonce contains a reminder of their planned trip to Europe. Edna's reply is not meant to mislead her husband, but it reflects that "she had abandoned herself to Fate."

Edna's response is a reminder of the naturalism that pervades the novel. Edna is no longer in control of her world. Naturalism, in the guise of destiny, now determines the course of events. Edna is described as awaiting with "indifference" for the events that will occur. In the past months, Edna has attempted to create her own destiny, but now she has abdicated her life to fate.

The third letter is a note from Arobin, which she burns, not because it displeases her, but because Arobin is unimportant to her life. Like her children, he enters and exits Edna's life with little notice. The days pass, and Robert fails to appear. However, Arobin does reappear, and the relationship with Edna resumes as it had prior to Robert's return—except that Edna greets each day without the hope that Robert will come back to her.

Finally, another awkward, unintentional meeting with Robert occurs when Edna visits a small garden for dinner. This garden is a place where Edna finds comfort and peace, and in this peaceful place, she has often dreamed of Robert.

As he was at the previous meeting, Robert is ill at ease. These accidental meetings cause him much more discomfort than they cause Edna. She is more accepting of their meetings; she sees them as part of the fate that has brought them together. Although Edna had planned to reveal nothing and treat him with the same indifference that he has treated her, she is happy to see him. She loves him, so she cannot take refuge in a false indifference. Edna will not permit Robert to hide his feelings in a subterfuge he cannot sustain, and she nearly forces him to admit that he loves her. Finally, she is satisfied.

After Robert walks Edna home, she makes the first move and kisses him. Edna has always had the courage to go after what she wants. Robert cannot help but respond, and finally, he is able to return her kiss and embrace her. All his resistance finally melts away, and he admits that he has been running away because of his feelings for her. Although Robert admits his love for Edna, he also admits that he has never forgotten that Edna is married. Edna replies that she is "no longer one of Mr. Pontellier's possessions." Her response shocks Robert, who realizes that she will not belong to him either. Edna may love Robert, but she will not be one of his possessions. She wants to love him as an equal. Her feelings confuse and even frighten Robert.

Edna is an idealist, who believes that, no matter the circumstances, their love for one another can overcome any obstacle. Before she leaves to attend Madame Ratignolle's childbirth, Edna tells Robert that he "awoke [her] last summer out of a life-long stupid dream." Her passion for him momentarily overwhelms Robert, but he is the weaker partner. His reluctance to allow Edna to leave reflects his awareness that he can only be strong when she can make him so. He pleads with Edna not to leave him because he knows his own weakness. He is also not as brave as Edna, and he will not be able to face the social ostracism that they will endure if they are seen as a couple. But Edna is not aware of Robert's fear when she leaves. She fully expects Robert to be waiting when she returns.

The birth of Madame Ratignolle's child is a traumatic event for Edna. This childbirth scene reminds Edna of her own childbirth experiences—"an ecstasy of pain, the heavy odor of chloroform, a stupor which had deadened sensation." Edna has repressed these memories, and more importantly, they represent obligations that Edna prefers not to remember. Madame Ratignolle's labor reminds Edna of her own children, who are safely hidden away at their father's family plantation. Edna may be able to leave her husband's house and her marriage physically, but she cannot ever leave motherhood. The dread she feels at this childbirth is a foreboding of her obligations and duties still to be met. Edna had always been sedated during childbirth; she "awaken[s] to find a new little life to which she had given being." Accordingly, childbirth had been abstract to her, but now, the experience is too real. Madame Ratignolle has yet another child to demand his or her attention, another child not unlike the two that Edna has been trying to forget.

Despite her agony, Edna does not leave, but her promise to stay with Madame Ratignolle has been replaced by an almost compulsive need to see the process through to the end. Edna is captive to "Nature," and in these moments, she realizes that she will always be captive to nature. Sensing that Edna may be near the edge of a precipice, Madame Ratignolle urges Edna to "[t]hink of the children, Edna. Oh think of the children! Remember them!" Adèle's warning, though, is unnecessary. The entire childbirth scene has reminded Edna of the children.

Once again, the naturalism theme in Chopin's work is evident; it emerges as the central focus in the childbirth scene. Nature shocks and repulses Edna. She has never witnessed childbirth; she was asleep when her own children were born, so she had an almost disassociated response. They appeared almost as if by magic, and Edna's motherly connection has always seemed a bit abstract. Now, the scene is described as evoking "an inward agony, with a flaming, outspoken revolt against the ways of Nature, she witnessed the scene of torture." The description seems more like a medieval torture chamber than a childbirth bed—a supposed scene of much joy in its conclusion. Now, Edna cannot ignore what nature has made abundantly clear—motherhood is not a role that she can easily escape. Edna has

recently awakened to her own promise as an individual, but she is reminded that she can never be *only* an individual.

While she leaves with Doctor Mandelet, Edna continues to reflect on the events of the past few hours. Madame Ratignolle's insistence that Edna be present has served its purpose—to remind Edna of the two small lives who depend on her. An almost philosophical Edna tells Doctor Mandelet that "[o]ne has to think of the children some time or other; the sooner the better." Eventually, Edna must deal with her children.

While considering her children, Edna believes that Robert is waiting for her, and she plans a future with him. Edna has clearly given the children little thought before this evening, and now, her speech of independence lacks conviction: "Nobody has any right—except children, perhaps—and even then, it seems to me—or it did seem." Before, her independence seemed so clear and easy, but Adèle has reminded Edna of what nature has made of her—a mother—and her situation is a prison that she cannot escape. Edna has awakened to life and to the need to be in control of her life, but she is reminded that, as a woman, she will always be a mother first and a woman second. When Edna declares that "I don't want anything but my own way," she still rebels against a society demanding that her own way is not an option. Nonetheless, Edna's declaration is a half-hearted one, and she acknowledges, "still I wouldn't want to trample upon the little lives." Suddenly, the children, so easily forgotten in the past months, loom as a huge presence that Edna cannot easily put away.

When left alone outside her own home, Edna begins to think again of Robert; she remembers the feel of him next to her. Edna has not forgotten about the children, but she compartmentalizes them. She will think of them again tomorrow; tonight she wants only to think of being with Robert. But when she enters the house, Robert is gone. He leaves only a note: "I love you. Good-by—because I love you." She would give up everything for Robert, perhaps even her children. But Robert is a coward. He has always been a coward; he ran off to Mexico and hid from her in New Orleans. Now, he does only what Edna should have expected. Her grief and pain are profound, but Chopin provides no hint of what Edna is thinking or planning while she passes the long, lonely night.

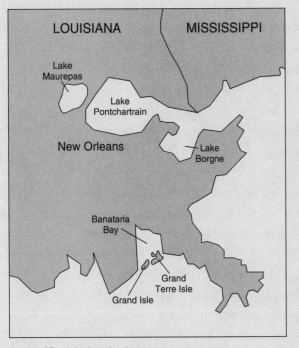

Location of Grande Isle in southern Louisiana.

In this final chapter, Edna returns to Grand Isle, the place where she first awoke to love and to life's promise.

When Edna appears suddenly on the island, Victor's exaggerated stories have somehow conjured her into being. Victor and Mariequita are astonished when this seeming apparition appears. Edna, has come to rest, but first, she wants to take a short swim in the ocean. As she walks to the beach, Edna's despondency is obvious. She is no longer able to think; she did all her thinking during the long night just passed. After she removes her clothing and enters the sea, Edna has never felt more alone.

Edna has little in common with other women. She is far different from Mademoiselle Reisz, who seems to hate all people and who has become a bitter, disappointed old woman. Nor is Edna at all like her only real woman friend, Adèle Ratignolle, a mother-woman who subordinates her life to the needs of her family. As for the men in her life, Edna fears that her nature will force her to turn to a succession of men to satisfy her sexual nature. She fears that "[t]oday it is Arobin; tomorrow it will be someone else." She does not worry about whether her husband will suffer because of her actions.

Nor is she concerned about Robert; she recognizes that, eventually, he will no longer matter to her. But Adèle has reminded Edna of her children's existence. She can cease to be Léonce's wife and Arobin's lover, but she cannot cease to be a mother. She cannot hurt her children.

In these final moments, Edna knows of only one way to escape her children, who seem like vultures that seek to "drag her into the soul's slavery for the rest of her days." Despite Edna's earlier proclamation to Adèle Ratignolle that she could never sacrifice herself for her children, she swims too far out in the ocean. Taking her own life is an easier sacrifice to make than the alternative sacrifice of her soul.

By returning to the water, Edna returns to the freedom of the past summer. For the first time in her life, Edna stands naked in the open air. She has cast aside the confines of the "pricking garments" of her life, just as she is about to cast aside the life that confines her. In the water, Edna is finally an individual who controls her own life. She can be completely in control only in this venue. After Robert ran away the previous summer, Edna took refuge in swimming, which represented a personal accomplishment that satisfied her as no other achievement had. She has freedom in the water—no husband beckons, and no children call her. She is alone, but not isolated. Edna has said many times that she just wants to be alone. The water provides a silence that soothes, a quiet that drowns out the world of civilization—a world that seems to offer so much to Edna, but actually offers her little. While she takes long, smooth strokes, Edna feels the "old terror" for a moment, and then she is no longer afraid. Previously, Mademoiselle Reisz warned Edna of the bird with the broken wing that, bruised and broken, flutters back to earth. The bird flutters overhead, but Edna, who has swum much farther than Mrs. Pontellier ever expected to swim, is much stronger than the broken bird.

Often readers don't understand Edna's suicide, which seems a final means of escaping from her children. Like the character of Susan Rawlings in Doris Lessing's *To Room Nineteen*, Edna Pontellier cannot find a room of her own in which to create her own life. Suicide is her only recourse.

For Edna, Susan, and many other women of the late nineteen and early twentieth centuries, motherhood is an inescapable bond that imprisons, controls, and

Edna disrobing on beach.
Everett Collection

ultimately defeats its victim. Edna feels power and control while swimming, so her choice of returning to Grand Isle is an appropriate escape to a time when she felt free of all the encumbrances of life that sought to possess her—Léonce, the children, and even Arobin and Robert. When Chopin tells readers that Edna lay awake all night, perhaps Edna is planning her actions or deliberating her choices, but she may also be remembering the brief months on her own with their illusion of freedom. When Edna arrives on Grand Isle, her manner is intentional, and she does not hesitate. She rejects society, but unlike a man, she cannot run away. She can escape to death.

The Awakening can be considered a naturalistic tragedy in which the impersonal forces of nature manipulate events. Edna is motivated by fate, as she

earlier reveals; the events in her life are beyond her control. She does not act of her own volition, and her walk to the beach is described as mechanical, with no self-awareness. She is not capable of thought, because she succumbs to the forces of naturalism, which determine her fate. Edna makes this choice because she is afraid that Arobin will be only the first in a succession of men. She acknowledges a fear that she will succumb again to her own animal desires—an inner nature beyond her control. With naturalism, Edna bears no responsibility for her death; nature controls everything. What Edna wants most is control over her own destiny, but in the end, she cannot escape nature or her children or the forces of naturalism.

Notes

Notes

CLIFFSCOMPLETE REVIEW

Use this CliffsComplete Review to gauge what you've learned and to build confidence in your understanding of the original text. After you work through the review questions, the problem-solving exercises, and the suggested activities, you're well on your way to understanding and appreciating the works of Kate Chopin.

IDENTIFY THE QUOTATION

Identify the following quotations by answering these questions:

* Who is the speaker of the quote?
* What does it reveal about the speaker's character?
* What does it tell us about other characters within the novel?
* Where does it occur within the novel?
* Where does it show us about the themes of the novel?
* What significant imagery do you see in the quote, and how do these images relate to the overall imagery of the novel?

1. "Oh! I was demented, dreaming of wild, impossible things, recalling men who had set their wives free, we have heard of such things."

2. She wondered if her husband had ever spoken to her like that before, and if she had submitted to his command.

3. "I am no longer one of Mr. Pontellier's possessions."

4. By the time she had regained the city the song no longer echoed in her soul.

5. "The bird that would soar above the level plain of tradition and prejudice must have strong wings."

6. "Woman, my dear friend, is a very peculiar and delicate organism—a sensitive and highly organized woman, such as I know Mrs. Pontellier to be, is especially peculiar."

7. He could not see that she was becoming herself and daily casting aside that fictitious self which we assume like a garment with which to appear before the world.

8. All sense of reality had gone out of her life; she had abandoned herself to Fate, and awaited the consequences with indifference.

TRUE/FALSE

1. T F Monsieur Pontellier is much older than Edna.

2. T F When Edna married, she had never before been in love and was swept away by her emotions.

3. T F Madame Ratignolle represents the perfect mother-woman, an idealized role.

4. T F Grand Isle is an idyllic paradise, an Eden in which freedom only appears to be possible.

5. T F Robert Lebrun often seduces women and initially sees Edna as just another conquest.

6. T F Creole women only appear to be sexually free; in reality, they are as conventional as are Edna's Presbyterian family in Kentucky.

7. T F Arobin intends to seduce Edna, but in the end, he falls in love with her.

8. T F Edna moves into the "pigeon house" because she hates cleaning the larger house.

9. T F Madame Ratignolle's confinement reminds Edna that she will always be a mother and can never escape her children.

10. T F Edna drowns because she unthinkingly swims out too far and is unable to return.

MULTIPLE CHOICE

1. What kind of a mother is Edna?
   a. Thoughtful and loving
   b. Doting and watchful of the children's every move
   c. Uncaring and cruel
   d. Concerned about her children when they are present and forgetful when they are gone

2. Léonce Pontellier expects his wife to be concerned with which of the following?
   a. The well-being of their children
   b. Running a smooth home and staff
   c. Adhering to the conventions of New Orleans society
   d. All the above

3. Edna's awakening occurs on Grand Isle because of which force?
   a. Madame Ratignolle's idealization of motherhood
   b. The unstructured environment that allows Edna to do what she wishes
   c. The realization of love and the possibilities of a life of one's making
   d. Léonce's absence during the week

4. Which three events make it easy for Edna to construct her own life?
   a. Léonce leaves for New York; the children go to their grandmother's plantation; the house is being remodeled

b. Léonce leaves for New York; the children go to their grandmother's plantation; Edna moves to the smaller "pigeon house"
   c. Léonce leaves for New York; the children's nurse assumes their care fulltime; the house is being remodeled
   d. Léonce leaves for Europe; the children go to their grandmother's plantation; the house is being remodeled

5. Why does Edna become involved with Arobin?
   a. He senses her vulnerability and sets out to seduce her.
   b. With Robert gone, Edna knows no other available men.
   c. He is exceptionally rich and handsome.
   d. Madame Ratignolle introduces them and endorses the relationship.

6. Mademoiselle Reisz plays what role in the book?
   a. She acts as a go-between, smuggling letters between Edna and Robert.
   b. She offers Edna and Robert a private place to meet.
   c. She allows Edna to read Robert's letters.
   d. She encourages Edna to leave her husband and marry Robert.

7. Which of the following items are important symbols in *The Awakening*?
   a. Trees and houses
   b. Birds and the sea
   c. Birds and cigars
   d. Dancers and pianists

8. Why is naturalism an important element of Chopin's novel?
   a. It determines Edna's fate.
   b. Much of the action takes place on the island.

c. Edna refuses to follow rules and acts in a natural manner.

d. All the important details make the book seem more real.

9. The mother-woman symbolizes the ideal Creole woman when she exhibits which of the following traits?

a. She puts her husband and children first, but she relies upon servants to actually take care of her children.

b. She puts her children first, and any extra time is devoted to her husband.

c. She puts her husband and children first, and she relies upon servants to perform the duties that do not directly involve personal care of her family—such as cleaning and cooking.

d. She devotes herself exclusively to her children.

10. Why does Edna commit suicide?

a. Robert leaves her.

b. She is depressed.

c. She realizes that she can never escape her children.

d. She realizes that she can never be as good a mother as Madame Ratignolle.

FILL IN THE BLANK

1. The _____ in the cage represents a caged Edna.

2. On a visit to the Lebrun's, _____ treats Edna with a too common familiarity.

3. Chopin's _____ is the piece that Mademoiselle Reisz plays when Edna comes to visit.

4. When Edna becomes faint on the visit to an old church, Robert takes her to _____ to rest.

5. The new little house that Edna moves to is called the _____.

6. When she learns that Edna is in love with Robert, Mademoiselle Reisz asks Edna if she has _____.

7. Edna's final, grand party at the Pontellier mansion is really a dinner for _____ people (insert a number into the blank).

8. Edna tells Robert that she is no longer one of Léonce's _____.

9. A young woman in Vera Cruz makes a _____ for Robert, and Edna becomes jealous.

10. Edna's husband is especially worried about Edna's neglect of social conventions when she ceases her _____.

ANSWERS

Identify the Quotation

1. The speaker is Robert Lebrun, in the scene in which he admits his love for Edna (Chapter 36). In this scene, Robert is admitting to Edna that, while in Mexico, he thought of her constantly, longed for her, and dreamed of the possibility of being with her.

2. These are Edna's thoughts following a particularly harsh argument with her husband (Chapter 11). During the argument, Léonce had insisted that Edna obey him and come to bed, but for the first time in their marriage, Edna refuses to obey. She has awakened to her own power and desire for control.

3. Edna is the speaker. Responding to Robert's caresses, she tells him that she is no longer property to be disposed of by any man. Edna's statement is significant for a woman, because all wives were regarded as a husband's personal property during this period (Chapter 36).

4. These are Edna's thoughts after she has been to visit her sons (Chapter 32). These thoughts illustrate that, while Edna enjoys her children and even loves them when they are at hand, as soon as she leaves them, she promptly forgets their existence.

5. The speaker is Mademoiselle Reisz, who upon discovering that Edna is moving from her husband's house, feels Edna's shoulder blades to ask if she is strong enough to fly. The old woman understands that Edna must be very strong to withstand the condemnation of society (Chapter 27).

6. The speaker is Doctor Mandelet, to whom Léonce voices concerns regarding Edna's recent behavior (Chapter 22). Ironically, this man pretends to understand the complexities of feminine unhappiness, and an even greater irony is that two men discuss a woman's problem, of which they know so little. That Edna no longer obeys her husband, as they assume she should, creates a problem for these men, one that they are not well suited to understand.

7. This sentence is the author inserting herself into the text to explain what Edna's husband cannot understand (Chapter 19). Edna has decided that she will never again pretend to be what she is not. She is rejecting the artificial conventions of society.

8. Edna has just responded to her husband's letter, in which he describes their future trip to Europe. Her response is not designed to deceive him, and it reflects, more accurately, Edna's inability to plan for future events. She has succumbed to naturalism and to its control over her life. As far as she is concerned, nature will now determine what is to happen to Edna (Chapter 35).

True/False

(1) T (2) F (3) T (4) T (5) F (6) T (7) F (8) F (9) T (10) F

Multiple Choice

(1) d. (2) d. (3) c. (4) b. (5) a. (6) c. (7) b. (8) a. (9) c. (10) c.

Fill in the Blank

(1) parrot (2) Victor (3) *Interlude* (4) Madame Antoine's (5) pigeon house (6) strong wings (7) ten (8) possessions (9) tobacco pouch (10) Tuesdays at home

DISCUSSION

Use the following questions to generate discussion:

1. *The Awakening* offers readers three contrasting pictures of how women function in a society. The most obvious differences are between the two wives—Edna Pontellier and Adèle Ratignolle—but Mademoiselle Reisz's role is also important. Discuss the depiction of these women and what Chopin is suggesting about each one's role in society.

2. Life is different on Grand Isle—freer and more relaxed—but there are still important social rules and conventions. Discuss the role of this vacation spot in Chopin's novel and its contribution to the tragic ending.

3. Edna becomes involved with both Robert Lebrun and Alcée Arobin, but these two men are very different. Robert makes a habit of flirting with women, but he is essentially unavailable and unprepared to take what he desires. On the other hand, Alcée is accustomed to having what he desires, and his approach to women is self-assured and deliberate. Discuss these differences and how each man contributes to the choices that Edna eventually makes.

4. Edna is a mother because having children is what married women do. It was never her choice, yet she makes her final decision based on her concern for her children. Discuss Edna's relationship with her children and her role as a mother.

5. Edna is Léonce Pontellier's wife, and because she is poorly suited for this role, Léonce is often depicted as a villain. But Léonce is more than a repressive husband and more than an ogre. At times he appears to love Edna, in spite of being frustrated at her inexplicable behavior. Discuss Léonce's role in the novel and his role as Edna's foil.

6. New Orleans society offers few choices for Edna. One of the possible choices may be the life of a single artist, a woman free to make her own choices. Mademoiselle Reisz offers one model of this single woman. Is Chopin suggesting that Edna may turn out to be a disagreeable old woman, given enough time? Discuss the elderly pianist and Chopin's depiction of single life.

7. Edna awakens to life's possibilities while at Grand Isle, but she undergoes other awakenings, as well. Discuss these awakenings and their importance in the choices that Edna makes about her life.

8. Chopin's novel is filled with significant use of symbolism—birds, water, and birth. Discuss this use of symbolism and its role in the novel.

IDENTIFYING ELEMENTS

Find examples of the following elements in the text of *The Awakening*:

Symbolism: Symbolism refers to the use of one object to mean another. A symbol retains its truth even when it is meant to refer to another object and does not take the place of the object.

Metaphor: A metaphor is a figure of speech that expresses an image through the use of another object. This differs from the symbol because a metaphor effectively takes the place of the object it suggests.

Irony: Irony in a text is often created when an author uses language to say one thing while meaning another. Its effect is subtle and not as obvious as sarcasm; thus, the reader may easily overlook irony in a text.

Epiphany: An epiphany is often that moment in a text when a character suddenly has a sudden revelation of truth, which is inspired by a seemingly small or unimportant event.

Foreshadowing: Foreshadowing is a literary device used to create an expectation on the part of the reader. An author may use foreshadowing to create tension in a text and to help keep a reader focused.

Zeitgeist: This is a German term referring to the spirit of the time, most commonly the intellectual and moral influences of a period.

ACTIVITIES

The following activities can springboard you into further discussions and projects:

1. Because *The Awakening* is relatively short and confined to only a few sets, the novel is an ideal vehicle for presentation as a play. Using Chopin's dialogue, create scenes and settings for the play. Devise your set directions to make the action clear and determine what roles could be successfully eliminated. Next, present your play with a few fellow students, and devote some time discussing how this text changes if presented on stage. Does it become a family drama, such as *A Doll's House*, or is it more a classical tragedy, such as *Oedipus*?

2. Chopin's text was written only a few years after Henrik Ibsen's *A Doll's House*, so the two works seem like almost natural companions for

comparison. In Ibsen's play, Nora must decide whether it is more important to know her own self or whether a secure life as an obedient wife and mother is the price a woman must pay for security and social acceptance. Make a poster comparing Chopin and Ibsen's two works, drawing parallels between Nora and Edna. What do you think that these two works suggest about the role of women in the late nineteenth century?

3. Chopin's biographers suggest that she often drew upon her own experiences to create her fiction. Certainly clear parallels exist between her life and Edna's. Find a good biography of Chopin (you may want to consider Emily Toth's *Unveiling Kate Chopin*) and try to find all the similarities between Chopin's life and Edna's. Then, consider why the ending is so different. What allows Chopin to survive, while Edna ends her life?

4. Consider the use of nature, and especially birds, in Chopin's work. Go through the novel, noting all the references to nature. How do these images relate to the themes in the book and why are they significant to fostering an understanding of Edna?

5. Go to the library and look in the microfilm section for some of the women's magazines popular at the end of the nineteenth century. What do the articles and advertisements suggest about the role of women in this world? How, then, is Chopin's book representative of this picture? If you combine the two images, do you get a composite picture of feminine life that is more accurate than if you view only one source?

6. Imagine for a moment that you are a married woman living in late-nineteenth-century New Orleans. Place yourself in Edna's shoes and consider how you might react if faced with her choices. In doing this exercise, try to forget all that you might have learned about being either a man or a woman in the early part of the twenty-first century. How might you adapt to the challenges of Chopin's world? What do you learn from this experience?

7. One of Chopin's key themes in *The Awakening* is the limitations that women faced during the late nineteenth century. Use Internet and library sources to find at least 10 to 12 authoritative sources on this topic. Prepare a short summary of this information and present it in class. Be prepared to make some connections to Chopin's text. Then consider whether Chopin left any room for debate on this topic or if her text is a unilateral condemnation of men and marriage.

8. Chopin creates two women who sought careers in art at a time when readers may think that women had few options. Edna finds only small success as an artist, but Mademoiselle Reisz is relatively successful as a pianist, although she is described negatively for the most part. Locate information about women artists and performers and determine how successful they were. Was it very difficult for women to succeed in this field, or was this one area where being a woman was less important?

9. Design a geographical web page for *The Awakening*. For one section, focus on the geographical locations that Chopin uses in the novel and create links to maps of these areas. Also provide links to some of the different kinds of buildings that Chopin uses, along with architectural examples from the period. Then consider finding some of the different socially oriented locations from the novel, such as the racetrack and the different neighborhoods depicted, and using the areas as a link. You may also want to include links to Chopin's life, such as the area where she was born and where she lived as an adult.

CLIFFSCOMPLETE RESOURCE CENTER

The learning doesn't need to stop here. Cliffs-Complete Resource Center shows you the best of the best: great links to information in print, on film, and online. And the following aren't all the great resources available to you; visit www.cliffsnotes.com for tips on reading literature, writing papers, giving presentations, locating other resources, and testing your knowledge.

BOOKS

Benfey, Christopher E. G. Degas in New Orleans: Encounters in the Creole World of Kate Chopin and George Washington Cable. New York: Alfred A. Knopf, 1998.

Benfey uses Degas' short visit to New Orleans in 1872 as a way to make connections between two American writers, Kate Chopin and George Washington Cable. Using these two American writers, Benfey tries to discover what it was about New Orleans culture that inspired Degas to create some of his finest work.

Boren, Lynda S. and Sara deSaussaure Davis, eds. *Kate Chopin Reconsidered: Beyond the Bayou*. Baton Rouge: Louisiana State University Press, 1992.

Boren and Davis have assembled a collection of fourteen essays that examine Chopin's life and writing from several different approaches, including feminist and biographical perspectives.

Petry, Alice Hall. *Critical Essays on Kate Chopin*. New York: Macmillan, 1996.

Petry reprints a collection of 37 essays and reviews of Chopin's work, covering the period from when Chopin was writing through recent scholarship. This book provides an opportunity to trace the way scholars and critics responded to Chopin during the past 100 years or more.

Seyerstad, Per. *Kate Chopin: Critical Biography*. Baton Rouge, Louisiana State University Press, 1969.

Seyersted provides a thorough examination of Chopin's life in a biography that scholars still find useful, in spite of its being more than 30 years old.

Toth, Emily. *Unveiling Kate Chopin*. Jackson: University Press of Mississippi, 1999.

Toth is considered one of the most important new scholars on Chopin's life and writing. This is a comprehensive discussion of Chopin's life and works, helpful to any student of Chopin.

Toth, Emily, Per Seyersted, and Cheyenne Bonnell, eds. *Kate Chopin's Private Papers*.

These papers are drawn from largely unpublished writings, including Chopin's diaries, letters, and manuscripts.

INTERNET

www.pbs.org/katechopin/

In 1999, PBS produced a film on Kate Chopin. This web site contains information about the film, as well as photos, scenes from the film, a transcript of the film's content, interviews, and a chronology of Chopin's life.

http://soleil.acomp.usf.edu/~smasturz/links.html

This web page includes many links helpful to anyone interested in Chopin's work or life. Topics include biography, criticism, character studies, literary genres, history, culture, philosophy, and religion.

www.vcu.edu/engweb/eng384/hourweb.htm

Here you can find links to many Chopin resources, including on-line works by Chopin, visits to Chopin's home, a biographical information, and student responses to Chopin's work.

www.csustan.edu/english/reuben/pal/chap6/chopin.html

Part of the PAL (Perspectives in American Literature) Research and Reference Guide, this site contains links to Chopin's works, a bibliography, and study questions on her work. It also provides links to other nineteenth-century authors.

www.literarytraveler.com/summer/south/chopin.htm

This web page belongs to the Literary Traveler, a site that provides information and photographs about the locations used in literature.

www.concord.tec.nh.us/library/authorresources/
chopinbib.htm

Features of this site include an annotated bibliography and biography for Chopin. It provides a helpful gateway to other authors and to literary timelines, as well.

www.gonzaga.edu/faculty/campbell/engl462/chopin.htm

Browse to this site for offerings that include a biographical sketch, a guide to other Internet resources on Chopin, and online texts of many of Chopin's works.

JOURNALS

Nineteen-Century Literature Criticism is a professional journal that offers literary criticism about issues that scholars are exploring relative to nineteenth-century authors and texts. This journal, with new issues offered quarterly since 1981, is published by Gale Research.

Nineteenth-Century Literature is a professional journal, first published in 1945 as *The Trollopian* and later as *Nineteenth-Century Fiction.* Each quarterly issue provides articles, reviews of new books, and bibliographies that examine nineteenth-century literature.

FILMS AND OTHER RECORDINGS

Grand Isle (1992). Directed by Mary Lambert, with performances by Kelly McGillis, Adrian Pasdar, Julian Sands, Jon deVries, Glenne Headly, Anthony De Dando, and Ellen Burstyn.

This film was made by Turner Broadcasting and was shown on cable television. For the most part, this film closely follows the text, adding little but eliminating some important scenes. However, over all, it is a better-than-average attempt to capture the essence of Chopin's novel.

Awakening. Naxos Audiobooks. Performed by Liza Ross, 157 minutes.

This recording is an abridged reading of Chopin's book.

Awakening and Selected Stories. Penguin Audiobooks. Performed by Joanna Adler, 360 minutes.

This recording is an abridged reading of Chopin's work.

Awakening. Blackstone Audiobooks. Performed by Walter Zimmerman, 360 minutes.

This is a full length reading of Chopin's novel.

OTHER MEDIA

Kate Chopin: A Re-Awakening (1999). Directed by Tika Laudun, with narration by Kelly McGillis, and JoBeth Williams reading passages from Chopin's works.

This film, produced by Public Broadcasting and shown on PBS, is an examination of Chopin's life and makes a very comprehensive effort to reveal Chopin for a modern audience who may not be familiar with her work.

CLIFFSCOMPLETE READING GROUP DISCUSSION GUIDE

Use the following questions and topics to enhance your reading group discussions. The discussion can help get you thinking—and hopefully talking—about Chopin in a whole new way!

DISCUSSION QUESTIONS

1. Throughout *The Awakening*, Chopin focuses on the relationship between husbands and wives, with both the Pontellier and Ratignolle families. How would you characterize these relationships? Do women have to completely subordinate themselves in this culture for them to find happiness, the way Madame Ratignolle does? Edna thinks that the Ratignolle marriage is empty and devoid of excitement—an unhappy representation of marriage. Do you agree? Do you think that this issue of control continues to be a serious problem between men and women?

2. Several times during the course of the novel, Edna relates that destiny is now in control of her future. This lack of choice is called *naturalism*, but a reader may also argue that blaming naturalism means that Edna does not have to take responsibility for the events that occur. Do you think this is true? And if so, is human nature never to blame when an individual, such as Edna, succumbs to the innate pressures that have built up inside? How much responsibility for Edna's tragedy can be blamed on environmental forces? How much on her family's history, especially her father?

3. Chopin's audience, especially her male audience, was deeply offended by Edna's rebellion, her affair, and her poor mothering of her children. But many women may reply that Edna knew her limitations. She is not a good mother and so her children are better off in the care of nurses and their grandmother. What are the pros and cons of her choices? Was she right to try to find some happiness in her life and leave the care of her children to others? Or should she have tried to make the best of her marriage and wait to see if this was just some sort of phase, as Doctor Mandelet suggests?

4. Readers are often deeply disturbed at Edna's suicide, arguing that she is a terrible mother who abandons her children by making a completely selfish decision that satisfies only her own needs. How do you feel about this view of Edna? Many readers may argue that a child is always better being cared for by the mother and that she should have stayed alive—even if she is unhappy. Would this generalization have worked in the Pontellier family? Would Edna's children have been better served if their mother had forgotten her own needs and concentrated on her children's needs? Or is Edna just a selfish, dysfunctional woman?

5. Often, readers try to argue that Edna did not really intend to commit suicide, in spite of the evidence in the text. Clearly, they are disturbed that such a vital, strong young woman would choose to end her own life. Why is suicide the only reasonable choice for Edna? What other choices may a young woman have during this period, considering the cultural and religious pressures of late nineteenth-century life?

6. Throughout the course of the novel, Edna is closely involved with three different men— Léonce, Robert, and Arobin. In addition, there are other men in her life—her father, Doctor Mandelet, Victor, and Monsieur Ratignolle. What kinds of conversations does Edna have with these men? Clearly the tone of her voice and the topics that she discusses with Robert and Arobin are very different than the way she talks to her husband. What can you learn about Edna from studying the way in which she speaks to these various men? What do her conversations with Arobin and Robert add to her life that the conversations with other men lack? And more importantly, what can the reader learn about his period from studying the conversations between men and women?

7. A key scene, and one filled with irony, occurs when Léonce visits Doctor Mandelet to discuss Edna's problems. There is much irony in having two men discuss the problems of a woman, and yet this scene would have seemed perfectly normal to the men in Chopin's audience, since it reveals how concerned Léonce is about his wife's well-being. Going to the doctor for marital advice implies that she is ill because her behavior is unacceptable. How do you feel about this implication? Is Léonce dealing with male-female social problems as a disease? The doctor's advice is designed to pacify Léonce, but is it dangerous for Edna?

8. Make a list of things important to Léonce. What does this list reveal about why he goes to Mandelet? Léonce worries that Edna has fallen in with feminists. How do you feel about this description of women as dangerous influences? Strictly speaking, Chopin was not a feminist, but is she exposing these issues for public discussion? And if so, could the banning of the book, or any book, act to stifle discussion of a controversial topic?

Index

continued

R

Notes

Notes